DORIS LESSING, Winner of the Nobel Prize for Literature 2007, is one of the most celebrated and distinguished writers of recent decades. A Companion of Honour and a Companion of Literature, she has been awarded the David Cohen Memorial Prize for British Literature, Spain's Prince of Asturias Prize, the International Catalunya Award and the S.T. Dupont Golden PEN Award for a Lifetime's Distinguished Service to Literature. She lives in north London.

By the same author

NOVELS
The Golden Notebook
Briefing for a Descent into Hell
The Summer Before the Dark
Memoirs of a Survivor
Diary of a Good Neighbour
If the Old Could . . .
The Good Terrorist
Love, Again
Mara and Dann
The Fifth Child
Ben, in the World
The Sweetest Dream
The Story of General Dann and Mara's
    Daughter, Griot and the Snow Dog
The Cleft

'Canopus in Argos: Archives' series
Re: Colonised Planet 5, Shikasta
The Marriages Between Zones
    Three, Four, and Five
The Sirian Experiments
The Making of the Representative for
    Planet 8
Documents Relating to the Sentimental
    Agents in the Volyen Empire

'Children of Violence' novel-sequence
Martha Quest
A Proper Marriage
A Ripple from the Storm
Landlocked
The Four-Gated City

OPERAS
The Marriages Between Zones Three,
    Four and Five (Music by Philip
    Glass)
The Making of the representative for
    Planet 8 (Music by Philip Glass)

SHORT STORIES
Five
The Habit of Loving
A Man and Two Women

The Story of a Non-Marrying Man
    and Other Stories
Winter in July
The Black Madonna
This Was the Old Chief's Country
    (Collected African Stories, Vol. 1)
The Sun Between Their Feet
    (Collected African Stories, Vol. 2)
To Room Nineteen
    (Collected Stories, Vol. 1)
The Temptation of Jack Orkney
    (Collected Stories, Vol. 2)
London Observed
The Old Age of El Magnifico
Particularly Cats
Rufus the Survivor
On Cats
The Grandmothers

POETRY
Fourteen Poems

DRAMA
Each His Own Wilderness
Play with a Tiger
The Singing Door

GRAPHIC NOVEL
Playing the Game
    (illustrated by Charlie Adlard)

NON-FICTION
In Pursuit of the English
Going Home
A Small Personal Voice
Prisons We Choose to Live Inside
The Wind Blows Away Our
    Words
African Laughter
Time Bites
Alfred and Emily

AUTOBIOGRAPHY
Under My Skin: Volume 1
Walking in the Shade: Volume 2

DORIS LESSING

The Grass is Singing

HARPER PERENNIAL
London, New York, Toronto, Sydney and New Delhi

Harper Perennial
An imprint of HarperCollins*Publishers*
77–85 Fulham Palace Road, Hammersmith, London W6 8JB

www.harperperennial.co.uk
Visit our authors' blog at www.fifthestate.co.uk

This Harper Perennial Modern Classics edition published 2007
13

Previously published in paperback by Grafton 1980, Paladin 1989 and
as a Flamingo Modern Classic 1994 (reprinted 9 times)

First published in Great Britain by Michael Joseph Ltd in 1950

Copyright © Doris Lessing 1950

Doris Lessing asserts the moral right
to be identified as the author of this work

A catalogue record for this book is available from the British Library

ISBN 978-0-586-08924-8

Set in Times

Printed and bound in Great Britain by Clays Ltd, St Ives plc

Mixed Sources
Product group from well-managed
forests and other controlled sources
www.fsc.org Cert no. SW-COC-1806
© 1996 Forest Stewardship Council

FSC is a non-profit international organisation established to promote the
responsible management of the world's forests. Products carrying the FSC
label are independently vertified to assure consumers that they come
from forests that are managed to meet the social, economic and
ecological needs of present and future generations.

Find out more about HarperCollins and the environment at
www.harpercollins.co.uk/green

To

Mrs GLADYS MAASDORP
of Southern Rhodesia
for whom I feel the greatest
affection and admiration

In this decayed hole among the mountains
In the faint moonlight, the grass is singing
Over the tumbled graves, about the chapel
There is the empty chapel, only the wind's home.
It has no windows, and the door swings,
Dry bones can harm no one.
Only a cock stood on the rooftree
Co co rico, co co rico
In a flash of lightning. Then a damp gust
Bringing rain

Ganga was sunken, and the limp leaves
Waited for rain, while the black clouds
Gathered far distant, over Himavant.
The jungle crouched, humped in silence.
Then spoke the thunder

From *The Waste Land* by T. S. ELIOT
with grateful acknowledgements to the
author and to Messrs Faber & Faber

'It is by the failures and misfits of a
civilization that one can best judge its
weaknesses.'

                    AUTHOR UNKNOWN

1

MURDER MYSTERY
By Special Correspondent
Mary Turner, wife of Richard Turner, a farmer at Ngesi, was found
murdered on the front verandah of their homestead yesterday morn-
ing. The houseboy, who has been arrested, has confessed to the crime.
No motive has been discovered.

It is thought he was in search of valuables.

The newspaper did not say much. People all over the country
must have glanced at the paragraph with its sensational heading
and felt a little spurt of anger mingled with what was almost
satisfaction, as if some belief had been confirmed, as if something had happened which could only have been expected.
When natives steal, murder or rape, that is the feeling white
people have.

And then they turned the page to something else.

But the people in 'the district' who knew the Turners, either
by sight, or from gossiping about them for so many years, did
not turn the page so quickly. Many must have snipped out the
paragraph, put it among old letters, or between the pages of a
book, keeping it perhaps as an omen or a warning, glancing at
the yellowing piece of paper with closed, secretive faces. For
they did not discuss the murder; that was the most extraordinary thing about it. It was as if they had a sixth sense which
told them everything there was to be known, although the three
people in a position to explain the facts said nothing. The
murder was simply not discussed. 'A bad business,' someone
would remark; and the faces of the people round about would
put on that reserved and guarded look. 'A very bad business,'
came the reply – and that was the end of it. There was, it

9

seemed, a tacit agreement that the Turner case should not be given undue publicity by gossip. Yet it was a farming district, where those isolated white families met only very occasionally, hungry for contact with their own kind, to talk and discuss and pull to pieces, all speaking at once, making the most of an hour or so's companionship before returning to their farms where they saw only their own faces and the faces of their black servants for weeks on end. Normally that murder would have been discussed for months; people would have been positively grateful for something to talk about.

To an outsider it would seem perhaps as if the energetic Charlie Slatter had travelled from farm to farm over the district telling people to keep quiet; but that was something that would have never have occurred to him. The steps he took (and he made not one mistake) were taken apparently instinctively and without conscious planning. The most interesting thing about the whole affair was this silent, unconscious agreement. Everyone behaved like a flock of birds who communicate – or so it seems – by means of a kind of telepathy.

Long before the murder marked them out, people spoke of the Turners in the hard, careless voices reserved for misfits, outlaws and the self-exiled. The Turners were disliked, though few of their neighbours had ever met them, or even seen them in the distance. Yet what was there to dislike? They simply 'kept themselves to themselves'; that was all. They were never seen at district dances, or fêtes, or gymkhanas. They must have had something to be ashamed of; that was the feeling. It was not right to seclude themselves like that; it was a slap in the face of everyone else; what had they got to be so stuck-up about? What, indeed! Living the way they did! That little box of a house – it was forgivable as a temporary dwelling, but not to live in permanently. Why, some natives (though not many, thank heavens) had houses as good; and it would give them a bad impression to see white people living in such a way.

And then it was that someone used the phrase 'poor whites'. It caused disquiet. There was no great money-cleavage in those days (that was before the era of the tobacco barons), but there was certainly a race division. The small community of Afrikaners had their own lives, and the Britishers ignored them. 'Poor whites' were Afrikaners, never British. But the person who said the Turners were poor whites stuck to it defiantly. What was the difference? What was a poor white? It was the way one lived, a question of standards. All the Turners needed were a drove of children to make them poor whites.

Though the arguments were unanswerable, people would still not think of them as poor whites. To do that would be letting the side down. The Turners were British, after all.

Thus the district handled the Turners, in accordance with that *esprit de corps* which is the first rule of South African society, but which the Turners themselves ignored. They apparently did not recognize the need for *esprit de corps*; that, really, was why they were hated.

The more one thinks about it, the more extraordinary the case becomes. Not the murder itself; but the way people felt about it, the way they pitied Dick Turner with a fine fierce indignation against Mary as if she were something unpleasant and unclean, and it served her right to get murdered. But they did not ask questions.

For instance, they must have wondered who that 'Special Correspondent' was. Someone in the district sent in the news, for the paragraph was not in newspaper language. But who? Marston, the assistant, left the district immediately after the murder. Denham, the policeman, might have written to the paper in a personal capacity, but it was not likely. There remained Charlie Slatter, who knew more about the Turners than anyone else, and was there on the day of the murder. One could say that he practically controlled the handling of the case, even taking precedence over the Sergeant himself. And people felt that to be quite right and proper. Whom should it concern, if not the white farmers, that a silly woman got herself murdered by a native for reasons people might think about, but never, never mentioned? It was their livelihood, their wives and families, their way of living, at stake.

But to the outsider it is strange that Slatter should have been allowed to take charge of the affair, to arrange that everything should pass over without more than a ripple of comment.

For there could have been no planning: there simply wasn't time. Why, for instance, when Dick Turner's farm boys came to him with the news, did he sit down to write a note to the Sergeant at the police camp? He did not use the telephone.

Everyone who has lived in the country knows what a branch telephone is like. You lift the receiver after you have turned the handle the required number of times, and then, click, click, click, you can hear the receivers coming off all over the district, and soft noises like breathing, a whisper, a subdued cough.

Slatter lived five miles from the Turners. The farm boys came to him first, when they discovered the body. And though it was an urgent matter, he ignored the telephone, but sent a personal letter by a native bearer on a bicycle to Denham at the police camp, twelve miles away. The Sergeant sent out half a dozen native policemen at once, to the Turners' farm, to see what they could find. He drove first to see Slatter, because the way that letter was worded roused his curiosity. That was why he arrived late on the scene of the murder. The native policemen did not have to search far for the murderer. After walking through the house, looking briefly at the body, and dispersing down the front of the little hill the house stood on, they saw Moses himself rise out of a tangled ant-heap in front of them. He walked up to them and said (or words to this effect): 'Here I am.' They snapped the handcuffs on him, and went back to the house to wait for the police cars to come. There they saw Dick Turner come out of the bush by the house with two whining dogs at his heels. He was off his head, talking crazily to himself, wandering in and out of the bush with his hands full of leaves and earth. They let him be, while keeping an eye on him, for he was a white man, though mad, and black men, even when policemen, do not lay hands on white flesh.

People did ask, cursorily, why the murderer had given himself up. There was not much chance of escape. But he did have a sporting chance. He could have run to the hills and hidden for a while. Or he could have slipped over the border to Portuguese territory. Then the District Native Commissioner, at a sundowner party, said that it was perfectly understandable. If one knew anything about the history of the country, or had read any of the memoirs or letters of the old missionaries and explorers, one would have come across accounts of the society Lobengula ruled. The laws were strict: everyone knew what they could or could not do. If someone did an unforgivable thing, like touching one of the King's women, he would submit fatalistically to punishment, which was likely to be impalement over an ant-heap on a stake, or something equally unpleasant. 'I have done wrong, and I know it,' he might say, 'therefore let me be punished.' Well, it was the tradition to face punishment, and really there was something rather fine about it. Remarks like these are forgiven from native commissioners, who have to study languages, customs, and so on; although it is not done to say things natives do are 'fine'. (Yet the fashion is changing: it is permissible to glorify the old ways sometimes, providing one says how depraved the natives have become since.)

So that aspect of the affair was dropped, yet it is not the least interesting, for Moses might not have been a Matabele at all. He was in Mashonaland; though of course natives do wander all over Africa. He might have come from anywhere: Portuguese territory, Nyasaland, the Union of South Africa. And it is a long time since the days of the great king Lobengula. But then native commissioners tend to think in terms of the past.

Well, having sent the letter to the police camp, Charlie Slatter went to the Turners' place, driving at a great speed over the bad farm roads in his fat American car.

Who *was* Charlie Slatter? It was he who, from the beginning of the tragedy to its end, personified Society for the Turners. He touches the story at half a dozen points; without him things would not have happened quite as they did, though sooner or later, in one way or another, the Turners were bound to come to grief.

Slatter had been a grocer's assistant in London. He was fond of telling his children that if it had not been for his energy and enterprise they would be running round the slums in rags. He was still a proper cockney, even after twenty years in Africa. He came with one idea: to make money. He made it. He made plenty. He was a crude, brutal, ruthless, yet kindhearted man, in his own way, and according to his own impulses, who could not help making money. He farmed as if he were turning the handle of a machine which would produce pound notes at the other end. He was hard with his wife, making her bear unnecessary hardships at the beginning; he was hard with his children, until he made money, when they got everything they wanted; and above all he was hard with his farm labourers. They, the geese that laid the golden eggs, were still in that state where they did not know there were other ways of living besides producing gold for other people. They know better now, or are beginning to. But Slatter believed in farming with the sjambok. It hung over his front door, like a motto on a wall: 'You shall not mind killing if it is necessary.' He had once killed a native in a fit of temper. He was fined thirty pounds. Since then he had kept his temper. But sjamboks are all very well for the Slatters; not so good for people less sure of themselves. It was he who had told Dick Turner, long ago, when Dick first started farming, that one should buy a sjambok before a plough or a harrow, and that sjambok did not do the Turners any good, as we shall see.

Slatter was a shortish, broad, powerful man, with heavy shoulders and thick arms. His face was broad and bristled; shrewd, watchful, and a little cunning. He had a crop of fair hair that made him look like a convict; but he did not care for appearances. His small blue eyes were hardly visible, because of the way he screwed them up, after years and years of South African sunshine.

Bent over the steering wheel, almost hugging it in his determination to get to the Turners quickly, his eyes were little blue chinks in a set face. He was wondering why Marston, the assistant, who was after all his employee, had not come to him about the murder, or at least sent a note. Where was he? The hut he lived in was only a couple of hundred yards from the house itself. Perhaps he had got cold feet and run away? Anything was possible, thought Charlie, from this particular type of young Englishman. He had a rooted contempt for soft-faced, soft-voiced Englishmen, combined with a fascination for their manner and breeding. His own sons, now grown up, were gentlemen. He had spent plenty of money to make them so; but he despised them for it. At the same time he was proud of them. This conflict showed itself in his attitude towards Marston: half hard and indifferent, half subtly deferential. At the moment he felt nothing but irritation.

Half-way he felt the car rock, and swearing, pulled it up. It was a puncture: no, two punctures. The red mud of the road held fragments of broken glass. His irritation expressed itself in the half-conscious thought, 'Just like Turner to have glass on his roads!' But Turner was now necessarily an object of passionate, protective pity, and the irritation was focused on Marston, the assistant who, Slatter felt, should somehow have prevented this murder. What was he being paid for? What had he been engaged for? But Slatter was a fair man in his own way, and where his own race was concerned. He restrained himself, and got down to mending one puncture and changing a tyre, working in the heavy red slush of the roads. This took him three-quarters of an hour, and by the time he was finished, and had picked the pieces of green glass from the mud and thrown them into the bush, the sweat was soaking his face and hair.

When he reached the house at last, he saw, as he approached through the bush, six glittering bicycles leaning against the walls. And in front of the house, under the trees, stood six native policemen, and among them the native Moses, his hands linked in front of him. The sun glinted on the handcuffs, on the bicycles, on the masses of heavy wet leaves. It was a wet, sultry morning. The sky was a tumult of discoloured clouds: it looked full of billowing dirty washing. Puddles on the pale soil held a sheen of sky.

Charlie walked up to the policemen, who saluted him. They were in fezes, and their rather fancy-dress uniform. This last thought did not occur to Charlie, who liked his natives either one way or the other: properly dressed according to their station, or in loincloths. He could not bear the half-civilized native. The policemen, picked for their physique, were a fine body of men, but they were put in the shade by Moses, who was a great powerful man, black as polished linoleum, and dressed in a singlet and shorts, which were damp and muddy. Charlie stood directly in front of the murderer and looked into his face. The man stared back, expressionless, indifferent. His own face was curious: it showed a kind of triumph, a guarded vindictiveness, and fear. Why fear? Of Moses, who was as good as hanged already? But he was uneasy, troubled. Then he seemed to shake himself into self-command, and turned and saw Dick Turner, standing a few paces away, covered with mud.

'Turner!' he said, peremptorily. He stopped, looking into the man's face. Dick appeared not to know him. Charlie took him by the arm and drew him towards his own car. He did not know he was incurably mad then; otherwise he might have been even more angry than he was. Having put Dick into the back seat of his car, he went into the house. In the front room stood Marston, his hands in his pockets, in a pose that seemed negligently calm. But his face was pale and strained.

'Where were you?' asked Charlie at once, accusingly.

'Normally Mr Turner wakes me,' said the youth calmly. 'This morning I slept late. When I came into the house I found Mrs Turner on the verandah. Then the policemen came. I was expecting you.' But he was afraid: it was the fear of death that sounded in his voice, not the fear that was controlling Charlie's actions: he had not been long enough in the country to understand Charlie's special fear.

Charlie grunted: he never spoke unless necessary. He looked long and curiously at Marston, as if trying to make out why it was the farm natives had not called a man who lay asleep a few yards off, but had instinctively sent for himself. But it was not with dislike or contempt he looked at Marston now; it was more the look a man gives a prospective partner who has yet to prove himself.

He turned and went into the bedroom. Mary Turner was a stiff shape under a soiled white sheet. At one end of the sheet protruded a mass of pale strawish hair, and at the other a crinkled yellow foot. Now a curious thing happened. The hate and contempt that one would have expected to show on his face when he looked at the murderer, twisted his features now, as he stared at Mary. His brows knotted, and for a few seconds his lips curled back over his teeth in a vicious grimace. He had his back to Marston, who would have been astonished to see him. Then, with a hard, angry movement, Charlie turned and left the room, driving the young man before him.

Marston said: 'She was lying on the verandah. I lifted her on to the bed.' He shuddered at the memory of the touch of the cold body. 'I thought she shouldn't be left lying there.' He hesitated and added, the muscles of his face contracting whitely: 'The dogs were licking at her.'

Charlie nodded, with a keen glance at him. He seemed indifferent as to where she might be lying. At the same time he approved the self-control of the assistant who had performed the unpleasant task.

'There was blood everywhere. I cleaned it up . . . I thought afterwards I should have left it for the police.'

'It makes no odds,' said Charlie absently. He sat down on one of the rough wood chairs in the front room, and remained in thought, whistling softly through his front teeth. Marston stood by the window, looking for the arrival of the police car. From time to time Charlie looked round the room alertly, flicking his tongue over his lips. Then he lapsed back into his soft whistling. It got on the young man's nerves.

At last, cautiously, almost warningly, Charlie said: 'What do *you* know of this?'

Marston noted the emphasized *you*, and wondered what Slatter knew. He was well in control of himself, but as taut as wire. He said: 'I don't know. Nothing really. It is all so difficult . . .' He hesitated, looking appealing at Charlie.

That look of almost soft appeal irritated Charlie, coming from a man, but it pleased him too: he was pleased the youth deferred to him. He knew the type so well. So many of them came from England to learn farming. They were usually ex-public school, very English, but extremely adaptable. From Charlie's point of view, the adaptability redeemed them. It was strange to see how quickly they accustomed themselves. At first they were diffident, though proud and withdrawn; cautiously learning the new ways, with a fine sensitiveness, an alert self-consciousness.

When old settlers say, 'One has to understand the country,' what they mean is, 'You have to get used to our ideas about the native.' They are saying, in effect, 'Learn our ideas, or otherwise get out: we don't want you.' Most of these young men were brought up with vague ideas about equality. They were shocked, for the first week or so, by the way natives were treated. They were revolted a hundred times a day by the casual way they were spoken of, as if they were so many cattle; or by a blow, or a look. They had been prepared to treat them as human beings. But they could not stand out against the society they were joining. It did not take them long to change. It was hard, of course, becoming as bad oneself. But it was not very long that they thought of it as 'bad'. And anyway, what had one's ideas amounted to? Abstract ideas about decency and goodwill, that was all: merely abstract ideas. When it came to the point, one never had contact with natives, except in the master–servant relationship. One never knew them in their own lives, as human beings. A few months, and these sensitive, decent young men had coarsened to suit the hard, arid, sun-drenched country they had come to; they had grown a new manner to match their thickened sunburnt limbs and toughened bodies.

If Tony Marston had been even a few more months in the country it would have been easy. That was Charlie's feeling. That was why he looked at the young man with a speculative frowning look, not condemning him, only wary and on the alert.

He said: 'What do you mean, it is all so difficult?'

Tony Marston appeared uncomfortable, as if he did not know his own mind. And for that matter he did not: the weeks in the Turners' houshold with its atmosphere of tragedy had not helped him to get his mind clear. The two standards – the one he had brought with him and the one he was adopting – conflicted still. And there was a roughness, a warning note, in

18

Charlie's voice, that left him wondering. What was he being warned against? He was intelligent enough to know he was being warned. In this he was unlike Charlie, who was acting by instinct and did not know his voice was a threat. It was all so unusual. Where were the police? What right had Charlie, who was a neighbour, to be fetched before himself, who was practically a member of the household? Why was Charlie quietly taking command?

His ideas of right were upset. He was confused, but he had his own ideas about the murder, which could not be stated straight out, like that, in black and white. When he came to think of it, the murder was logical enough; looking back over the last few days he could see that something like this was bound to happen, he could almost say he had been expecting it, some kind of violence or ugliness. Anger, violence, death, seemed natural to this vast, harsh country . . . he had done a lot of thinking since he had strolled casually into the house that morning, wondering why everyone was so late, to find Mary Turner lying murdered on the verandah, and the police boys outside, guarding the houseboy; and Dick Turner muttering and stumbling through the puddles, mad, but apparently harmless. Things he had not understood, he understood now, and he was ready to talk about them. But he was in the dark as to Charlie's attitude. There was something here he could not get hold of.

'It's like this,' he said. 'When I first arrived I didn't know much about the country.'

Charlie said, with a good-humoured but brutal irony, 'Thanks for the information.' And then, 'Have you any idea why this nigger murdered Mrs Turner?'

'Well, I have a sort of idea, yes.'

'We had better leave it to the Sergeant, when he comes then.'

It was a snub; he had been shut up. Tony held his tongue, angry but bewildered.

When the Sergeant came, he went over to look at the murderer, glanced at Dick through the window of Slatter's car, and then came into the house.

'I went to your place, Slatter,' he said, nodding at Tony, giving him a keen look. Then he went into the bedroom. And his reactions were as Charlie's had been: vindictiveness towards the murderer, emotional pity for Dick, and for Mary, a bitter contemptuous anger: Sergeant Denham had been in the country for a number of years. This time Tony saw the expression on the face, and it gave him a shock. The faces of the two men as they stood over the body, gazing down at it, made him feel uneasy, even afraid. He himself felt a little disgust, but not much; it was mainly pity that agitated him, knowing what he knew. It was the disgust that he would feel for any social irregularity, no more than the distaste that comes from failure of the imagination. This profound instinctive horror and fear astonished him.

The three of them went silently into the living-room.

Charlie Slatter and Sergeant Denham stood side by side like two judges, as if they had purposely taken up this attitude. Opposite them was Tony. He stood his ground, but he felt an absurd guiltiness taking hold of him, simply because of their pose, standing like that, looking at him with subtle reserved faces that he could not read.

'Bad business,' said Sergeant Denham briefly.

No one answered. He snapped open a notebook, adjusted elastic over a page, and poised a pencil.

'A few questions, if you don't mind,' he said. Tony nodded.

'How long have you been here?'

'About three weeks.'

'Living in this house?'

'No, in a hut down the path.'

'You were going to run this place while they were away?'

'Yes, for six months.'

'And then?'

'And then I intended to go on a tobacco farm.'

'When did you know about this business?'

'They didn't call me. I woke and found Mrs Turner.'

Tony's voice showed he was now on the defensive. He felt wounded, even insulted that he had not been called: above all, that these two men seemed to think it right and natural that he should be bypassed in this fashion, as if his newness to the country unfitted him for any kind of responsibility. And he resented the way he was being questioned. They had no right to do it. He was beginning to simmer with rage, although he knew quite well that they themselves were quite unconscious of the patronage implicit in their manner, and that it would be better for him to try and understand the real meaning of this scene, rather than to stand on his dignity.

'You had your meals with the Turners?'

'Yes.'

'Apart from that, were you ever here – socially, so to speak?'

'No, hardly at all. I have been busy learning the job.'

'Get on well with Turner?'

'Yes, I think so. I mean, he was not easy to know. He was absorbed in his work. And he was obviously very unhappy at leaving the place.'

'Yes, poor devil, he had a hard time of it.' The voice was suddenly tender almost maudlin, with pity, although the Sergeant snapped out the words, and then shut his mouth tight, as if to present a brave face to the world. Tony was disconcerted: the unexpectedness of these men's responses was taking him right out of his depth. He was feeling nothing that they were feeling: he was an outsider in this tragedy, although both the Sergeant and Charlie Slatter seemed to feel personally implicated, for they had unconsciously assumed poses of weary dignity, appearing bowed down with unutterable burdens, because of poor Dick Turner and his sufferings.

Yet it was Charlie who had literally turned Dick off his farm; and in previous interviews, at which Tony had been present, he had shown none of this sentimental pity.

There was a long pause. The Sergeant shut his notebook. But he had not yet finished. He was regarding Tony cautiously, wondering how to frame the next question. Or that was how it appeared to Tony, who could see that here was the moment that was the crux of the whole affair. Charlie's face: wary, a little cunning, a little afraid, proclaimed it.

'See anything out of the ordinary while you were here?' asked the Sergeant, apparently casual.

'Yes, I did,' blurted Tony, suddenly determined not to be bullied. For he knew he was being bullied, though he was cut off from them both by a gulf in experience and belief. They looked up at him, frowning; glanced at each other swiftly – then away, as if afraid to acknowledge conspiracy.

'What did you see? I hope you realize the – unpleasantness – of this case?' The last question was a grudging appeal.

'Any murder is surely unpleasant,' remarked Tony drily.

'When you have been in the country long enough, you will understand that we don't like niggers murdering white women.'

The phrase, 'When you have been in the country', stuck in Tony's gullet. He had heard it too often, and it had come to jar on him. At the same time it made him feel angry. Also callow. He would have liked to blurt out the truth in one overwhelming, incontrovertible statement; but the truth was not like that. It never was. The fact he knew, or guessed, about Mary, the fact these two men were conspiring to ignore, could be stated easily enough. But the important thing, the thing that really mattered, so it seemed to him, was to understand the background, the circumstances, the characters of Dick and Mary, the pattern of their lives. And it was not so easy to do. He had arrived at the truth circuitously: circuitously it would have to be explained. And his chief emotion, which was an impersonal pity for Mary and Dick and the native, a pity that was also rage against circumstances, made it difficult for him to know where to begin.

'Look,' he said, 'I'll tell you what I know from the beginning, only it will take some time, I am afraid . . .'

'You mean you know why Mrs Turner was murdered?' The question was a quick, shrewd parry.

'No, not just like that. Only I can form a theory.' The choice of words was most unfortunate.

'We don't want theories. We want facts. And in any case, you should remember Dick Turner. This is all most unpleasant for him. You should remember him, poor devil.'

Here it was again: the utterly illogical appeal, which to these two men was clearly not illogical at all. The whole thing was preposterous! Tony began to lose his temper.

'Do you or do you not want to hear what I have to say?' he asked, irritably.

'Go ahead. Only remember, I don't want to hear your fancies. I want to hear facts. Have you ever seen anything *definite* which would throw light on this murder? For instance, have you seen this boy attempting to get at her jewellery, or something like that? Anything that is definite. Not something in the air.'

Tony laughed. The two men looked at him sharply.

'You know as well as I do this case is not something that can be explained straight off like that. You know that. It's not something that can be said in black and white, straight off.'

It was pure deadlock; no one spoke. As if Sergeant Denham had not heard those last words, a heavy frown on his face, he said at last: 'For instance, how did Mrs Turner treat this boy? Did she treat her boys well?'

The angry Tony, fumbling for a foothold in this welter of emotion and half-understood loyalties, clutched at this for a beginning.

'Yes, she treated him badly, I thought. Though on the other hand . . .'

'Nagged at him, eh? Oh well, women are pretty bad that way, in this country, very often. Aren't they, Slatter?' The voice was easy, intimate, informal. 'My old woman drives me mad – it's something about this country. They have no idea how to deal with niggers.'

'Needs a man to deal with niggers,' said Charlie. 'Niggers don't understand women giving them orders. They keep their own women in their right place.' He laughed. The Sergeant laughed. They turned towards each other, even including Tony, in an unmistakable relief. The tension had broken; the danger was over: once again, he had been bypassed, and the interview, it seemed, was over. He could hardly believe it.

'But look here,' he said. Then he stopped. Both men turned to look at him, a steady, grave, irritated look on their faces. And the warning was unmistakable! It was the warning that might have been given to a greenhorn who was going to let *himself* down by saying too much. This realization was too much for Tony. He gave in; he washed his hands of it. He watched the other two in utter astonishment: they were together in mood and emotion, standing there in perfect understanding; the understanding was unrealized by themselves, the sympathy unacknowledged; their concerted handling of this affair had been instinctive: they were completely unaware of there being anything extraordinary, even anything illegal. And was there anything illegal, after all? This was a casual talk, on the face of it, nothing formal about it now that the notebook was shut – and it had been shut ever since they had reached the crisis of the scene.

Charlie said, turning towards the sergeant, 'Better get her out of here. It is too hot to wait.'

'Yes,' said the policeman, moving to give orders accordingly.

And that brutally matter-of-fact remark, Tony realized afterwards, was the only time poor Mary Turner was referred to directly. But why should she be? – except that this was really a friendly talk between the farmer who had been her next neighbour, the policeman who had been in her house on his rounds as a guest, and the assistant who had lived there for some weeks. It wasn't a formal occasion, this: Tony clung to the thought. There was a court case to come yet, which would be properly conducted.

'The case will be a matter of form, of course,' said the Sergeant, as if thinking aloud, with a look at Tony. He was standing by the police car, watching the native policemen lift the body of Mary Turner, which was wrapped in a blanket, into the back seat. She was stiff; a rigid outstretched arm knocked horribly against the narrow door; it was difficult to get her in. At last it was done and the door shut. And then there was another problem: they could not put Moses the murderer into the same car with her; one could not put a black man close to a white woman, even though she were dead, and murdered by him. And there was only Charlie's car, and mad Dick Turner was in that, sitting staring in the back. There seemed to be a feeling that Moses, having committed a murder, deserved to be taken by car; but there was no help for it, he would have to walk, guarded by the policemen, wheeling their bicycles, to the camp.

All these arrangements completed, there was a pause.

They stood there beside the cars, in the moment of parting, looking at the red-brick house with its shimmering hot roof, and the thick encroaching bush, and the group of black men moving off under the trees on their long walk. Moses was quite impassive, allowing himself to be directed without any movement of his own. His face was blank. He seemed to be staring straight into the sun. Was he thinking he would not see it much longer? Impossible to say. Regret? Not a sign of it. Fear? It did not seem so. The three men looked at the murderer, thinking their own thoughts, speculative, frowning, but not as if he were important now. No, he was unimportant: he was the constant, the black man who will thieve, rape, murder, if given half a chance. Even for Tony he no longer mattered; and his knowledge of the native mind was too small to give him any basis for conjecture.

'And what about him?' asked Charlie, jerking his thumb at Dick Turner. He meant: where does he come in, as far as the court case is concerned?

'He looks to me as if he won't be good for much,' said the Sergeant, who after all had plenty of experience of death, crime and madness.

No, for them the important thing was Mary Turner, who had let the side down; but even she, since she was dead, was no longer a problem. The one fact that remained still to be dealt with was the necessity for preserving appearances. Sergeant Denham understood that: it was part of his job, though it would not appear in regulations, was rather implicit in the spirit of the country, the spirit in which he was soaked. Charlie Slatter understood it, none better. Still side by side, as if one impulse, one regret, one fear, moved them both, they stood together in that last moment before they left the place, giving their final silent warning to Tony, looking at him gravely.

And he was beginning to understand. He knew now, at least, that what had been fought out in the room they had just left was nothing to do with the murder as such. The murder, in itself, was nothing. The struggle that had been decided in a few brief words – or rather, in the silences between the words – had had nothing to do with the surface meaning of the scene. He would understand it all a good deal better in a few months, when he had 'become used to the country'. And then he would do his best to forget the knowledge, for to live with the colour bar in all its nuances and implications means closing one's mind to many things, if one intends to remain an accepted member of society. But, in the interval, there would be a few brief moments when he would see the thing clearly, and understand that it was 'white civilization' fighting to defend itself that had been implicit in the attitude of Charlie Slatter and the Sergeant, 'white civilization' which will never, never admit that a white person, and most particularly, a white woman, can have a human relationship, whether for good or for evil, with a black person. For once it admits that, it crashes, and nothing can save it. So, above all, it cannot afford failures, such as the Turners' failure.

For the sake of those few lucid moments, and his half-confused knowledge, it can be said that Tony was the person present who had the greatest responsibility that day. For it would never have occurred to either Slatter or the Sergeant that they might be wrong: they were upheld, as in all their dealings with the black–white relationship, by a feeling of almost martyred responsibility. Yet Tony, too, wanted to be accepted by this new country. He would have to adapt himself, and if he did not conform, would be rejected: the issue was clear to him, he had heard the phrase 'getting used to our ideas' too often to have any illusions on the point. And, if he had acted according to his by now muddled ideas of right and wrong, his feeling that a monstrous injustice was being done, what difference would it make to the only participant in the tragedy who was neither dead or mad? For Moses would be hanged in any case; he had committed a murder, that fact remained. Did he intend to go on fighting in the dark for the sake of a principle? And if so, which principle? If he had stepped forward then, as he nearly did, when Sergeant Denham climbed finally into the car, and had said: 'Look here, I am just not going to shut up about this,' what would have been gained? It is certain that the Sergeant would not have understood him. His face would have contracted, his brow gone dark with irritation, and, taking his foot off the clutch, he would have said, 'Shut up about what? Who has asked you to shut up?' And then, if Tony had stammered out something about responsiblity, he would have looked significantly at Charlie and shrugged. Tony might have continued, ignoring the shrug and its implication of his wrongmindedness: 'If you must blame somebody, then blame Mrs Turner. You can't have it both ways. Either the white people are responsible for their behaviour, or they are not. It takes two to make a murder – a murder of this kind. Though, one can't really blame her either. She can't help being what she is. I've lived here, I tell you, which neither of you has done, and the whole thing is so difficult it is impossible to say who is to blame.' And then the Sergeant would have said, 'You can say what you think right in court.' That is what he would have said, just as if the issue had not been decided – though ostensibly it had never been mentioned – less than ten minutes before. 'It's not a question of blame,' the Sergeant might have said. 'Has anyone said anything about blame? But you can't get away from the fact that this nigger has murdered her, can you?'

So Tony said nothing and the police car went off through the trees. Charlie Slatter followed in his car with Dick Turner. Tony was left in the empty clearing, with an empty house.

He went inside, slowly, obsessed with the one clear image that remained to him after the events of the morning, and which seemed to him the key to the whole thing: the look on the Sergeant's and Slatter's faces when they looked down at the body; that almost hysterical look of hate and fear.

He sat down, his hand to his head, which ached badly; then got up again and fetched from a dusty shelf in the kitchen a medicine bottle marked 'Brandy'. He drank it off. He felt shaky in the knees and in the thighs. He was weak, too, with repugnance against this ugly little house which seemed to hold within its walls, even in its very brick and cement, the fears and horror of the murder. He felt suddenly as if he could not bear to stay in it, not for another moment.

He looked up at the bare crackling tin of the roof, that was warped with the sun, at the faded gimcrack furniture, at the dusty brick floors covered with ragged animal skins, and wondered how those two, Mary and Dick Turner, could have borne to live in such a place, year in and year out, for so long. Why, even the little thatched hut were he lived at the back was better than this! Why did they go on without even so much as putting in ceilings? It was enough to drive anyone mad, the heat in this place.

And then, feeling a little muddle-headed (the heat made the brandy take effect at once), he wondered how all this had begun, where the tragedy had started. For he clung obstinately to the belief, in spite of Slatter and the Sergeant, that the causes of the murder must be looked for a long way back, and that it was they which were important. What sort of woman had Mary Turner been, before she came to this farm and had been driven slowly off balance by heat and loneliness and poverty? And Dick Turner himself – what had he been? And the native – but here his thoughts were stopped by lack of knowledge. He could not even begin to imagine the mind of a native.

Passing his hand over his forehead, he tried desperately, and for the last time, to achieve some sort of a vision that would lift the murder above the confusions and complexities of the morning, and make of it, perhaps, a symbol, or a warning. But he failed. It was too hot. He was still exasperated by the attitude of the two men. His head was reeling. It must be over a hundred in this room, he thought angrily, getting up from his chair, and finding that his legs were unsteady. And he had drunk, at the most, two tablespoons of brandy! This damned country, he thought, convulsed with anger. Why should this happen to me, getting involved with a damned twisted affair like this, when I have only just come; and I really can't be expected to act as judge and jury and compassionate God into the bargain!

He stumbled on to the verandah, where the murder had been

committed the night before. There was a ruddy smear on the brick, and a puddle of rainwater was tinged pink. The same big shabby dogs were licking at the edges of the water, and cringed away when Tony shouted at them. He leaned against the wall and stared over the soaked greens and browns of the veld to the kopjes, which were sharp and blue after the rain; it had poured half the night. He realized, as the sound grew loud in his ears, that cicadas were shrilling all about him. He had been too absorbed to hear them. It was a steady, insistent screaming from every bush and tree. It wore on his nerves. 'I am getting out of this place,' he said suddenly. 'I am getting out of it altogether. I am going to the other end of the country. I wash my hands of the thing. Let the Slatters and the Denhams do as they like. What has it got to do with me?'

That morning, he packed his things and walked over to the Slatters' to tell Charlie he would not stay. Charlie seemed indifferent, even relieved; he had been thinking there was no need of a manager now that Dick would not come back.

After that the Turners' farm was run as an overflow for Charlie's cattle. They grazed all over it, even up to the hill where the house stood. It was left empty: it soon fell down.

Tony went back into town, where he hung round the bars and hotels for a while, waiting to hear of some job that would suit him. But his early carefree adaptability was gone. He had grown difficult to please. He visited several farms, but each time went away: farming had lost its glitter for him. At the trial, which was as Sergeant Denham had said it would be, a mere formality, he said what was expected of him. It was suggested that the native had murdered Mary Turner while drunk, in search of money and jewellery.

When the trial was over, Tony loafed about aimlessly until his money was finished. The murder, those few weeks with the Turners, had affected him more than he knew. But his money being gone, he had to do something in order to eat. He met a man from Northern Rhodesia, who told him about the copper mines and the wonderfully high salaries. They sounded fantastic to Tony. He took the next train to the copper belt, intending to save some money and start some business on his own account. But the salaries, once there, did not seem so good as they had from a distance. The cost of living was high, and then, everyone drank so much . . . Soon he left underground work and was a kind of manager. So, in the end, he sat in an office and did paperwork, which was what he had come to Africa to avoid. But it wasn't so bad really. One should take things as they came. Life isn't as one expects it to be – and so on; these were the things he said to himself when depressed, and was measuring himself against his early ambitions.

For the people in 'the district', who knew all about him by hearsay, he was the young man from England who hadn't the guts to stand more than a few weeks of farming. No guts, they said. He should have stuck it out.

2

As the railway lines spread and knotted and ramified all over Southern Africa, along them, at short distances of a few miles, sprang up little dorps that to a traveller appear as insignificant clusters of ugly buildings, but which are the centres of farming districts perhaps a couple of hundred miles across. They contain the station building, the post office, sometimes a hotel, but always a store.

If one was looking for a symbol to express South Africa, the South Africa that was created by financiers and mine magnates, the South Africa which the old missionaries and explorers who charted the Dark Continent would be horrified to see, one would find it in the store. The store is everywhere. Drive ten miles from one and you come on the next; poke your head out of the railway carriage, and there it is; every mine has its store, and many farms.

It is always a low single-storeyed building divided into segments like a strip of chocolate, with grocery, butchery and bottle-store under one corrugated iron roof. It has a high dark wooden counter, and behind the counter shelves hold anything from distemper mixture to toothbrushes, all mixed together. There are a couple of racks holding cheap cotton dresses in brilliant colours, and perhaps a stack of shoe-boxes, or a glass case for cosmetics or sweets. There is the unmistakable smell, a smell compounded of varnish, dried blood from the killing yards behind, dried hides, dried fruit and strong yellow soap. Behind the counter is a Greek, or a Jew, or an Indian. Sometimes the children of this man, who is invariably hated by the whole district as a profiteer and an alien, are playing among the vegetables because the living quarters are just behind the shop.

For thousands of people up and down Southern Africa the store is the background to their childhood. So many things centred round it. It brings back, for instance, memories of those nights when the car, after driving endlessly through a chilly, dusty darkness, stopped unexpectedly in front of a square of light where men lounged with glasses in their hands, and one was carried out into the brilliantly-lit bar for a sip of searing liquid 'to keep the fever away'. Or it might be the place where one drove twice a week to collect mail, and to see all the farmers from miles around buying their groceries, and reading letters from Home with one leg propped on the running-board of the car, momentarily oblivious to the sun, the square of red dust where the dogs lay scattered like flies on meat and the groups of staring natives – momentarily transported back to the country for which they were so bitterly homesick, but where they would not choose to live again: 'South Africa gets into you,' these self-exiled people would say, ruefully.

For Mary, the word 'Home' spoken nostalgically, meant England, although both her parents were South Africans and had never been to England. It mean 'England' because of those mail-days, when she slipped up to the store to watch the cars come in, and drive away again laden with stores and letters and magazines from overseas.

For Mary, the store was the real centre of her life, even more important to her than to most children. To begin with, she always lived within sight of it, in one of those little dusty dorps. She was always having to run across to bring a pound of dried peaches or a tin of salmon for her mother, or to find out whether the weekly newspaper had arrived. And she would linger there for hours, staring at the piles of sticky coloured sweets, letting the fine grain stored in the sacks round the walls trickle through her fingers, looking covertly at the little Greek girl whom she was not allowed to play with, because her mother said her parents were dagos. And later, when she grew older, the store came to have another significance: it was the place where her father bought his drink. Sometimes her mother

worked herself into a passion of resentment, and walked up to
the barman, complaining that she could not make ends meet,
while her husband squandered his salary in drink. Mary knew,
even as a child, that her mother complained for the sake of
making a scene and parading her sorrows: that she really
enjoyed the luxury of standing there in the bar while the casual
drinkers looked on, sympathetically; she enjoyed complaining
in a hard sorrowful voice about her husband. 'Every night he
comes home from here,' she would say, 'every night! And I am
expected to bring up three children on the money that is left
over when he chooses to come home.' And then she would
stand still, waiting for the condolences of the man who pock-
eted the money which was rightly hers to spend for the children.
But he would say at the end, 'But what can I do? I can't refuse
to sell him drink, now can I?' And at last, having played out
her scene and taken her fill of sympathy, she would walk away
across the expanse of red dust to her house, holding Mary by
the hand – a tall, scrawny woman with angry, unhealthy
brilliant eyes. She made a confidante of Mary early. She used
to cry over her sewing while Mary comforted her miserably,
longing to get away, but feeling important too, and hating her
father.

This is not to say that he drank himself into a state of
brutality. He was seldom drunk as some men were, whom
Mary saw outside the bar, frightening her into a real terror of
the place. He drank himself every evening into a state of
cheerful fuddled good humour, coming home late to a cold
dinner, which he ate by himself. His wife treated him with a
cold indifference. She reserved her scornful ridicule of him for
when her friends came to tea. It was as if she did not wish to
give her husband the satisfaction of knowing that she cared
anything for him at all, or felt anything for him, even contempt
and derision. She behaved as if he were simply not there for
her. And for all practical purposes he was not. He brought
home the money, and not enough of that. Apart from that he
was a cipher in the house, and knew it. He was a little man,
with dull ruffled hair, a baked-apple face, and an air of uneasy
though aggressive jocularity. He called visiting petty officials

'sir'; and shouted at the natives under him; he was on the railway, working as a pumpman.

And then, as well as being the focus of the district, and the source of her father's drunkenness, the store was the powerful, implacable place that sent in bills at the end of the month. They could never be fully paid: her mother was always appealing to the owner for just another month's grace. Her father and mother fought over these bills twelve times a year. They never quarrelled over anything but money; sometimes, in fact, her mother remarked drily that she might have done worse: she might, for instance, be like Mrs Newman, who had seven children; she had only three mouths to fill, after all. It was a long time before Mary saw the connection between these phrases, and by then there was only one mouth to feed, her own; for her brother and sister both died of dysentery one very dusty year. Her parents were good friends because of this sorrow for a short while: Mary could remember thinking that it was an ill wind that did no one good; because the two dead children were both so much older than she that they were no good to her as playmates, and the loss was more than compensated by the happiness of living in a house where there were suddenly no quarrels, with a mother who wept, but who had lost that terrible hard indifference. That phase did not last long, however. She looked back on it as the happiest time of her childhood.

The family moved three times before Mary went to school; but afterwards she could not distinguish between the various stations she had lived in. She remembered an exposed dusty village that was backed by a file of bunchy gum trees, with a square of dust always swirling and settling because of passing ox-waggons; with hot sluggish air that sounded several times a day with the screaming and coughing of trains. Dust and chickens; dust and children and wandering natives; dust and the store – always the store.

Then she was sent to boarding school and her life changed. She was extremely happy, so happy that she dreaded going home at holiday-times to her fuddled father, her bitter mother, and the fly-away little house that was like a small wooden box on stilts.

At sixteen she left school and took a job in an office in town: one of those sleepy little towns scattered like raisins in a dry cake over the body of South Africa. Again, she was very happy. She seemed born for typing and shorthand and book-keeping and the comfortable routine of an office. She liked things to happen safely one after another in a pattern, and she liked, particularly, the friendly impersonality of it. By the time she was twenty she had a good job, her own friends, a niche in the town. Then her mother died and she was virtually alone in the world, for her father was five hundred miles away, having been transferred to yet another station. She hardly saw him: he was proud of her, but (which was more to the point) left her alone. They did not even write; they were not the writing sort. Mary was pleased to be rid of him. Being alone in the world had no terrors for her at all, she liked it. And by dropping her father she seemed in some way to be avenging her mother's sufferings. It had never occurred to her that her father, too, might have suffered. 'About what?' she would have retorted, had anyone suggested it. 'He's a man, isn't he? He can do as he likes.' She had inherited from her mother an arid feminism, which had no meaning in her own life at all, for she was leading the comfortable carefee existence of a single woman in South Africa, and she did not know how fortunate she was. How could she know? She understood nothing of conditions in other countries, had no measuring rod to assess herself with.

It had never occurred to her to think, for instance, that she, the daughter of a petty railway official and a woman whose life had been so unhappy because of economic pressure that she had literally pined to death, was living in much the same way as the daughters of the wealthiest in South Africa, could do as she pleased – could marry, if she wished, anyone she wanted. These things did not enter her head. 'Class' is not a South African word; and its equivalent, 'race', meant to her the office boy in the firm where she worked, other women's servants, and the amorphous mass of natives in the streets, whom she hardly noticed. She knew (the phrase was in the air) that the natives were getting 'cheeky'. But she had nothing to do with them really. They were outside her orbit.

Till she was twenty-five nothing happened to break the smooth and comfortable life she led. Then her father died. That removed the last link that bound her to a childhood she hated to remember. There was nothing left to connect her with the sordid little house on stilts, the screaming of trains, the dust, and the strife between her parents. Nothing at all! She was free. And when the funeral was over, and she had returned to the office, she looked forward to a life that would continue as it had so far been. She was very happy: that was perhaps her only positive quality, for there was nothing else distinctive about her, though at twenty-five she was at her prettiest. Sheer contentment put a bloom on her: she was a thin girl, who moved awkwardly, with a fashionable curtain of light-brown hair, serious blue eyes, and pretty clothes. Her friends would have described her as a slim blonde: she modelled herself on the more childish-looking film stars.

At thirty nothing had changed. On her thirtieth birthday she felt a vague surprise that did not even amount to discomfort – for she did not feel any different – that the years had gone past so quickly. Thirty! It sounded a great age. But it had nothing to do with her. At the same time she did not celebrate this birthday; she allowed it to be forgotten. She felt almost outraged that such a thing could happen to her, who was no different from the Mary of sixteen.

She was by now the personal secretary of her employer, and was earning good money. If she had wanted, she could have taken a flat and lived the smart sort of life. She was quite presentable. She had the undistinguished, dead-level appearance of South African white democracy. Her voice was one of thousands: flattened, a little sing-song, clipped. Anyone could have worn her clothes. There was nothing to prevent her living by herself, even running her own car, entertaining on a small scale. She could have become a person on her own account. But this was against her instinct.

She chose to live in a girls' club, which had been started, really, to help women who could not earn much money, but she had been there so long no one thought of asking her to leave. She chose it because it reminded her of school, and she had hated leaving school. She liked the crowds of girls, and eating in a big dining-room, and coming home after the pictures to find a friend in her room waiting for a little gossip. In the Club she was a person of some importance, out of the usual run. For one thing she was so much older than the others. She had come to have what was almost the rôle of a comfortable maiden aunt to whom one can tell one's troubles. For Mary was never shocked, never condemned, never told tales. She seemed impersonal, above the little worries. The stiffness of her manner, her shyness, protected her from many spites and jealousies. She seemed immune. This was her strength, but also a weakness that she would not have considered a weakness: she felt disinclined, almost repelled, by the thought of intimacies and scenes and contacts. She moved among all those young women with a faint aloofness that said as clear as words: I will not be drawn in. And she was quite unconscious of it. She was very happy in the Club.

Outside the girls' club, and the office, where again she was a person of some importance, because of the many years she had worked there, she led a full and active life. Yet it was a passive one, in some respects, for it depended on other people entirely. She was not the kind of woman who initiates parties, or who is the centre of a crowd. She was still the girl who is 'taken out'.

Her life was really rather extraordinary: the conditions which produced it are passing now, and when the change is complete, women will look back on them as on a vanished Golden Age.

She got up late, in time for the office (she was very punctual) but not in time for breakfast. She worked efficiently, but in a leisurely way, until lunch. She went back to the club for lunch. Two more hours' work in the afternoon and she was free. Then she played tennis, or hockey or swam. And always with a man, one of those innumerable men who 'took her out', treating her like a sister: Mary was such a good pal! Just as she seemed to have a hundred women friends, but no particular friend, so she had (it seemed) a hundred men, who had taken her out, or were taking her out, or who had married and now asked her to their homes. She was friend to half the town. And in the evening she always went to sundowner parties that prolonged themselves till midnight, or danced, or went to the pictures. Sometimes she went to the pictures five nights a week. She was never in bed before twelve or later. And so it had gone on, day after day, week after week, year after year. South Africa is a wonderful place: for the unmarried white woman. But she was not playing her part, for she did not get married. The years went past; her friends got married; she had been bridesmaid a dozen times; other people's children were growing up; but she went on as companionable, as adaptable, as aloof and as heart-whole as ever, working as hard enjoying herself as she ever did in the office, and never for one moment alone, except when she was asleep.

She seemed not to care for men. She would say to her girls, 'Men! They get all the fun.' Yet outside the office and the club her life was entirely dependent upon men, though she would have most indignantly repudiated the accusation. And perhaps she was not so dependent upon them really, for when she listened to other people's complaints and miseries she offered none of her own. Sometimes her friends felt a little put off, and let down. It was hardly fair, they felt obscurely, to listen, to advise, to act as a sort of universal shoulder for the world to weep on, and give back nothing of her own. The truth was she had no troubles. She heard other people's complicated stories with wonder, even a little fear. She shrank away from all that. She was a most rare phenomenon: a woman of thirty without love troubles, headaches, backaches, sleeplessness or neurosis. She did not know how rare she was.

And she was still 'one of the girls'. If a visiting cricket team came to town and partners were needed, the organizers would ring up Mary. That was the kind of thing she was good at: adapting herself sensibly and quietly to any occasion. She would sell tickets for a charity dance or act as a dancing partner for a visiting full-back with equal amiability.

And she still wore her hair little-girl fashion on her shoulders, and wore little-girl frocks in pastel colours, and kept her shy, naïve manner. If she had been left alone she would have gone on, in her own way, enjoying herself thoroughly, until people found one day that she had turned imperceptibly into one of those women who have become old without ever having been middle-aged: a little withered, a little acid, hard as nails, sentimentally kindhearted, and addicted to religion or small dogs.

They would have been kind to her, because she had 'missed the best things of life'. But then there are so many people who don't want them: so many for whom the best things have been poisoned from the start. When Mary thought of 'home' she remembered a wooden box shaken by passing trains; when she thought of marriage she remembered her father coming home red-eyed and fuddled; when she thought of children she saw her mother's face at her children's funeral – anguished, but as dry and as hard as rock. Mary liked other people's children but shuddered at the thought of having any of her own. She felt sentimental at weddings, but she had a profound distaste for sex; there had been little privacy in her home and there were things she did not care to remember; she had taken good care to forget them years ago.

She certainly did feel, at times, a restlessness, a vague dissatisfaction that took the pleasure out of her activities for a while. She would be going to bed, for instance, contentedly, after the pictures, when the thought would strike her, 'Another day gone!' And then time would contract and it seemed to her only a breathing space since she left school and came into town to earn her own living; and she would feel a little panicky, as if an invisible support had been drawn away from underneath her. But then, being a sensible person, and firmly convinced that thinking about oneself was morbid, she would get into bed and turn out the lights. She might wonder, before drifting off to sleep, 'Is this all? When I get to be old will this be all I have to look back on?' But by morning she would have forgotten it, and the days went round, and she would be happy again. For she did not know what she wanted. Something bigger, she would think vaguely – a different kind of life. But the mood never lasted long. She was so satisfied with her work, where she felt sufficient and capable; with her friends, whom she relied on; with her life at the Club, which was as pleasant and as gregarious as being in a giant twittering aviary, where there was always the excitement of other people's engagements and weddings: and with her men friends, who treated her just like a good pal, with none of this silly sex business.

But all women become conscious, sooner or later, of that impalpable but steel-strong pressure to get married, and Mary, who was not at all susceptible to atmosphere, or the things people imply, was brought face to face with it suddenly, and most unpleasantly.

She was in the house of a married friend, sitting on the verandah, with a lighted room behind her. She was alone; and heard people talking in low voices, and caught her own name. She rose to go inside and declare herself: it was typical of her that her first thought was, how unpleasant it would be for her friends to know she had overheard. Then she sank down again, and waited for a suitable moment to pretend she had just come in from the garden. This was the conversation she listened to, while her face burned and her hands went clammy.

'She's not fifteen any longer: it is ridiculous! Someone should tell her about her clothes.'

'How old is she?'

'Must be well over thirty. She has been going strong for years. She was working long before I began working, and that was a good twelve years ago.'

'Why doesn't she marry? She must have had plenty of chances.'

There was a dry chuckle. 'I don't think so. My husband was keen on her himself once, but he thinks she will never marry. She just isn't like that, isn't like that at all. Something missing somewhere.'

'Oh, I don't know.'

'She's gone off so much, in any case. The other day I caught sight of her in the street and hardly recognized her. It's a fact! The way she plays all those games, her skin is like sandpaper, and she's got so thin.'

'But she's such a nice girl.'

'She'll never set the rivers on fire, though.'

'She'd make someone a good wife. She's a good sort, Mary.'

'She should marry someone years older than herself. A man of fifty would suit her . . . you'll see, she will marry someone old enough to be her father one of these days.'

'One never can tell!'

There was another chuckle, good-hearted enough, but it sounded cruelly malicious to Mary. She was stunned and outraged; but most of all deeply wounded that her friends could discuss her thus. She was so naïve, so unconscious of herself in relation to other people, that it had never entered her head that people could discuss her behind her back. And the things they had said! She sat there writhing, twisting her hands. Then she composed herself and went back into the room to join her treacherous friends, who greeted her as cordially as if they had not just that moment driven knives into her heart and thrown her quite off balance; she could not recognize herself in the picture they had made of her!

That little incident, apparently so unimportant, which would have had no effect on a person who had the faintest idea of the kind of world she lived in, had a profound effect on Mary. She who had never had time to think of herself, took to sitting in her room for hours at a time, wondering: 'Why did they say those things? What is the matter with me? What did they mean when they said that I am *not like that*?' And she would look warily, appealingly, into the faces of friends to see if she could find there traces of their condemnation of her. And she was even more disturbed and unhappy because they seemed just as usual, treating her with their ordinary friendliness. She began to suspect double meanings where none were intended, to find maliciousness in the glance of a person who felt nothing but affection for her.

Turning over in her mind the words she had by accident listened to, she thought of ways to improve herself. She took the ribbon out of her hair, though with regret, because she thought she looked very pretty with a mass of curls round her rather long thin face; and bought herself tailor-made clothes, in which she felt ill at ease, because she felt truly herself in pinafore frocks and childish skirts. And for the first time in her life she was feeling uncomfortable with men. A small core of contempt for them, of which she was quite unconscious, and which had protected her from sex as surely as if she had been truly hideous, had melted, and she had lost her poise. And she began looking around for someone to marry. She did not put it to herself like that; but, after all, she was nothing if not a social being, though she had never thought of 'society', the abstraction; and if her friends were thinking she should get married, then there might be something in it. If she had ever learned to put her feelings into words, that was perhaps how she would have expressed herself. And the first man she allowed to approach her was a widower of fifty-five with half-grown children. It was because she felt safer with him . . . because she did not associate ardours and embraces with a middle-aged gentleman whose attitude towards her was almost fatherly.

He knew perfectly well what he wanted: a pleasant companion, a mother for his children and someone to run his house for him. He found Mary good company, and she was kind to his children. Nothing, really, could have been more suitable: since apparently she had to get married, this was the kind of marriage to suit her best. But things went wrong. He underestimated her experience; it seemed to him that a woman who had been on her own so long should know her own mind and understand what he was offering her. A relationship developed which was clear to both of them, until he proposed to her, was accepted, and began to make love to her. Then a violent revulsion overcame her and she ran away; they were in his comfortable drawing room, and when he began to kiss her, she ran out of his house into the night and all the way home through the streets to the club. There she fell on the bed and wept. And his feeling for her was not one to be enhanced by this kind of foolishness, which a younger man, physically in love with her, might have found charming. Next morning, she was horrified at her behaviour. What a way to behave; she, who was always in command of herself, and who dreaded nothing more than scenes and ambiguity. She apologized to him, but that was the end of it.

And now she was left at sea, not knowing what it was she

needed. It seemed to her that she had run from him because he was 'an old man', that was how the affair arranged itself in her mind. She shuddered, and avoided men over thirty. She was over that age herself; but in spite of everything, she thought of herself as a girl still.

And all the time, unconsciously, without admitting it to herself, she was looking for a husband.

During those few months before she married, people were discussing her in a way which would have sickened her, had she suspected it. It seems hard that Mary, whose charity towards other people's failures and scandals grew out of a genuine, rock-bottom aversion towards the personal things like love and passion, was doomed all her life to be the subject of gossip. But so it was. At this time, too, the shocking and rather ridiculous story of that night when she had run away from her elderly lover was spreading round the wide circle of her friends, though it is impossible to say who could have known about it in the first place. But when people heard it they nodded and laughed as if it confirmed something they had known for a long time. A woman of thirty behaving like that! They laughed, rather unpleasantly; in this age of scientific sex, nothing seems more ridiculous than sexual gaucherie. They didn't forgive her; they laughed, and felt that in some way it served her right.

She was so changed, they said; she looked so dull and dowdy, and her skin was bad; she looked as if she were going to be ill; she was obviously having a nervous breakdown and at her age it was to be expected, with the way she lived and everything; she was looking for a man and couldn't get one. And then, her manner was so odd, these days . . . These were some of the things they said.

It is terrible to destroy a person's picture of himself in the interests of truth or some other abstraction. How can one know he will be able to create another to enable him to go on living? Mary's idea of herself was destroyed and she was not fitted to recreate herself. She could not exist without that impersonal, casual friendship from other people; and now it seemed to her there was pity in the way they looked at her, and a little impatience, too, as if she were really rather a futile woman after all. She felt as she had never done before; she was hollow inside, empty, and into this emptiness would sweep from nowhere a vast panic, as if there were nothing in the world she could grasp hold of. And she was afraid to meet people, afraid, above all, of men. If a man kissed her (which they did, sensing her new mood), she was revolted; on the other hand she went to the pictures even more frequently than before and came out feverish and unsettled. There seemed no connection between the distorted mirror of the screen and her own life; it was impossible to fit together what she wanted for herself, and what she was offered.

At the age of thirty, this woman who had had a 'good' State education, a thoroughly comfortable life enjoying herself in a civilized way, and access to all knowledge of her time (only she read nothing but bad novels) knew so little about herself that she was thrown completely off her balance because some gossiping women had said she ought to get married.

Then she met Dick Turner. It might have been anybody. Or rather, it would have been the first man she met who treated her as if she were wonderful and unique. She needed that badly. She needed it to restore her feeling of superiority to men, which was really, at bottom, what she had been living from all these years.

They met casually at the cinema. He was in for the day from his farm. He very rarely came into town, except when he had to buy goods he could not get at his local store, and that happened perhaps once or twice a year. On this occasion he ran into a man he had not seen for years and was persuaded to stay the night in town and go to the cinema. He was almost amused at himself for agreeing: all this seemed so very remote from him. His farm lorry, heaped with sacks of grain and two harrows, stood outside the cinema, looking out of place and cumbersome; and Mary looked through the back window at these unfamiliar objects and smiled. It was necessary for her to smile when she saw them. She loved the town, felt safe there, and associated the country with her childhood, because of those little dorps she had lived in, and the way they were all

44

surrounded by miles and miles of nothingness – miles and miles of veld.

Dick Turner disliked the town. When he drove in from the veld he knew so well, through those ugly scattered suburbs that looked as if they had come out of housing catalogues; ugly little houses stuck anyhow over the veld, that had no relationship with the hard brown African soil and the arching blue sky, cosy little houses meant for cosy little countries – and then on into the business part of the town with the shops full of fashions for smart women and extravagant imported food, he felt ill at ease and uncomfortable and murderous.

He suffered from claustrophobia. He wanted to run away – either to run away or to smash the place up. So he always escaped as soon as possible back to his farm, where he felt at home.

But there are thousands of people in Africa who could be lifted bodily out of their suburb and put into a town the other side of the world and hardly notice the difference. The suburb is as invincible and fatal as factories, and even beautiful South Africa, whose soil looks outraged by those pretty little suburbs creeping over it like a disease, cannot escape. When Dick Turner saw them, and thought of the way people lived in them, and the way the cautious suburban mind was ruining *his* country, he wanted to swear and to smash and to murder. He could not bear it. He did not put these feelings into words; he had lost the habit of word-spinning, living the life he did, out on the soil all day. But the feeling was the strongest he knew. He felt he could kill the bankers and the financiers and the magnates and the clerks – all the people who built prim little houses with hedged gardens full of English flowers for preference.

And above all, he loathed the cinema. When he found himself inside the picture-house on this occasion, he wondered what had possessed him that he had agreed to come. He could not keep his eyes on the screen. The long-limbed, smooth-faced women bored him; the story seemed meaningless. And it was hot and stuffy. After a while he ignored the screen altogether, and looked round the audience. In front of him, around him, behind him, rows and rows of people staring and leaning away from each other up at the screen – hundreds of people flown out of their bodies and living in the lives of those stupid people posturing there. It made him feel uneasy.

He fidgeted, lit a cigarette, gazed at the dark plush curtains that masked the exits. And then, looking along the row he was sitting in, he saw a shaft of light fall from somewhere above, showing the curve of a cheek and a sheaf of fairish glinting hair. The face seemed to float, yearning upwards, ruddily gold in the queer greenish light. He poked the man next to him, and said, 'Who is that?' 'Mary,' was the grunted reply, after a brief look. But 'Mary' did not help Dick much. He stared at that lovely floating face and the falling hair, and after the show was over, he looked for her hurriedly in the crush outside the door. But he could not see her. He supposed, vaguely, that she had gone with someone else. He was given a girl to take home whom he hardly glanced at. She was dressed in what seemed to him a ridiculous way, and he wanted to laugh at her high heels, in which she tiptapped beside him across the street. In the car she looked over her shoulder at the piled back of the lorry, and asked in a hurried affected voice: 'What are those funny things at the back?'

'Have you never seen a harrow?' he asked. He dropped her, without regret, at the place where she lived – a big building, which was full of light and people. He forgot her immediately.

But he dreamed about the girl with the young uptilted face and the wave of loose gleaming hair. It was a luxury, dreaming about a woman, for he had forbidden himself such things. He had started farming five years before, and was still not making it pay. He was indebted to the Land Bank, and heavily mortgaged, for he had had no capital at all, when he started. He had given up drink, cigarettes, all but the necessities. He worked as only a man possessed by a vision can work, from six in the morning till seven at night, taking his meals on the lands, his whole being concentrated on the farm. His dream was to get married and have children. Only he could not ask a woman to share such a life. First he would have to get out of debt, build a house, be able to afford the little luxuries. Having driven himself for years, it was part of his dream to spoil a wife. He knew exactly what sort of a house he would build: not one of those meaningless block-like buildings stuck on top of the soil. He wanted a big thatched house with wide verandahs open to the air. He had even chosen the ant-heaps that he would dig to make his bricks, and had marked the parts of the farm where the grass grew tallest, taller than a big man, for the thatch. But it seemed to him sometimes that he was very far from getting what he wanted. He was pursued by bad luck. The farmers about him, he knew, called him 'Jonah'. If there was a drought he seemed to get the brunt of it, and if it rained in swamps then his farm suffered most. If he decided to grow cotton for the first time, cotton slumped that year, and if there was a swarm of locusts, then he took it for granted, with a kind of angry but determined fatalism, that they would make straight for his most promising patch of mealies. His dream had become a little less grandiose of late. He was lonely, he wanted a wife, and above all, children; and the way things were it would be years before he had them. He was beginning to think that if he could pay off *some* of the mortgage, and add an extra room to his house, perhaps get some furniture, then he could think of getting married. In the meantime he thought of the girl in the cinema. She became the focus of his work and imaginings. He cursed himself for it, for he knew thinking about women, particularly one woman, was as dangerous as drink to him, but it was no good. Just over a month after his visit to town, he found himself planning another. It was not necessary and he knew it. He gave up even persuading himself that it was necessary. In town, he did the little business he had to do quickly, and went in search of someone who could tell him 'Mary's' surname.

When he drove up to the big building, he recognized it, but did not connect the girl he had driven home that night with the girl of the cinema. Even when she came to the door, and stood in the hall looking to see who he was, he did not recognize her. He saw a tall, thin girl, with deeply blue, rather evasive eyes that looked hurt. Her hair was in tight ridges round her head; she wore trousers. Women in trousers did not seem to him females at all: he was properly old-fashioned. Then she said,

'Are you looking for me?' rather puzzled and shy; and at once he remembered that silly voice asking about the harrows and stared at her incredulously. He was so disappointed he began to stammer and shift his feet. Then he thought that he could not stand there for ever, staring at her, and he asked her to go for a drive. It was not a pleasant evening. He was angry with himself for his self-delusion and weakness; she was flattered but puzzled as to why he had sought her out, since he hardly spoke now he had got her into the car and was driving aimlessly around the town. But he wanted to find in her the girl who had haunted him, and he had done so, by the time he had to take her home. He kept glancing at her sideways as they passed street lamps, and he could see how a trick of light had created something beautiful and strange from an ordinary and not very attractive girl. And then, he began to like her, because it was essential for him to love somebody; he had not realized how very lonely he had been. And when he left her that night, it was with regret, saying he would come again soon.

Back on the farm, he took himself to task. This would end in marriage if he were not careful, and he simply could not afford it. That was the end of it, then; he would forget her, put the whole thing out of his mind. Besides, what did he know about her? Nothing at all! Except that she was obviously, as he put it, 'thoroughly spoiled'. She was not the kind to share a struggling farmer's life. So he argued with himself, working harder than he had ever done before, and thinking sometimes, 'After all, if I have a good season this year I might go back and see her.' He took to walking ten miles over the veld with his gun after his day's work to exhaust himself. He wore himself out, grew thin and haunted-looking. He fought with himself for two months, until at last one day he found himself preparing to take the car into town, exactly as if he had decided it long ago, and as if all his exhortations and self-discipline had been nothing but a shield to hide from himself his real intention. As he dressed he whistled jauntily, but with a crestfallen undertone; and his face wore a curious little defeated smile.

As for Mary, those two months were a long nightmare. He had come all the way in from his farm after meeting her once for five minutes, and then, having spent an evening with her, had not thought it worth his while to come back. Her friends were right, she lacked something. There was something wrong with her. But she clung to the thought of him, in spite of the fact that she said to herself she was useless, a failure, a ridiculous creature whom no one wanted. She gave up going out in the evenings, and remained in her room waiting for him to call for her. She sat for hours and hours by herself, her mind numb with misery; and at night she dreamed long grey dreams in which she struggled through sand, or climbed staircases which collapsed as she reached the top, letting her slide back to the bottom again. She woke in the mornings tired and depressed, unable to face the day. Her employer, used to her inevitable efficiency, told her to take a holiday and not to come back till she felt better. She left the office, feeling as if she had been thrown out (though he could not have been nicer about her breakdown) and stayed all day in the club. If she went away for a holiday she might miss Dick. Yet what was Dick to her, really? Nothing. She hardly knew him. He was a spare, sunburnt, slow-voiced, deep-eyed young man who had come into her life like an accident, and that was all she could say about him. And yet, she would have said it was for his sake she was making herself ill. All her restlessness, her vague feelings of inadequacy, centred on him, and when she asked herself, in chilly dismay, why it should be he, rather than any of the other men she knew, there was no satisfactory reply.

Weeks after she had given up hope, and had gone to the doctor for a prescription because 'she was feeling tired' and had been told she must take a holiday at once, if she wanted to avoid complete breakdown; when she had reached a stage of misery that made it impossible for her to meet any of her old friends, because of her obsession that their friendship was a cloak for malicious gossip and real dislike of her, she was called to the door again one evening. She was not thinking about Dick. When she saw him it took all her self-control to greet him calmly; if she had shown her emotion he might after all have given her up. By now he had persuaded himself into believing she was a practical. adaptable, serene person, who would need only a few weeks on the farm to become what he wanted her to be. Tears of hysteria would have shocked him, ruined his vision of her.

It was to an apparently calm, maternal Mary that he proposed. He was adoring, self-abasing, and grateful when she accepted him. They were married by special licence two weeks later. Her desire to get married as quickly as possible surprised him; he saw her as a busy and popular woman with a secure place in the social life of the town, and thought it would take her some time to arrange her affairs: this idea of her was part of her attraction for him. But a quick marriage fell in with his plans, really. He hated the idea of waiting about the town while a woman fussed with clothes and bridesmaids. There was no honeymoon. He explained he was too poor really to afford one, though if she insisted he would do what he could. She did not insist. She was very relieved to escape a honeymoon.

3

It was a long way from the town to the farm – well over a hundred miles; and by the time he told her they had crossed the boundary, it was late at night. Mary, who was half asleep, roused herself to look at his farm, and saw the dim shapes of low trees, like great soft birds, flying past; and beyond it a hazy sky that was cracked and seamed with stars. Her tiredness relaxed her limbs, quietened her nerves. Reaction from the strained state of the last few months was a dulled acquiescence, a numbness, that was almost indifference. She thought it would be pleasant to live peacefully for a change; she had not realized how exhausted she was, after those years of living geared to a perpetual demand for the next thing. She said to herself, with determination to face it, that she would 'get close to nature'. It was a phrase that took away the edge of her distaste for the veld. 'Getting close to nature', which was sanctioned, after all, by the pleasant sentimentality of the sort of books she read, was a reassuring abstraction. At the week-ends, when she worked in town, she had often gone out for picnics with crowds of young people, to sit all day on hot rocks in the shade, listening to a portable gramophone playing dance music from America, and had thought of that, too, as 'getting close to nature'. 'It is nice to get out of the town,' she would say. But like most people, the things she said bore no relation at all to the things she felt: she was always profoundly relieved to get back to hot and cold water in taps and the streets and the office.

Still, she would be her own mistress: that was marriage, what her friends had married for – to have homes of their own and no one to tell them what to do. She felt vaguely that she had been right to marry – everyone had been right. For, looking back, it seemed to her that all the people she had met were secretly, silently but relentlessly, persuading her to marry. She was going to be happy. She had no idea of the life she had to lead. Poverty, which Dick had warned her of with a scrupulous humility, was another abstraction, nothing to do with her pinched childhood. She saw it as a rather exhilarating fight against odds.

The car stopped at last and she roused herself. The moon had gone behind a great luminous white cloud, and it was suddenly very dark – miles of darkness under a dimly starlit sky. All around were trees, the squat, flattened trees of the highveld, which seem as if pressure of sun has distorted them, looking now like vague dark presences standing about the small clearing where the car had stopped. There was a small square building whose corrugated roof began to gleam whitely as the moon slowly slid out from behind the cloud and drenched the clearing with brilliance. Mary got out of the car and watched it drive away round the house to the back. She looked round her, shivering a little, for a cold breath blew out of the trees and down in the vlei beyond them hung a cold white vapour. Listening in the complete silence, innumerable little noises rose from the bush, as if colonies of strange creatures had become still and watchful at their coming and were now going about their own business. She glanced round at the house; it looked shut and dark and stuffy, under that wide streaming moonlight. A border of stones glinted whitely in front of her, and she walked along them, away from the house and towards the trees, seeing them grow large and soft as she approached. Then a strange bird called, a wild nocturnal sound, and she turned and ran back, suddenly terrified, as if a hostile breath had blown upon her, from another world, from the trees. And as she stumbled in her high heels over the uneven ground and regained balance, there was a stir and a cackle of fowls that had been wakened by the lights of the car, and the homely sound comforted her. She stopped before the house, and put out her hand to touch the leaves of a plant standing in a tin on the wall of the verandah. Her fingers were fragrant with the dry scent of geraniums. Then a square of light appeared in the blank wall of the house, and she saw Dick's tall shape stooping inside, hazed by the candle he held in front of him. She went up the steps to the door, and stood waiting. Dick had vanished again, leaving the candle on the table. In the dim yellow light the room seemed tiny, tiny; and very low; the roof was the corrugated iron she had seen from outside; there was a strong musty smell, almost animal-like. Dick came back holding an old cocoa tin flattened at the rim to form a funnel, and climbed on the chair under the hanging lamp to fill it. The paraffin dripped greasily down and pattered on the floor, and the strong smell sickened her. The light flared up, flickered wildly, then settled into a low yellow flame. Now she could see the skins of animals on the red brick floor: some kind of wildcat, or perhaps a small leopard, and a big fawn-coloured skin of some buck. She sat down, bewildered by the strangeness of it all. Dick was watching her face, she knew, for signs of disappointment, and she forced herself to smile, though she felt weak with foreboding: this tiny stuffy room, the bare brick floor, the greasy lamp, were not what she had imagined. Apparently satisfied, Dick smiled at her gratefully, and said, 'I will make some tea.' He disappeared again. When he came back, she was standing by the wall, looking at two pictures that hung there. One was of a chocolate-box lady with a rose in her hand; and the other was of a child of about six, torn off a calendar.

He flushed when he saw her, and stripped the pictures from the walls. 'I haven't looked at them for years,' he said, tearing them across. 'But leave them,' she said, feeling an intruder on this man's intimate life: the two pictures, stuck up roughly on the wall with tintacks, had given her for the first time an insight into his loneliness, and made her understand his hurried courtship and blind need for her. But she felt alien to him, unable to fit herself to his need. Looking to the floor, she saw the pretty childish face, topped with curls, torn across, lying where he had thrown it. She picked it up, thinking that he must be fond of children. They had never discussed children; there had not been time to discuss much. She looked for a waste-paper basket, for it offended her to see the scraps of paper on the floor, but Dick took it from her, squeezed it into a ball, and flung it into the corner. 'We can put up something else,' he said shyly. It was his shyness, his deference towards her, that enabled her to hold her own. Feeling protectively towards him, which she did when he looked like that, bashful and appealing, she need not think of him as the man she had married who had claims on her. She sat herself down, with composure, in front of the tray he had brought in, and watched him pour tea. On a tin tray was a stained, torn cloth, and two enormous cracked cups. Across her wave of distaste came his voice: 'But that is your job now'; and she took the teapot from him, and poured, feeling him watching her with proud delight.

Now she was here, the woman, clothing his bare little house with her presence, he could hardly contain himself with pleasure and exaltation. It seemed to him that he had been a fool to wait so long, living alone, planning a future that was so easily attainable. And then he looked at her town clothes, her high heels, her reddened nails, and was uneasy again. To hide it, he began talking about the house, with diffidence because of his poverty, never taking his eyes off her face. He told her how he had built it himself, laying the bricks, although he had known nothing about building, to save the wages of a native builder; how he had furnished it slowly, at first with only a bed to sleep in and a packing-case to eat off; how a neighbour had given him a table, and another a chair, and gradually the place had taken shape. The cupboards were petrol boxes painted and covered with curtains of flowered stuff. There was no door between this room and the next, but a heavy curtain of sacking hung there, which had been embroidered all over in red and black wool by Charlie Slatter's wife, on the next farm. And so on; she heard the history of each thing, and saw that what seemed so pathetic and frail to her represented to him victories over discomfort; and she began to feel, slowly, that it was not in this house she was sitting, with her husband, but back with her mother, watching her endlessly contrive and patch and mend – till suddenly she got to her feet with an awkward scrambling movement, unable to bear it; possessed with the thought that her father, from his grave, had sent out his will and forced her back into the kind of life he had made her mother lead.

'Let's go next door,' she said abruptly, her voice harsh. Dick rose also, surprised and a little hurt, cut off in the middle of his histories. Next door was the bedroom. There was a hanging cupboard, again of embroidered sacking; a stack of shelves, petrol boxes with a mirror balanced on top; and the bed which Dick had bought for the occasion. It was a proper old-fashioned bed, high and massive: that was his idea of marriage. He had bought it at a sale, feeling, as he put down the money, that he was capturing happiness itself.

Seeing her stand there, looking about her with a lost pathetic face, unconsciously holding her hands to her cheeks as if in pain, he was sorry for her, and left her alone to undress. Undressing himself beyond the curtain he felt again a bitter pang of guilt. He had no right to marry, no right, no right. He said it under his breath, torturing himself with the repetition; and when he knocked timidly on the wall and went in to find her lying in bed with her back turned, he approached her with the timid adoration which was the only touch she could have borne.

It was not so bad, she thought, when it was all over: not as bad as *that*. It meant nothing to her, nothing at all. Expecting outrage and imposition, she was relieved to find she felt nothing. She was able maternally to bestow the gift of herself on this humble stranger, and remain untouched. Women have an extraordinary ability to withdraw from the sexual relationship, to immunize themselves against it, in such a way that their men can be left feeling let down and insulted without having anything tangible to complain of. Mary did not have to learn this, because it was natural to her, and because she had expected nothing in the first place – at any rate, not from this man, who was flesh and blood, and therefore rather ridiculous – not the creature of her imagination whom she endowed with hands and lips but left bodiless. And if Dick felt as if he had been denied, rebuffed, made to appear brutal and foolish, then his sense of guilt told him that it was no more than he deserved. Perhaps he *needed* to feel guilty? Perhaps it was not such a bad marriage after all? There are innumerable marriages where two people, both twisted and wrong in their depths, are well matched, making each other miserable in the way they need, in the way the pattern of their lives demands. In any event, when he leaned over to turn out the light, and saw her little spiked shoes tumbled sideways on the skin of the leopard he had shot the year before, he repeated to himself again, but with a thrill of satisfaction in his abasement, 'I had no right.'

Mary watched the wildly flickering flame of the dying lamp leap over walls and roof and the glittering window panes, and fell asleep holding his hand protectively, as she might have held a child's whom she had wounded.

4

When she woke she found she was alone in the bed, and there was the clanging of a gong somewhere at the back of the house. She could see a tender gold light on the trees through the window, and faint rosy patches of sun lay on the white walls, showing up the rough grain of the whitewash. As she watched they deepened and turned vivid yellow, barring the room with gold, which made it look smaller, lower, and more bare than it had at night, in the dim lamplight. In a few moments Dick came back in pyjamas, and touched her cheek with his hand, so that she felt the chill of early morning on his skin.

'Sleep well?'

'Yes, thank you.'

'Tea is coming now.'

They were polite and awkward with each other, repudiating the contacts of the night. He sat on the edge of the bed eating biscuits. Presently an elderly native brought in the tray, and put it on the table.

'This is the new missus,' said Dick to him.

'This is Samson, Mary.'

The old boy kept his eyes on the ground and said, 'Good morning, missus.' Then he added politely to Dick, as if this was expected of him, 'Very nice, very nice, boss.'

Dick laughed, saying, 'He'll look after you: he is not a bad old swine.'

Mary was rather outraged at this casual stockmarket attitude; then she saw that it was only a matter of form, and calmed herself. She was left with a feeling of indignation, saying to herself, 'And who does he think *he* is?' Dick, however, was unaware, and foolishly happy.

He drank two cups of tea in a rush, and then went out to dress, coming back in khaki shorts and shirt to say goodbye before going down to the lands. Mary got up, too, when he had gone, and looked around her. Samson was cleaning the room into which they had come first the night before, and all the furniture was pushed into the middle, so she stepped past him on to the small verandah which was merely an extension of the iron roof, held up by three brick pillars with a low wall about it. There were some petrol tins painted a dark green, the paint blistered and broken, holding geraniums and flowering shrubs. Beyond the verandah wall was a space of pale sand, and then the low scrubby bush, which sloped down in a vlei full of tall shining grass. Beyond that again stretched bush, undulating vleis and ridges, bounded at the horizon by kopjes. Looking round she saw that the house was built on a low rise that swelled up in a great hollow several miles across, and ringed by kopjes that coiled blue and hazy and beautiful, a long way off in front, but close to the house at the back. She thought, it will be hot here, closed in as it is. But she shaded her eyes and gazed across the vleis, finding it strange and lovely with the dull green foliage, the endless expanses of tawny grass shining gold in the sun, and the vivid arching blue sky. And there was a chorus of birds, a shrilling and cascading of sound such as she had not heard before.

She walked round the house to the back. She saw it was a rectangle: the two rooms she had already seen in the front, and behind them the kitchen, the storeroom and the bathroom. At the end of a short path, screened off with a curving break of grass, was a narrow sentry-box building, which was the lavatory. On one side was a fowlhouse, with a great wire run full of scrawny white chickens, and across the hard bare ground scraped and gobbled a scattering of turkeys. She entered the house from the back through the kitchen, where there was a wood stove and a massive table of scrubbed bush timber, taking up half the floor space. Samson was in the bedroom, making the bed.

She had never come into contact with natives before, as an employer on her own account. Her mother's servants she had been forbidden to talk to; in the club she had been kind to the waiters; but the 'native problem' meant for her other women's complaints of their servants at tea parties. She was afraid of them, of course. Every woman in South Africa is brought up to be. In her childhood she had been forbidden to walk out alone, and when she had asked why, she had been told in the furtive, lowered, but matter-of-fact voice she associated with her mother, that they were nasty and might do horrible things to her.

And now she had to face it, this business of struggling with natives – she took it for granted it would be a struggle – and felt reluctant, though determined not to be imposed upon. But she was disposed to like Samson, who was a kind-faced respectful old native, who asked her, as she entered the bedroom, 'Missus like to see the kitchen?'

She had hoped Dick would show her round, but seeing that the native was eager to, she agreed. He padded out of the room in front of her on his bare feet and took her to the back. There he opened the pantry for her – a dim, high-windowed place full of provisions of all kinds, with great metal bins for sugar, flour and meal, standing on the floor.

'Boss has keys,' he explained; and she was amused at his matter-of-fact acceptance of a precaution that could only be against his stealing.

Between Samson and Dick there was a perfect understanding. Dick locked up everything, but put out for use a third as much again as was required, which was used by Samson, who did not regard this as stealing. But there was not much to steal in that bachelor household, and Samson hoped for better things now there was a woman. With deference and courtesy he showed Mary the thin supplies of linen, the utensils, the way the stove worked, the wood-pile at the back – all with the air of a faithful caretaker handing over keys to the rightful owner. He also showed her, when she asked, the old plough disc hung on the bough of a tree over the wood-pile, with the rusting iron bolt from a waggon with which it was beaten. It was this that she had heard on waking that morning; it was beaten at half-past five to rouse the boys in the compound close by and again at twelve-thirty and two, to mark the dinner break. It was a heavy, clanging, penetrating noise that carried miles over the bush.

She went back into the house while the boy prepared breakfast; already the song of the birds had been quenched by the deepening heat; at seven in the morning Mary found her forehead damp and her limbs sticky.

Dick came back half an hour later, glad to see her, but preoccupied. He went straight through the house into the back, and she heard him shouting at Samson in kitchen kaffir. She did not understand a word of it. Then he came back and said:

'That old fool has let those dogs go again. I told him not to.'

'What dogs?'

He explained: 'They get restless and go out by themselves, for hunting trips, if I am not here. Sometimes for days. Always when I am not here. He let them out. Then they get into trouble in the bush. Because he is too damned lazy to feed them.'

He sat heavy and silent through the meal, a nervous tension between his eyes. The planter had broken down, a water cart had lost a wheel, the waggon had been driven up a hill with the brake on, in sheer lighthearted carelessness. He was back in it, over his head in it, with the familiar irritations and the usual sense of helplessness against cheerful incompetence. Mary said nothing: this was all too strange for her.

Immediately after breakfast he took his hat off the chair and went off again. Mary looked for a cooking book and took it to the kitchen. Half-way through the morning the dogs returned, two large mongrels, cheerfully apologetic to Samson for their truancy, but ignoring her, the stranger. They drank deeply, slobbering trails of water over the kitchen floor, then went to sleep on the skins in the front room smelling heavily of the kill in the bush.

When her cooking experiments were over – which the native Samson watched with an air of polite forbearance – she settled down on the bed with a handbook on kitchen kaffir. This was clearly the first thing she had to learn: she was unable to make Samson understand her.

5

With her own saved money Mary bought flowered materials, and covered cushions and made curtains; bought a little linen, crockery, and some dress lengths. The house gradually lost its air of bleak poverty, and put on an inexpensive prettiness, with bright hangings and some pictures. Mary worked hard, and looked for Dick's look of approval and surprise when he came back from work and noted every new change. A month after she had arrived she walked through the house, and saw there was nothing more to be done. Besides, there was no more money.

She had settled easily into the new rhythm. She found the change so embracing that it was as if she were an entirely new person. Every morning she woke with the clanging of the plough disc, and drank tea in bed with Dick. When he had gone down on the lands she put out groceries for the day. She was so conscientious that Samson found things had worsened rather than improved: even his understood one-third allowance had gone, and she wore the store keys tied to her belt. By breakfast time what work she had to do in the house was finished except for light cooking; but Samson was a better cook than she, and after a while she left it to him. She sewed all morning, till lunchtime; sewed after lunch, and went to bed immediately after supper, sleeping like a child all night.

In the first flush of energy and determination she really enjoyed the life, putting things to rights and making a little go a long way. She liked, particularly, the early mornings before the heat numbed and tired her; liked the new leisure; liked Dick's approval. For his pride and affectionate gratitude for what she was doing (he would never have believed that his forlorn house could look like this) overshadowed his patient disappointment. When she saw that puzzled hurt look on his face, she pushed away the thought of what he must be suffering, for it made him repulsive to her again.

Then, having done all she could to the house, she began on dress materials, finishing an inexpensive trousseau. A few months after her marriage she found there was nothing more to do. Suddenly, from one day to the next, she found herself unoccupied. Instinctively staving off idleness as something dangerous, she returned to her underwear, and embroidered everything that could possibly be embroidered. There she sat all day, sewing and stitching, hour after hour, as if fine embroidery would save her life. She was a good needle-woman, and the results were admirable. Dick praised her work and was amazed, for he had expected a difficult period while she was settling down, thinking she would take the lonely life hard at first. But she showed no signs of being lonely, she seemed perfectly satisfied to sew all day. And all this time he treated her like a brother, for he was a sensitive man, and was waiting for her to turn to him of her own accord. The relief she was unable to hide that his endearments were no more than affectionate, hurt him deeply, but he still thought: It will come right in the end.

There came an end to embroidery; again she was left empty-handed. Again she looked about for something to do. The walls, she decided, were filthy. She would whitewash them all herself, to save money. So, for two weeks, Dick came back to the house to find furniture stacked in the middle of rooms and pails of thick white stuff standing on the floor. But she was very methodical. One room was finished before another was begun; and while he admired her for her capability and self-assurance, undertaking this work she had no experience or knowledge of, he was alarmed too. What was she going to do with all this energy and efficiency? It undermined his own self-assurance even further, seeing her like this, for he knew, deep down, that this quality was one he lacked. Soon, the walls were dazzling blue-white, every inch of them painted by Mary herself, standing on a rough ladder for days at a time.

And now she found she was tired. She found it pleasant to let go a little, and to spend her time sitting with her hands folded, on the big sofa. But not for long. She was restless, so restless she did not know what to do with herself. She unpacked the novels she had brought with her, and turned them over. These were the books she had collected over years from the mass that had come her way. She had read each one a dozen times, knowing it by heart, following the familiar tales as a child listens to his mother telling him a well-known fairy tale. It had been a drug, a soporific, in the past, reading them; now, as she turned them over listlessly, she wondered why they had lost their flavour. Her mind wandered as she determinedly turned the pages; and she realized, after she had been reading for perhaps an hour, that she had not taken in a word. She threw the book aside and tried another, but with the same result. For a few days the house was littered with books in faded dust covers. Dick was pleased: it flattered him to think he had married a woman who read books. One evening he picked up a book called *The Fair Lady*, and opened it in the middle.

'. . . The trekkers trekked North, towards the Land of Promise where never the cold grasping hand of the hated British could reach them. Like a cold snake through the hot landscape the column coiled. Prunella Van Koetzie skirmished lightly on her horse on the perimeter of the column, wearing a white *kappie* over her dainty sweat pearled face and close clustering ringlets. Piet Van Friesland watched her, his heart throbbing in time to the great blood-stained heart of South Africa itself. Could he win her, the sweet Prunella, who bore herself like a queen among these burghers and mynheers and buxom fraus in their *doeks* and *veldschoens*? Could he? He stared and stared. Tant' Anna, putting out the *koekies* and the *biltong* for the midday meal, in a red *doek* the colour of the *kaffir-boom* trees, shook her fat sides in laughter and said to herself, "That will be a match yet."'

He put it down, and looked across at Mary, who was sitting with a book in her lap, staring up at the roof.

'Can't we have ceilings, Dick?' she asked fretfully.

'It would cost so much,' he said doubtfully. 'Perhaps next year, if we do well.'

In a few days Mary gathered up the books and put them away; they were not what she wanted. She took up the handbook on kitchen kaffir again, and spent all her time on it, practising on Samson in the kitchen, disconcerting him with her ungood-humoured criticisms, but behaving with a cold-dispassionate justice.

Samson became more and more unhappy. He had been so used to Dick, and they understood each other very well. Dick swore at him often, but laughed with him afterwards. This woman never laughed. She put out, carefully, so much meal, and so much sugar; and watched the left-overs from their own food with an extraordinary, humiliating capacity for remembering every cold potato and every piece of bread, asking for them if they were missing.

Shaken out of his comparatively comfortable existence, he grew sulky. There were several rows in the kitchen, and once Dick found Mary in tears. She knew there had been enough raisins put out for the pudding, but when they came to eat it, there were hardly any. And the boy denied stealing them . . .

'Good heavens,' said Dick, amused, 'I thought there was something really wrong.'

'But I *know* he took them,' sobbed Mary.

'He probably did, but he's a good old swine on the whole.'

'I am going to take it out of his wages.'

Dick, puzzled at her emotional state, said: 'If you think it is really necessary.' He reflected that this was the first time he had seen her cry.

So Samson, who earned a pound a month, was docked two shillings. He accepted the information with a shut sullen face, saying nothing to her, but appealing to Dick, who told him that he was to take orders from Mary. Samson gave notice that evening, on the grounds that he was needed in his kraal. Mary began to question him closely as to why he was needed; but Dick touched her arm warningly and shook his head.

'Why shouldn't I ask him?' she demanded. 'He's lying, isn't he?'

'Of course he's lying,' said Dick irritably. 'Of course. That is not the point. You can't keep him against his will.'

'Why should I accept a lie?' said Mary. 'Why should I? Why can't he say straight out that he doesn't like working for me, instead of lying about his kraal?'

Dick shrugged, looking at her with impatience; he could not understand her unreasonable insistence: he knew how to get on with natives; dealing with them was a sometimes amusing, sometimes annoying game in which both sides followed certain unwritten rules.

'You would be angry if he did say so,' he remarked ruefully, but with affection still; he could not take her seriously, she seemed to him a child when she behaved like this. And he was genuinely grieved that this old native, who had worked for him all these years, was going now. 'Well,' he said at last, philosophically, 'I should have expected it. I should have got a new boy right from the beginning. There's always trouble with a change of management.'

Mary watched the farewell scene, that took place on the back steps, from the doorway. She was filled with wonder, and even repulsion. Dick was really sorry to see the end of this nigger! She could not understand any white person feeling anything personal about a native; it made Dick seem really horrible to her. She heard him say, 'When your work in the kraal is finished, you will come back and work for us again?' The native answered, 'Yes, baas,' but he was already turned to go; and Dick came back into the house silent and glum. 'He won't come back,' he said.

'There are plenty of other munts, aren't there?' she asked snappily, disliking him.

'Yes,' he assented, 'oh yes.'

It was several days before a new cook offered himself for work, and Mary did the house herself. She found it unexpectedly heavy, although there was not, really, so much to do. Yet she liked the feeling of being alone there all day, responsible for it. She scrubbed and swept and polished; housework was quite a new thing to her; all her life natives had done the work for her, as silently and as unobtrusively as fairies. Because it was new, she really enjoyed it. But when everything was clean and polished, and the pantry was full of food, she used to sit on the old greasy sofa in the front room, suddenly collapsing on it as if her legs had been drained of strength. It was so hot! She had never imagined it could be so hot. The sweat poured off her all day; she could feel it running down her ribs and thighs under her dress, as if ants were crawling over her. She used to sit quite, quite still, her eyes closed, and feel the heat beating down from the iron over her head. Really, it was so bad she should wear a hat even in the house. If Dick had ever really lived in this house, she thought, instead of being down on the lands all day, he would have put in ceilings. Surely they did not cost so much? As the days passed, she found herself thinking fretfully that she had been foolish to spend her little store of money on curtains rather than on ceilings. If she asked Dick again, and explained to him what it meant to her, perhaps he would relent and find the money? But she knew she could not easily ask, and bring that heavy tormented look on his face. For by now she had become used to that look. Though really, she liked it: deep down, she liked it very much. When he took her hand endearingly, and kissed it submissively, and said pleadingly, 'Darling, do you hate me for bringing you here?' she replied, 'No, dear, you know I don't.' It was the only time she could bring herself to use endearments to him, when she was feeling victorious and forgiving. His craving for forgiveness, and his abasement before her was the greatest satisfaction she knew, although she despised him for it.

So she used to sit on that sofa, her eyes shut, suffering because of the heat, and feeling at the same time tenderly sorrowful and queenly . . . because of her willingness to suffer.

And then, suddenly, the heat became intolerable. Outside in the bush the cicadas shrilled incessantly, and her head ached; her limbs were heavy and tense. She would get up and go into the bedroom, and examine her clothes, to see if there was nothing she could do: no bit of embroidery, or an alteration. She looked through Dick's things for darning and mending; but he wore nothing but shirts and shorts, and if she sometimes found a button off she was lucky. With nothing to do, she would wander on to the verandah, to sit watching the lights change on the distant blue kopjes; or she would go to the back of the house where the little kopje stood, a rough heap of giant boulders, and watch the heat-waves beat up out of the hot stone, where the heat-lizards, vivid red and blue and emerald, darted over the rocks like flames. Until at last her head began to swim, and she had to go back to the house to get a glass of water.

Then came a native to the back door, asking for work. He wanted seventeen shillings a month. She beat him down by two, feeling pleased with herself because of her victory over him. He was a native straight from his kraal, a youth, probably not out of his 'teens, thin with the long, long walk through the bush from his home in Nyasaland, hundreds of miles away. He was unable to understand her, and very nervous. He carried himself stiffly, his shoulders rigid, in a hunched attentive attitude, never taking his eyes off her, afraid to miss her slightest look. She was irritated by this subservience and her voice was hard. She showed him all over the house, corner by corner, cupboard by cupboard, explaining to him how things should be done in her by now fluent kitchen kaffir. He followed her like a scared dog. He had never seen forks and knives and plates before, though he had heard legends of these extraordinary objects from friends returning from service in the white men's houses. He did not know what to do with them; and she expected him to know the difference between a pudding plate and a dinner plate. She stood over him while he laid the table; and all the afternoon she kept him at it, explaining, exhorting and spurring him on. That night, at supper, he laid the table badly, and she flew at him, in a frenzy of annoyance, while Dick sat and watched her uneasily. When the native had gone out, he said: 'You have to take things easy, you know, with a new boy.'

'But I told him! If I have told him once I have told him fifty times!'

'But this is probably the first time he has ever been in a white man's house!'

'I don't care. I told him what to do. Why doesn't he do it?'

He looked at her attentively, his forehead contracted, his lips tight. She seemed possessed by irritation, not herself at all.

'Mary, listen to me for a moment. If you get yourself into a state over your boys, then you are finished. You will have to let go your standards a little. You must go easy.'

'I won't let go my standards. I won't! Why should I? It's bad enough . . .' She stopped herself. She had been going to say, 'It is bad enough living in a pigsty like this . . .'

He sensed that was what she had been going to say, and he dropped his head and stared at his plate. But this time he did not appeal to her. He was angry; he did not feel submissive and in the wrong; and when she went on : 'I told him how to lay this table,' speaking in a hot, blind, tired voice, he got up from the meal and went outside; and she could see the spurt of a match and the rapid glowing of a cigarette. So! He was annoyed, was he? So annoyed that he broke his rule about never smoking until after dinner! Well, let him be annoyed.

The next day at lunch, the servant dropped a plate through nervousness, and she dismissed him at once. Again she had to do her own work, and this time she felt aggrieved, hating it, and blaming it on the offending native whom she had sacked without payment. She cleaned and polished tables and chairs and plates, as if she were scrubbing skin off a black face. She was consumed with hatred. At the same time, she was making a secret resolution not to be quite so pernickety with the next servant she found.

The next boy was quite different. He had had years of experience working for white women who treated him as if he were a machine; and he had learned to present a blank, neutral surface, and to answer in a soft neutral voice. He replied gently, to everything she said, 'Yes, missus; yes, missus,' not looking at her. It made her angry that he would never meet her eyes. She did not know it was part of the native code of politeness not to look a superior in the face; she thought it was merely further evidence of their shifty and dishonest nature. It was simply as if he were not really there, only a black body ready to do her bidding. And that enraged her too. She felt she would like to pick up a plate and throw it in his face so as to make it human and expressive, even with pain. But she was icily correct this time; and though she never for a moment took her eye off him, and followed him round after the work was finished, calling him back for every speck of dust or smear of grease, she was careful not to go too far. This boy she would keep: so she said to herself. But she never relaxed her will; her will that he would do as she said, as she wanted, in every tiny thing.

Dick saw all this with increasing foreboding. What was the matter with her? With him she seemed at ease, quiet, almost maternal. With the natives she was a virago. He asked her – in order to get her away from the house – to come down on the lands with him to see how he worked. He felt that if she could be really close to him in his problems and worries, they would be drawn closer together. Besides, it was lonely for him, all those hours and hours of walking, walking round the lands by himself, watching the labourers work.

She assented, rather dubiously, for she did not really want to go. When she thought of him down there in the heat mirage close to the heavy steaming red soil, beside the reeking bodies of the working natives, it was as if she thought of a man in a submarine, someone who voluntarily descended into a strange and alien world. But she fetched her hat and dutifully accompanied him in the car.

For the whole of one morning she followed him around, from field to field, from one gang of boys to the next; and all the time, at the back of her mind, was the thought that the new servant was alone in the house and probably getting up to all sorts of mischief. He was certainly stealing while her back was turned: he might be handling her clothes, looking through her personal things! While Dick was patiently explaining about soils and drains and native wages, she was thinking with half her mind about that native alone with *her* things. When she got back at lunchtime the first thing she did was to go round the house, looking for what he had left undone, and examining her drawers, which looked untouched. But then, one never knew – they were such cunning swine! Next day, when Dick asked her if she would come again, she said nervously, 'No, Dick, if you don't mind. It is so hot down there. You are used to it.' And really it seemed to her that she could not stand another morning with the hot sun on her neck, with the dazzle of heat in her eyes, although she felt sick with the heat when she stayed in the house. But then, she had something to do in the house, supervising that native.

As time passed, the heat became an obsession. She could not bear the sapping, undermining waves that beat down from the iron roof. Even the usually active dogs used to lie all day on the verandah, moving from place to place as the bricks grew warm under them, their tongues lolling wetly, so that the floor was covered by small pools. Mary could hear them panting softly, or whining with exasperation because of the flies. And when they came to put their heads on her knee, pleading for sympathy because of the heat, she would shoo them off crossly: the enormous, rank-smelling animals were an irritation to her, getting under her feet as she moved about the little house, leaving hairs on the cushions, snuffling noisily for fleas when she was trying to rest. She would lock them out of the house, and in the middle of the morning she would tell the boy to carry a petrol tin full of lukewarm water into the bedroom, and, having made sure he was out of the house, she stripped herself and stood in a basin on the brick floor, pouring it over her. The scattering drops fell on the porous brick, which hissed with dryness.

'When is it going to rain?' she asked Dick.

'Oh, not for another month yet,' he answered easily, but looking surprised at her question. Surely she knew when the rains were likely to fall? She had been in the country longer than he had. But it seemed to her that in the town there had been no seasons, really, not as there were here. She had been out of the rhythm of cold and heat and rain. It had been hot, it had rained, the cold weather had come – yes, certainly; but it was something extraneous to her, something happening independent of her. Here body and mind were subservient to the slow movement of the seasons; she had never in her life watched an implacable sky for signs of rain, as she did now, standing on the verandah, and screwing up her eyes at the great massed white clouds, like blocks of glittering crystal quartz sailing through the blue.

'The water is going very quickly,' said Dick, one day, frowning.

It was fetched twice a week from the bottom of the hill where the well was. Mary would hear shouting and yelling, as if someone were in agonized pain, and going out to the front of the house, she watched the water-cart come through the trees, drawn by two slow-moving beautiful oxen, straining with their hindquarters up the slope. The cart was two petrol drums lashed to a frame, and in front the disselboom rested on yokes on the necks of the big powerful beasts. She watched the thick muscles surging under the hide, and saw how branches of trees had been laid over the drums to keep the water cool. Sometimes it splashed up and made a fine sparkling spray falling through the sunshine, and the oxen tossed their heads and blew out their nostrils, smelling the water. And all the time the native driver yelled and howled, dancing beside his beasts and lashing with his long whip that coiled and hissed in the air, but never touched them.

'What are you using it for?' asked Dick. She told him. His face darkened, and he looked at her in incredulous horror, as if she had committed a crime.

'What, wasting it like that?'

'I am not wasting it,' she said coldly. 'I am so hot I can't stand it. I want to cool myself.'

Dick swallowed, trying to keep calm. 'Listen to me,' he said angrily, in a voice he had never before used to her. 'Listen to me! Every time I order the watercart to fetch water for the house, it means a driver, and two waggon boys, and two oxen off other work for a whole morning. It costs money to fetch water. And then you go and throw it away! Why don't you fill the bath with water and get into it, instead of wasting it and throwing it away each time?'

She was furious. This seemed the last straw. Here was she, living here uncomplainingly, suffering these hardships; and then she could not use a couple of gallons of water! She opened her mouth to shout at him, but before she could, he had become suddenly contrite because of the way he had spoken to

her; and there was another of those little scenes which comforted and soothed her: he apologizing, abasing himself, and
she forgiving him.

But when he had gone, she went into the bathroom, and
stared down at the bath, still hating him for what he had said.
The bathroom had been built on after the house was finished.
It was a lean-to with mud walls (mud plastered over bush poles)
and a tin roof. Where the rain had run through the joins in the
roof, the whitewash was discoloured and the mud cracked. The
bath itself was of zinc, a shallow zinc shape set into a dried mud
base. The metal had been dazzling once; she could see how it
had been because the scratches on the dull surface glittered
brightly. Over many years a patina of grease and dirt had
formed, and now, when it was scrubbed, it wore thin in patches
only. It was filthy, filthy! Mary stared down at it, stiff with
distaste. When she bathed, which was only twice a week
because of the trouble and cost of fetching water, she sat
gingerly at the extreme end of the bath, trying to touch it as
little as possible, and getting out as soon as she could. Here a
bath was like medicine, which had to be taken, not a luxury to
be enjoyed.

The arrangements for the bath were unbelievable, she cried,
tearing herself to pieces with her own anger. On bath nights
two petrol tins of water were heated on the stove, and carried
into the bathroom and set down on the floor. They were
covered over with thick farm sacks to keep the water hot, and
the sacks were hot and steamy and sent up a musty smell.
Across the tops of the tins pieces of bushwood had been
wedged, to carry them by, and the wood was greasy with much
handling. She just would not put up with it, she said at last,
turning to leave the bathroom in angry distaste. She called the
boy and told him to scrub the bath, to scrub it until it was
clean. He thought she meant the usual scrubbing, and in five
minutes had finished. She went to examine it: it was just the
same. Stroking her fingers over the zinc, she could feel the crust
of dirt. She called him back and told him to clean, to clean it
properly, to go on scrubbing till it shone, every inch of it.

That was about eleven in the morning.

It was an unfortunate day for Mary. It was on that day that she made her first contact with 'the district', in the shape of Charlie Slatter and his wife. It is worthwhile explaining in detail what happened that day, because so many things can be understood by it: she went from mistake to mistake, with her head held high and her mouth set tight, rigid with pride and the determination not to show weakness. When Dick returned to lunch, he found her cooking in the kitchen, looking positively ugly with anger, her face flushed and her hair untidy.

'Where is the boy?' he asked, surprised to find her doing his work.

'Cleaning the bath,' she said shortly, snapping out the words angrily.

'Why now?'

'It's dirty,' she said.

Dick went into the bathroom, from where he could hear the sluish, sluish of a scrubbing brush, and found the native bent over the bath, rubbing away, but making little impression. He returned to the kitchen.

'Why start him on it now?' he asked. 'It's been like that for years. A zinc bath goes like that. It's not dirt, Mary, not really. It changes colour.'

Without looking at him she piled a tray with food and marched into the front room. 'It's dirt,' she said. 'I will never get into that bath again until it is really clean. How you can allow your things to be so filthy I cannot understand.'

'You have used it yourself for some weeks without complaining,' he said drily, automatically reaching for a cigarette and sticking it between his lips. But she did not reply.

He shook his head when she said the food was ready and went off to the fields again, calling for the dogs. When she was in this mood, he could not bear to be near her. Mary cleared the table, without eating herself, and sat down to listen to the sound of the scrubbing brush. She remained there for two hours, her head aching, listening with every muscle of her tensed body. She was determined he should not scamp his work. At half-past three there was sudden silence, and she sat up, alertly ready to go to the bathroom and make him begin again. But the door opened and he entered. Without looking at her, addressing her invisible double that stood to one side of her, he said that he was going to his hut for some food, and would go on with the bath when he came back. She had forgotten about his food. She never thought of natives as people who had to eat or sleep: they were either there, or they were not, and what their lives were when they were out of her sight she had never paused to think. She nodded, feeling guilty. Then she smothered her guilt, thinking, 'It's his fault for not keeping it properly clean in the first place.'

The tension of listening to his working relaxed, she went out to look at the sky. There were no clouds at all. It was a low dome of sonorous blue, with an undertone of sultry sulphur-colour, because of the smoke that dimmed the air. The pale sandy soil in front of the house dazzled up waves of light, and out of it curved the gleaming stems of the poinsettia bushes, bursting into irregular slashes of crimson. She looked away over the trees, which were dingy and brownish, over the acres of shining wavy grass to the hills. They were hazy and indistinct. The veld fires had been burning for weeks, all round, and she could taste the smoke on her tongue. Sometimes a tiny fragment of charred grass fell on her skin, and left a greasy black smudge. Columns of smoke rose in the distance, heavy bluish coils hanging motionless, making a complicated architecture in the dull air.

The week before a fire had swept over part of their farm, destroying two cowsheds and acres of grazing. Where it had burnt, lay black expanses of desolation, and still, here and there, fallen logs smoked in the blackness, faint tendrils of smoke showing grey against the charred landscape. She turned her eyes away, because she did not want to think of the money that had been lost, and saw in front of her, where the road wound, clouds of reddish dust. The course of that road could always be marked, because the trees along it were rust-coloured as if locusts had settled on them. She watched the dust spurt up as if a beetle were burrowing through the trees, and thought, 'Why, it is a car!' And a few minutes later she realized it was coming to them, and felt quite panicky. Callers! But Dick had said she must expect people to come. She ran into the back of the house, to tell the boy to get tea. He wasn't there. It was then four: she remembered that half an hour before she had told him he could go. She ran out over the shifting mass of chips and bark-strips of the wood-pile, and, drawing the rusty wooden bolt from the crotch of the tree, beat the plough disc. Ten resonant clanging beats were the signal that the houseboy was wanted. Then she returned to the house. The stove was out; she found it difficult to light; and there was nothing to eat. She did not bother to cook cakes when Dick was never there for tea. She opened a packet of store biscuits and looked down at her frock. She could not possibly be seen in such a rag! But it was too late. The car was droning up the hill. She rushed out into the front, wringing her hands. She might have been isolated for years, and unused to people, from the way she behaved, rather than a woman who for years and years had never, not for a minute, been alone. She saw the car stop, and two people get out. They were a short, powerfully-built, sandy-coloured man, and a dark full-bodied woman with a pleasant face. She waited for them, smiling shyly to answer their cordial faces. And then, with what relief she saw Dick's car coming up the hill! She blessed him for his consideration, coming to help her out on this first visit. He had seen the dust-trail over the trees, too, and had come as soon as he could.

The man and the woman shook her hand, and greeted her. But it was Dick who asked them inside. The four of them sat in the tiny room, so that it appeared even more crowded than ever. Dick and Charlie Slatter talked on one side, and she and Mrs Slatter on the other. Mrs Slatter was a kindly soul, and sorry for Mary who had married a good-for-nothing like Dick. She had heard she was a town girl, and knew herself what hardship and loneliness was, though she was long past the struggling state herself. She had, now, a large house, three sons at university, and a comfortable life. But she remembered only too well the sufferings and humiliations of poverty. She looked at Mary with real tenderness, remembering her own past, and was prepared to make friends. But Mary was stiff with resentment, because she had noticed Mrs Slatter looking keenly round the room, pricing every cushion, noticing the new whitewash and the curtains.

'How pretty you have made it,' she said, with genuine admiration, knowing what it was to use dyed flour sacks for curtains and painted petrol boxes for cupboards. But Mary misunderstood her. She would not soften at all. She would not discuss her house with Mrs Slatter, who was patronizing her. After a few moments Mrs Slatter looked closely at the girl's face, flushed, and in a changed voice that was formal and distant, began to talk of other things. Then the boy brought in the tea, and Mary suffered fresh agonies over the cups and the tin tray. She tried to think of something to discuss that was not connected with the farm. Films? She cast her mind over the hundreds she had seen in the last few years, and could not remember the names of more than two or three. Films, which had once been so important to her, were now a little unreal; and in any case Mrs Slatter went to the pictures perhaps twice a year, when she was in town on her rare shopping trips. The shops in town? No, that was a question of money again, and she was wearing a faded cotton frock she was ashamed of. She looked across to Dick for help, but he was absorbed in conversation with Charlie, discussing crops, prices, and – above all – native labour. Whenever two or three farmers are gathered together, it is decreed that they should discuss nothing but the shortcomings and deficiencies of their natives. They talk about their labourers with a persistent irritation sounding in their voices: individual natives they might like, but as a genus, they loathe them to the point of neurosis. They never cease complaining about their unhappy lot, having to deal with natives who are so exasperatingly indifferent to the welfare of the white man, working only to please themselves. They had no idea of the dignity of labour, no idea of improving themselves by hard work.

Mary listened to the male conversation with wonder. It was the first time she had heard men talk farming, and she began to see that Dick was hungry for it, and felt a little mean that she knew so little, and could not help relieve his mind by discussing the farm with him. She turned back to Mrs Slatter, who was silent, feeling wounded because Mary would not accept her sympathy and her help. At last the visit came to an end, with regret on Dick's side, but relief from Mary. The two Turners went out to say good-bye, and watched the big expensive car slide down the hill, and away into the trees amid puffs of red dust.

Dick said, 'I am glad they came. It must be lonely for you.'

'I am not lonely,' said Mary truthfully. Loneliness, she thought, was craving for other people's company. But she did not know that loneliness can be an unnoticed cramping of the spirit for lack of companionship.

'But you must talk women's talk sometimes,' said Dick, with awkward jocularity.

She glanced at him in surprise: this tone was new to her. He was staring after the departing car, his face regretful. He was not regretting Charlie Slatter, whom he did not like, but the talk, the masculine talk which gave him self-assurance in his relations with Mary. He felt as though he had been given an injection of new vigour, because of that hour spent in the little room, the two men on one side, discussing their own concerns, and the two women on the other, talking, presumably, about clothes and servants. For he had not heard a word of what Mrs Slatter and Mary had said. He had not noticed how awkward it had been for both of them.

'You must go and see her, Mary,' he announced. 'I'll give you the car one afternoon when work is slack, and you can go and have a good gossip.' He spoke quite jauntily and freely, his face clear from that load of worry, his hands in his pockets.

Mary did not understand why he seemed alien and hostile to her, but she was piqued at this casual summing up of her needs. And she had no desire for Mrs Slatter's company. She did not want anyone's company.

'I don't want to,' she said childishly.

'Why not?'

But at this point the servant came out on to the verandah behind them, and held out, without speaking, his contract of service. He wanted to leave: he was needed by his family in the kraal. Mary immediately lost her temper; her irritation found a permissible outlet in this exasperating native. Dick simply pulled her back, as if she were a thing of no account, and went out to the kitchen with the native. She heard the boy complain that he had been working since five o'clock that morning with no food at all, because he was only in the compound a few moments before he had been summoned back by the gong. He could not work like that; his child in his kraal was ill; he wanted to go at once. Dick replied, ignoring the unwritten rules for once, that the new missus did not know much about running a house yet, and that she would learn and that it would not happen again. Speaking like this to a native, appealing to him, was contrary to Dick's ideas of relationship between white and black, but he was furious with Mary for her lack of consideration and tact.

Mary was quite stupefied with rage. How dare he take the native's part against her! When Dick returned she was standing on the verandah with her hands clenched and her face set.

'How dare you!' she said, her voice stifled.

'If you must do these things, then you must take the consequences,' said Dick wearily. 'He's a human being, isn't he? He's got to eat. Why must that bath be done all at once? It can be done over several days, if it means all that to you.'

'It's my house,' said Mary. 'He's my boy, not yours. Don't interfere.'

'Listen to me,' said Dick curtly. 'I work hard enough, don't I? All day I am down on the lands with these lazy black savages, fighting them to get some work out of them. You know that. I won't come back home to this damned fight, fight, fight in the house. Do you understand? I will not have it. And you should learn sense. If you want to get work out of them you have to know how to manage them. You shouldn't expect too much. They are nothing but savages after all.' Thus Dick, who had never stopped to reflect that these same savages had cooked for him better than his wife did, had run his house, had given him a comfortable existence, as far as his pinched life could be comfortable, for years.

Mary was beside herself. She said, wanting to hurt him, really wanting to hurt him for the first time, because of this new arrogance of his, 'You expect a lot from me, don't you?' On the brink of disaster, she pulled herself up, but could not stop completely, and after a hesitation went on, 'You expect such a lot! You expect me to live like a poor white in this pokey little place of yours. You expect me to cook myself every day because you won't put in ceilings . . .' She was speaking in a new voice for her, a voice she had never used before in her life. It was taken direct from her mother, when she had had those scenes over money with her father. It was not the voice of Mary, the individual (who after all really did not care so much about the bath or whether the native stayed or went), but the voice of the suffering female, who wanted to show her husband she just would not be treated like that. In a moment she would begin to cry, as her mother had cried on these occasions, in a kind of dignified, martyred rage.

Dick said curtly, white with fury, 'I told you when I married you what you could expect. You can't accuse me of telling you lies. I explained everything to you. And there are farmers' wives all over the country living no better, and not making such a fuss. And as for ceilings, you can whistle for them. I have lived in this house for six years and it hasn't hurt me. You can make the best of it.'

She gasped in astonishment. Never had he spoken like that to her. And inside she went hard and cold against him, and nothing would melt her until he said he was sorry and craved her forgiveness.

'That boy will stay now, I've seen to that. Now treat him properly and don't make a fool of yourself again,' said Dick.

She went straight into the kitchen, gave the boy the money he was owed, counting out the shillings as if she grudged them, and dismissed him. She returned cold and victorious. But Dick did not acknowledge her victory.

'It is not me you are hurting, it is yourself,' he said. 'If you go on like this, you'll never get any servants. They soon learn the women who don't know how to treat their boys.'

She got the supper herself, struggling with the stove, and

afterwards when Dick had gone to bed early, as he always did, she remained alone in the little front room. After a while, feeling caged, she went out into the dark outside the house, and walked up and down the path between the borders of white stones which gleamed faintly through the dark, trying to catch a breath of cool air to soothe her hot cheeks. Lightning was flickering gently over the kopjes; there was a dull red glow where the fire burned; and overhead it was dark and stuffy. She was tense with hatred. Then she began to picture herself walking there up and down in the darkness, with the hated bush all around her, outside that pigsty he called a house, having to do all her own work – while only a few months ago she had been living her own life in town, surrounded by friends who loved her and needed her. She began to cry, weakening into self-pity. She cried for hours, till she could walk no more. She staggered back into bed, feeling bruised and beaten. The tension between them lasted for an intolerable week, until at last the rains fell, and the air grew cool and relaxed. And he had not apologized. The incident was simply not mentioned. Unresolved and unacknowledged, the conflict was put behind them, and they went on as if it had not happened. But it had changed them both. Although his assurance did not last long, and he soon lapsed back into his old dependence on her, a faint apology always in his voice, he was left with a core of resentment against her. For the sake of their life together she had to smother her dislike of him because of the way he had behaved, but then, it was not so easy to smother; it was put against the account of the native who had left, and, indirectly, against all natives.

Towards the end of that week a note came from Mrs Slatter, asking them both for an evening party.

Dick was really reluctant to go, because he had got out of the way of organized jollification; he was ill at ease in crowds. But he wanted to accept for Mary's sake. She, however, refused to go. She wrote a formal note of thanks, saying she regretted, etc.

Mrs Slatter had asked them on an impulse of real friendliness, for she was still sorry for Mary, in spite of her stiff angular pride. But the note offended her: it might have been copied out of a letter-writing guide. This kind of formality did not fit in with the easy manners of the district, and she showed the note to her husband with raised eyebrows, saying nothing.

'Leave her,' said Charlie Slatter. 'She'll come off her high horse. Got ideas into her head, that's what's wrong with her. She'll come to her senses. Not that she's much loss. The pair of them need some sense shaken into them. Turner is in for trouble. He is so up in the air that he doesn't even burn fireguards! And he is planting trees. Trees! He is wasting money planting trees while he is in debt.'

Mr Slatter's farm had hardly any trees left on it. It was a monument to farming malpractice, with great gullies cutting through it, and acres of good dark earth gone dead from misuse. But he made the money, that was the thing. It enraged him to think it was so easy to make money, and that damned fool Dick Turner played the fool with trees. On a kindhearted impulse, that was half exasperation, he drove over one morning to see Dick, avoiding the house (because he did not want to meet that stuck-up idiot Mary) looking for him on the lands. He spent three hours trying to persuade Dick to plant tobacco, instead of mealies and little crops. He was very sarcastic about those 'little crops', the beans and cotton and sunhemp that Dick liked. And Dick steadily refused to listen to Charlie. He liked his crops, the feeling of having his eggs in several baskets. And tobacco seemed to him an inhuman crop: it wasn't farming at all, it was a sort of factory thing, with the barns and the grading sheds and the getting up at nights to watch barn temperatures.

'What are you going to do when the family starts coming along?' asked Charlie brusquely, his matter-of-fact little blue eyes fixed on Dick.

'I'll get out of the mess my own way,' said Dick obstinately.

'You are a fool,' said Charlie. 'A fool. Don't say I didn't tell you. Don't come to me for loans when your wife's belly begins to swell and you need cash.'

'I have never asked you for anything,' replied Dick, wounded, his face dark with pride. There was a moment of sheer hatred between the two men. But somewhere, somehow, they respected each other, in spite of their difference in temperament – perhaps because they shared the same life, after all? And they parted cordially enough, although Dick could not bring himself to match Charlie's bluff good-humour.

When Charlie had gone he went back to the house, sick with worry. Sudden strain and anxiety always went to the nerves of his stomach, and he wanted to vomit. But he concealed it from Mary, because of the cause of his worry. Children were what he wanted now that his marriage was a failure and seemed impossible to right. Children would bring them close together and break down this invisible barrier. But they simply could not afford to have children. When he had said to Mary (thinking she might be longing for them) that they would have to wait, she had assented with a look of relief. He had not missed that look. But perhaps when he got out of the wood, she would be pleased to have children.

He drove himself to work harder, so that things could be better and children would be possible. He planned and schemed and dreamed all day, standing on his land watching the boys work. And in the meantime matters in the house did not improve. Mary just could not get on with natives, and that was the end of it. He had to accept it; she was made like that, and could not be altered. A cook never lasted longer than a month, and all the time there were scenes and storms of temper. He set his teeth to bear it, feeling obscurely that it was in some way his fault, because of the hardships of her life; but sometimes he would rush from the house, inarticulate with irritation. If only she had something to fill her time – that was the trouble.

6

It was by chance that Mary picked up a pamphlet on bee-keeping from the counter of the store one day, and took it home with her; but even if she had not, no doubt it would have happened some other way. But it was that chance which gave her her first glimpse into Dick's real character: that, and a few words she overheard the same day.

They seldom went into the station seven miles away; but sent in a native twice a week to fetch their post and groceries. He left at about ten in the morning, with an empty sugar sack swung over his shoulders, and returned after dusk with the sack bulging, and oozing blood from the parcel of meat. But a native, although conveniently endowed by nature with the ability to walk long distances without feeling fatigue, cannot carry sacks of flour and mealiemeal; and once a month the trip was made by car.

Mary had given her order, seen the things put into the car, and was standing on the long verandah of the store among piled crates and sacks, waiting for Dick to finish his business. As he came out, a man she did not know stopped him and said, 'Well, Jonah, your farm flooded again this season, I suppose?' She turned sharply to look: a few years ago she would not have noticed the undertone of contempt in the lazy rallying voice. Dick smiled and said, 'I have had good rains this year, things are not too bad.'

'Your luck changed, eh?'

'Looks like it.'

Dick came towards her, the smile gone, his face strained.

'Who was that?' she asked.

'I borrowed two hundred pounds from him three years ago, just after we were married.'

'You didn't tell me?'

'I didn't want to worry you.'

After a pause she asked, 'Have you paid it back?'

'All but fifty pounds.'

'Next season, I suppose?' Her voice was too gentle, too considerate.

'With a bit of luck.'

She saw on his face that queer grin of his, more a baring of the teeth than a smile: self-critical, assessing, defeated. She hated to see it.

They finished what they had to do: collecting mail from the post office and buying meat for the week. Walking over caked dried mud, which showed where puddles lay from the beginning of the rainy season to its end, shading her eyes with her hand, Mary refrained from looking at Dick, and made sprightly remarks in a strained voice. He attempted to reply, in the same tone; which was so foreign to them both that it deepened the tension between them. When they returned to the verandah of the store, which was crowded with sacks and packing-cases, he knocked his leg against the pedal of a leaning bicycle, and began to swear with a violence out of proportion to the small accident. People turned to look; and Mary walked on, her colour deepening. In complete silence they got into the car and drove away over the railway lines and past the post office on the way home. In her hand she had the pamphlet on bees. She picked it up from the counter because most days, at about lunch-time, she heard a soft swelling roar over the house, and Dick had told her it was swarming bees passing. She had thought she might make some pocket money from bees. But the pamphlet was written for English conditions, and was not very helpful. She used it as a fan, waving away the flies that buzzed round her head and clustered at last on the canvas roof. They had come in from the butchery with the meat. She was thinking uneasily of that note of contempt in the man's voice, which contradicted all her previous ideas of Dick. It was not even contempt, more amusement. Her own attitude towards him was fundamentally one of contempt, but only as a man; as a man she paid no attention to him, she left him out of account altogether. As a farmer she respected him. She respected his ruthless driving of himself, his absorption in his work. She believed that he was going through a necessary period of struggle before achieving the moderate affluence enjoyed by most farmers. In her feeling for him, in relation to his work, was admiration, even affection.

She who had once taken everything at its face value, never noticing the inflection of a phrase, or the look on a face which contradicted what was actually being said, spent the hour's drive home considering the implications of that man's gentle amusement at Dick. She wondered for the first time, whether she had been deluding herself. She kept glancing sideways at Dick, noticing little things about him she blamed herself for not noticing before. As he gripped the steering wheel, his lean hands, burnt coffee-coloured by the sun, shook perpetually, although almost imperceptibly. It seemed to her a sign of weakness, that trembling; the mouth was too tight-set. He was leaning forward, gripping the wheel, gazing down the narrow winding bush track as if trying to foresee his own future.

Back in the house, she flung the pamphlet down on the table and went to unpack the groceries. When she came back, Dick was absorbed in the pamphlet. He did not hear her when she spoke. She was used to this absorption of his: he would sometimes sit through a meal without speaking, not noticing what he ate, sometimes laying down his knife and fork before the plate was empty, thinking about some farm problem, his brow heavy with worry. She had learned not to trouble him at these times. She took refuge in her own thoughts; or, rather, she lapsed into her familiar state, which was a dim mindlessness. Sometimes they hardly spoke for days at a time.

After supper, instead of going to bed as usual at about eight, he sat himself down at the table under the gently-swaying, paraffin-smelling lamp, and began making calculations on a piece of paper. She sat and watched him, her hands folded. This was now her characteristic pose: sitting quietly, as though waiting for something to wake her into movement. After an hour or so, he pushed away the scraps of paper, and hitched up his trousers with a gay, boyish movement she had not seen before.

'What do you say about bees, Mary?'

'I don't know anything about them. It's not a bad idea.'

'I'll go over tomorrow to see Charlie. His brother-in-law kept bees in the Transvaal, he told me once.' He spoke with new energy; he seemed to have new life.

'But this book is for England,' she said, turning it over dubiously. It seemed to her a flimsy foundation for such a change in him; a flimsy basis for even a hobby like bees.

But after breakfast next day Dick drove off to see Charlie Slatter. He returned frowning, his face obstinate but whistling jauntily. Mary was struck by that whistle: it was so familiar. It was a trick of his; he stuck his hands in his pockets, little-boy fashion, and whistled with a pathetic jauntiness when she lost her temper and raged at him because of the house, or because of the clumsiness of the water arrangements. It always made her feel quite mad with irritation, because he could not stand up to her and hold his own.

'What did he say?' she asked.

'He's wet-blanketing the whole thing. Because his brother-in-law failed it's no reason I will.'

He went off to the farm instinctively making his way to the tree plantation. This was a hundred acres of some of the best ground on his farm, which he had planted with young gums a couple of years before. It was this plantation that had so annoyed Charlie Slatter – perhaps because of an unacknowledged feeling of guilt that he himself never put back in his soil what he took from it.

Dick often stood at the edge of the field, watching the wind flow whitely over the tops of the shining young trees, that bent and swung and shook themselves all day. He had planted them apparently on an impulse; but it was really the fruition of a dream of his. Years before he bought the farm, some mining company had cut out every tree on the place, leaving nothing but coarse scrub and wastes of grass. The trees were growing up again, but over the whole three thousand acres of land there was nothing to be seen but stunted second growth: short, ugly little trees from mutilated trunks. There wasn't a good tree left on the farm. It wasn't much, planting a hundred acres of good trees that would grow into straight white-stemmed giants; but it was a small retribution; and this was his favourite place on the farm. When he was particularly worried, or had quarrelled with Mary, or wanted to think clearly, he stood and looked at his trees; or strolled down the long aisles between light swaying branches that glittered with small polished leaves like coins. Today he considered bees; until, quite late, he realized he had not been near the farm-work all day, and with a sigh he left his plantation and went to the labourers.

At lunch-time he did not speak at all. He was obsessed by bees. At last he explained to the doubtful Mary that he reckoned he could make a good two hundred pounds a year. This was a shock to her; she had imagined he was thinking of a few beehives as a profitable hobby. But it was no good arguing with him: one cannot argue against figures, and his calculations were impeccable proof that those two hundred pounds were as good as made. And what could she say? She had no experience of this kind of thing; only her instinct told her to distrust bees on this occasion.

For a good month Dick was oblivious, gone into a beautiful dream of rich honeycombs and heavy dark clusters of fruitful bees. He built twenty beehives himself; and planted an acre of a special kind of grass near the bee-allotment. He took some of his labourers off their usual work, and sent them over the veld to find swarming bees, and spent hours every evening in the golden dusk, smoking out swarms to try and catch the queen bee. This method, he had been told, was the correct one. But a great many of the bees died, and he did not find the queens. Then he began planting his hives all over the veld near swarms he located, hoping they would be tempted. But not a bee ever went near his hives; perhaps because they were African bees, and did not like hives made after an English pattern. Who knows? Dick certainly did not. At last a swarm settled in a hive. But one cannot make two hundred a year from one swarm of bees. Then Dick got himself badly stung, and it seemed as if the poison drove the obsession from his system. Mary, amazed and even angry, saw that the brooding abstraction had gone from his face, for he had spent weeks of time and quite a lot of money. Yet, from one day to the next, he lost interest in bees. On the whole, Mary was relieved to see him go back to normal, thinking about his crops and his farm again. It had been like a temporary madness, when he was quite unlike himself.

It was about six months later that the whole thing happened again. Even then she could not really believe it when she saw him poring over a farming magazine, where there was a particularly tempting article about the profitability of pigs, and heard him say, 'Mary, I am going to buy some pigs from Charlie.'

She said sharply, 'I hope you are not going to start that again.'

'Start what again?'

'You know very well what I mean. Castles in the air about making money. Why don't you stick to your farm?'

'Pigs are farming, aren't they? And Charlie does very well from his pigs.' Then he began to whistle. As he walked across the room to the verandah, to escape her angry accusing face, it seemed to her that it was not a tall, spare, stooping man whom she saw, only; but also a swaggering little boy, trying to keep his end up after cold water had been poured over his enthusiasm. She could distinctly see that little boy, swaggering with his hips and whistling, but with a defeated look about his knees and thighs. She heard the whistling from the verandah, a little melancholy noise, and suddenly felt as if she wanted to cry. But why, why? He might very well make money from pigs. Other people did. But all the same, she pinned her hopes to the end of the season, when they would see how much money they had made. It ought not to be so bad: the season had been good, and the rains kind to Dick.

He built the pigstyes up behind the house among the rocks of the kopje. This was to save bricks, he said; the rocks supplied part of the walls; he used big boulders as a framework on which to tack screens of grass and wood. He had saved pounds of money, he told her, building them this way.

'But won't it be very hot here?' asked Mary. They were standing among the half-built styes, on the kopje. It was not very easy to climb up here, through tangled grass and weeds that clung to one's legs, leaving them stuck all over with tiny green burs, as clinging as cat's claws. There was a big euphorbia tree branching up into the sky from the top of the kopje, and Dick said it would provide shade and coolness. But they were now standing in a warm shade from the thick, fleshy, candle-like branches, and Mary could feel her head beginning to ache. The boulders were too hot to touch: the accumulated sunshine of months seemed stored in that granite. She looked at the two farm dogs, who lay prostrate at their feet, panting, and remarked: 'I hope pigs don't feel the heat.'

'But I tell you, it won't be hot,' he said. 'Not when I have put up some sunbreaks.'

'The heat seems to beat out of the ground.'

'Well, Mary, it's all very well to criticize, but this way I have saved money. I couldn't have afforded to spend fifty pounds on cement and bricks.'

'I am not criticizing,' she said hastily, because of the defensive note in his voice.

He bought six expensive pigs from Charlie Slatter, and installed them in the rock-girt styes. But pigs have to be fed; and this is a costly business, if food has to be bought for the purpose. Dick found that he would have to order many sacks of maize. And he decided they should have all the milk his cows produced except for the very minimum required for the house. Mary, then, went to the pantry each morning to see the milk brought up from the cowsheds, and to pour off perhaps a pint for themselves. The rest was set to go sour on the table in the kitchen; because Dick had read somewhere that sour milk had bacon-making qualities fresh milk lacked. The flies gathered over the bubbling crusty white stuff, and the whole house smelled faintly acrid.

And then, when the little piglets arrived, and grew, it would be a question of transporting them and selling them, and so on . . . These problems, however, did not arise, for the piglets, when born, died again almost immediately. Dick said disease had attacked his pigs: it was just his luck; but Mary remarked drily that she thought they disliked being roasted before their time. He was grateful to her for the grimly humorous remark: it made laughter possible and saved the situation. He laughed with relief, scratching his head ruefully, hitching up his pants; and then began to whistle his melancholy little plaint. Mary walked out of the room, her face hard. The women who marry men like Dick learn sooner or later that there are two things they can do: they can drive themselves mad, tear themselves to pieces in storms of futile anger and rebellion; or they can hold themselves tight and go bitter. Mary, with the memory of her own mother recurring more and more frequently, like an older, sardonic double of herself walking beside her, followed the course her upbringing made inevitable. To rage at Dick seemed to her a failure in pride; her formerly pleasant but formless face was setting into lines of endurance; but it was as if she wore two masks, one contradicting the other; her lips were becoming thin and tight, but they could tremble with irritation; her brows drew together, but between them there was a vulnerable sensitive patch of skin that would flame a sullen red when she was in conflict with her servants. Sometimes she would present the worn visage of an indomitable old woman who has learnt to expect the worst from life, and sometimes the face of defenceless hysteria. But she was still able to walk from the room, silent in wordless criticism.

It was only a few months after the pigs had been sold that she noticed one day, with a cold sensation in her stomach, that familiar rapt expression on Dick's face. She saw him standing on the verandah, staring out over the miles of dull tawny veld to the hills, and wondered what vision possessed him now. She remained silent, however, waiting for him to turn to her, boyishly excited because of the success he already knew in imagination. And even then she was not really, not finally, despairing. Arguing against her dull premonitions, she told herself that the season had been good, and Dick quite pleased; he had paid a hundred pounds off the mortgage, and had enough in hand to carry them over the next year without borrowing. She had become adjusted, without knowing it, to his negative judging of a season by the standard of the debts he had *not* incurred. And when he remarked one day, with a defiant glance at her, that he had been reading about turkeys, she forced herself to appear interested. She said to herself that other farmers did these things and made money. Sooner or later Dick would strike a patch of luck: the market would favour him, perhaps; or the climate of his farm particularly suit turkeys, and he would find he had made a good profit. Then he began to remind her, already defending himself against the accusations she had not made, that he had lost very little over the pigs, after all (he had apparently forgotten about the bees); and it had been a costless experiment. The styes had cost nothing at all, and the boys' wages amounted only to a few shillings. The food they had grown themselves, or practically all of it. Mary remembered the sacks of maize they had bought, and that finding money to pay boys' wages was his greatest worry, but still kept her mouth shut and her eyes turned away, determined not to provoke him into further passions of hostile self-defence.

She saw more of Dick during the few weeks of the turkey-obsession than she had since she married him, or ever would again. He was hardly down on the farm at all; but spent the whole day supervising the building of the brick houses and the great wire runs. The fine-meshed wire cost over fifty pounds. Then the turkeys were bought, and expensive incubators, and weighing machines, and all the rest of the paraphernalia Dick thought essential; but before even the first lot of eggs were hatched, he remarked one day that he thought of using the runs and the houses, not for turkeys, but for rabbits. Rabbits could be fed on a handful of grass, and they breed like – well, like rabbits. It was true that people did not have much taste for rabbit-flesh (this is a South African prejudice), but tastes could be acquired, and if they sold the rabbits at five shillings each, he reckoned they could make a comfortable fifty or sixty pounds a month. Then, when the rabbits were established, they could buy a special breed of Angora rabbits, because he had heard the wool fetched six shillings a pound.

At this point, unable to control herself and hating herself for it, Mary lost her temper – lost it finally and destructively. Even as she raged against him, her feeling was of cold self-condemnation because she was giving him the satisfaction of seeing her thus. But it was a feeling he would not have understood. Her anger was terrible to him, though he told himself continually that she was in the wrong and had no right to thwart his well-meant but unfortunate efforts. She raged and wept and swore, till at last she was too weak to stand, and remained lolling in the corner of the sofa, sobbing, trying to get her breath. And Dick did not hitch up his pants, start to whistle or look like a harried little boy. He looked at her for a long time as she sat there, sobbing; and then said sardonically, 'OK boss.' Mary did not like that; she did not like it at all; for his sarcastic remark said more about their marriage than she had ever allowed herself to think, and it was unseemly that her contempt of him should be put so plainly into words: it was a condition of the existence of their marriage that she should pity him generously, not despise him.

But there was no more talk about rabbits or turkeys. She sold the turkeys, and filled the wire runs with chickens. To make some money to buy herself some clothes, she said. Did he expect her to go about in rags like a kaffir. He did not expect anything, apparently, for he did not even reply to her challenge. He was again preoccupied. There was no hint of apology or defensiveness in his manner when he informed her that he intended to start a kaffir store on his farm. He simply stated the fact, not looking at her, in a matter-of-fact take-it-or-leave-it voice. Everyone knew that kaffir stores made a pile of money, he said. Charlie Slatter had a store on his farm; a lot of farmers did. They were goldmines of profit. Mary shrank from the word 'goldmines' because she had found a series of crumbling weed-covered trenches behind the house one day, which he had told her he had dug years before in an effort to discover the Eldorado he had been convinced was hidden beneath the soil of his farm. She said quietly, 'If there is a store on Slatter's place, only five miles off, there is no point in having another here.'

'I have a hundred natives here always.'

'If they earn fifteen bob a month you are not going to become a Rockefeller on what they spend.'

'There are always natives passing through,' he said stubbornly.

He applied for a trading licence and got it without difficulty. Then he built a store. It seemed to Mary a terrible thing, an omen and a warning, that the store, the ugly menacing store of her childhood, should follow her here, even to her home.

But it was built a few hundred yards from the house itself, consisting of a small room bisected by a counter, with a bigger room behind to hold the stock. To begin with what stock they needed could be contained on the shelves of the store itself, but as the thing expanded, they would need the second room.

Mary helped Dick lay out the goods, sick with depression, hating the feel of the cheap materials that smelled of chemicals, and the blankets that seemed rough and greasy on the fingers even before they were used. They hung up the jewellery of garish glass and brass and copper, and she set them swinging and tinkling, with a tight-lipped smile, because of her memories of childhood, when it had been her greatest delight to watch the brilliant strings of beads swaying and shimmering. She was thinking that these two rooms added to the house would have made their life comfortable: the money spent on the store, the turkey-runs, the pigstyes, the beehives, would have put ceilings into the house, would have taken the terror out of the thought of the approaching hot season. But what was the use of saying it? She felt like dissolving in hopeless foreboding tears; but she said not a word, and helped Dick with the work till it was finished.

When the store was ready, and filled to the roof with kaffir goods, Dick was so pleased he went into the station and bought twenty cheap bicycles. It was ambitious, because rubber rots; but then, he said, his natives were always asking him for advances to buy bicycles; they could buy them from him. Then the question arose who was to run the store? When it really gets going, he said, we can engage a storeman. Mary shut her eyes and sighed. Before they had even started, when it looked as if it would be a long time before they had paid off the capital spent on it, he was talking about a storeman who would cost at the very least thirty pounds a month. Why not engage a native? she asked. You can't trust niggers further than you can kick them, he said, as far as money is concerned. He said that he had taken it for granted that she would run the store; she hadn't anything to do in any case. He made this last remark in the harsh resentful voice that was, at this time, his usual way of addressing her.

Mary replied sharply that she would rather die than set foot inside it. Nothing would make her, nothing.

'It wouldn't hurt you,' said Dick. 'Are you too good to stand behind a counter, then?'

'Selling kaffir truck to stinking kaffirs,' she said.

But that was not her feeling – not then, before she had started the work. She could not explain to Dick how that store smell made her remember the way she had stood, as a very small girl, looking fearfully up at the rows of bottles on the shelves, wondering which of them her father would handle that night; the way her mother had taken coins out of his pockets at nights, when he had fallen asleep in a chair snoring, mouth open, legs sprawling; and how the next day she would be sent up to the store to buy food that would not appear on the account at the month's end. These things she could not explain to Dick, for the good reason that he was now associated in her mind with the greyness and misery of her childhood, and it would have been like arguing with destiny itself. At last she agreed to serve in the store; there was nothing else she could do.

Now, as she went about her work, she could glance out of the back door and see the new shining roof among the trees; and from time to time she walked far enough along the path to see whether there was anyone waiting to buy. By ten in the morning half a dozen native women and their children were sitting under the trees. If she disliked native men, she loathed the women. She hated the exposed fleshiness of them, their soft brown bodies and soft bashful faces that were also insolent and inquisitive, and their chattering voices that held a brazen fleshy undertone. She could not bear to see them sitting there on the grass, their legs tucked under them in that traditional timeless pose, as peaceful and uncaring as if it did not matter whether the store was opened, or whether it remained shut all day and they would have to return tomorrow. Above all, she hated the way they suckled their babies, with their breasts hanging down for everyone to see; there was something in their calm satisfied maternity that made her blood boil. 'Their babies hanging on to them like leeches,' she said to herself shuddering, for she thought with horror of suckling a child. The idea of a child's lips on her breasts made her feel quite sick; at the thought of it she would involuntarily clasp her hands over her breasts, as if protecting them from a violation. And since so many white women are like her, turning with relief to the bottle, she was in good company, and did not think of herself, but rather of these black women, as strange; they were alien and primitive creatures with ugly desires she could not bear to think about.

When she saw there were perhaps ten or twelve of them waiting there, making a bright-coloured group against the green trees and grass, with their chocolate flesh and vivid headcloths and metal ear-rings, she took the keys off the hook in the wardrobe (they were put there so the native servant should not know where they were and take himself to the store to steal when she was not looking) and shading her eyes with her hand, she marched off along the path to get the unpleasant business finished. She would open the door with a bang, letting it swing back hard against the brick wall, and enter the dark store, her nose delicately crinkled against the smell. Then the women slowly crowded in, fingering the stuffs, and laying the brilliant beads against their dark skins with little exclamations of pleasure, or of horror, because of the price. The children hung to their mothers' backs (like monkeys, Mary thought) or clutched their skirts, staring at the white-skinned Mary, clusters of flies in the corners of their eyes. Mary would stand there for half an hour perhaps, holding herself aloof, drumming with her fingers on the wood, answering questions about price and quality briefly. She would not give the women the pleasure of haggling over the price. And after a few moments she felt she could not stay there any longer, shut into the stuffy store with a crowd of these chattering evil-smelling creatures. She said sharply, in the kitchen kaffir, 'Hurry up now!' One by one, they drifted away, their gaiety and the pleasure quite subdued, sensing her dislike of them.

'Have I got to stand there for hours just so that one of them can spend sixpence on a string of beads?' she asked.

'Gives you something to do,' he replied, with that new brutal indifference, without even looking at her.

It was the store that finished Mary: the necessity for serving behind the counter, and the knowledge that it was there, always there, a burden on her, not five minutes' walk down the path where ticks would crawl on her legs from the crowding bushes and grass. But ostensibly she broke down over the bicycles. For some reason they were not sold after all. Perhaps they were not the types the natives wanted; it was difficult to say. One was sold at last, but the rest remained in the back room, propped upside-down like steel skeletons in a welter of rubber tubing. The rubber rotted; when one stretched it, there were grey flakes on the canvas base. So that was another fifty pounds or so gone! And while they were not actually losing on the store, they were not making anything much. Taking the bicycles, and the cost of the building, the venture was a heavy loss, and they could expect to do no more than keep a balance on the goods remaining on the shelves. But Dick would not give it up.

'It's there now,' he said. 'We can't lose any more. You can go on with it, Mary. It won't hurt you.'

But she was thinking of the fifty pounds lost on the bicycles. It would have meant ceilings, or a good suite of furniture to replace the gimcrack stuff in their house, or even a week's holiday.

Thinking of that holiday, that she was always planning, but which never seemed to become possible, turned Mary's thoughts in a new direction. Her life, for a while, had a new meaning.

In the afternoons, these days, she always slept. She slept for hours and hours: it was a way to make time pass quickly. At one o'clock she lay down, and it was after four when she woke.

But Dick would not be home for two hours yet, so she lay half-clothed on the bed, drugged with sleep, her mouth dry and her head aching. It was during those two hours of half-consciousness that she allowed herself to dream about that beautiful lost time when she worked in an office . . . and lived as she pleased, before 'people made her get married'. That was how she put it to herself. And she began to think, during those grey wastes of time, how it would be when Dick at last made some money and they could go and live in town again; although she knew, in her moments of honesty, that he would never make money. Then came the thought that there was nothing to prevent her running away and going back to her old life. Here the memory of her friends checked her: what would they say, breaking up a marriage like that? The conventionality of her ethics, which had nothing to do with her real life, was restored by the thought of those friends, and the memory of their judgments on other people. It hurt her, the thought of facing them again, with her record of failure; for she was still, at bottom, haunted by a feeling of inadequacy, because 'she was not like that'. That phrase had stuck in her mind all these years, and still rankled. But her desire to escape her misery had become so insupportable, that she pushed out of her mind the idea of her friends. She thought, now, of nothing but getting away, of becoming again what she had been. But then, there was such a gulf between what she now was, and that shy, aloof, yet adaptable girl with the crowds of acquaintances. She was conscious of that gulf, but not as unredeemable alteration in herself. She felt, rather, as if she had been lifted from the part fitted to her, in a play she understood, and made suddenly to act one unfamiliar to her. It was a feeling of being out of character that chilled her, not knowledge that she had changed. The soil, the black labourers, always so close to their lives but also so cut off, Dick in his farm clothes with his hands stained with oil – these things did not belong to her, they were not real. It was monstrous that they should have been imposed upon her.

Slowly, slowly, over weeks, she persuaded herself into the belief that she would only need to get into the train and go back into town for that lovely peaceful life, the life she was made for, to begin again.

And, one day, when the boy returned from the station with his heavy sack of groceries and meat and mail, and she took out the weekly newspaper and looked as usual, at the announcements of the births and marriages (to see what her old friends were doing – this was the only part of the paper she read), she noticed that her old firm, the one she had worked for all those years, were advertising for a shorthand typist. She was standing in the kitchen, that was lit dimly by a flickering candle and the ruddy glimmer from the stove, beside the table loaded with soap and meat, the cookboy just behind her, preparing supper – yet, in a moment, she was transported away from the farm back into her old life. All night the illusion persisted, and she lay awake breathless with thoughts of this easily achievable future, that was also her past. And when Dick had gone off to the lands, she dressed, packed a suitcase, and left a note for him, quite in the traditional way, but saying merely that she was going back to her old job: exactly as if Dick had known her mind and approved of her decision.

She walked the five miles between their homestead and the Slatters' farm in just over an hour. She was running half the way, her suitcase swinging heavily in her hand and bumping against her legs, her shoes filling with the soft gritty dust, sometimes stumbling over the sharp ruts. She found Charlie Slatter standing at the gully that marked the boundary between the farms, seemingly doing nothing at all. He was looking down the road along which she came, humming at the back of his throat, his eyes screwed up. It struck her, as she stopped in front of him, that it was odd he should be idle, he who was always busy. She did not imagine he was planning how he would buy up that fool Dick Turner's farm when he went bankrupt; he needed extra grazing for his cattle. Remembering that she had only met him two or three times, and that each time he had not troubled to hide his dislike, she drew herself up, and tried to speak slowly, although she was breathless. She asked him if he would drive her into the station in time to catch the morning train; there would not be another for three days, and it was urgent. Charlie looked at her shrewdly, and appeared to be calculating.

'Where's your old man?' he asked with brusque jocularity.

'He's working . . .' stammered Mary.

He grunted, looked suspicious, but lifted her suitcase into his car which was standing under a big tree beside the road. He got into the car, and she climbed in beside him, fumbling with the door, while he stared ahead down the road, whistling between his teeth: Charlie did not believe in pampering women by waiting on them. At last she got herself settled, clutching her suitcase as if it were a passport.

'Hubby too busy to take you to the station?' asked Charlie at last, turning to look at her shrewdly. She coloured up, and nodded, feeling guilty; but she did not consciously reflect she was putting him in a false position; her mind was on that train.

He put down the accelerator and the big powerful car tore along the track, closely missing the trees, and skidding badly in the dust. The train was standing in the station, panting and dribbling water, and she had no time to spare. She thanked Charlie briefly, and had forgotten him before the train started. She had just enough money to get her into town: not enough for a taxi.

She walked from the station, carrying her suitcase, through the town she had not entered since she left it after her marriage; on the few occasions Dick had had to make the trip, she had refused to accompany him, shrinking from exposing herself to the chance of meeting people she had known. Her heart lifted as she neared the Club.

It was such a lovely, lovely day, with its gusts of perfumed wind, and its gay glittering sunshine. Even the sky looked different, seen from between the well-known buildings, that seemed so fresh and clean with their white walls and red roofs. It was not the implacable blue dome that arched over the farm, enclosing it in a cycle of unalterable seasons; it was a soft flower-blue, and she felt, in her exaltation, that she could run off the pavement into the blue substance and float there, at ease and peaceful at last. The street she walked along was lined with bauhinea trees, with their pink and white blossoms perched on the branches like butterflies among leaves. It was an avenue of pink and white, with the fresh blue sky above. It was a different world! It was her world.

At the Club she was met by a new matron who told her they did not take married women. The woman looked at her curiously, and that look destroyed Mary's sudden irresponsible happiness. She had forgotten about the rule against married women; but then, she had not been thinking of herself as married. She came to her senses, as she stood in the hall where she had faced Dick Turner all those years ago, and looked about her at the unchanged setting, which was yet so very strange to her. Everything looked so glossy, and clean and ordered.

Soberly she went to an hotel, and tidied her hair when she reached the room she had been given. Then she walked to the office. None of the girls working there knew her. The furniture had been changed; the desk where she had sat was moved, and it seemed outrageous that her things should have been tampered with. She looked at the girls in their pretty frocks, with their dressed hair, and thought for the first time that she hardly looked the part. But it was too late now. She was being shown into her old employer's office, and immediately she saw on his face the look of the woman at the Club. She found herself glancing down at her hands, which were crinkled and brown; and hid them under her bag. The man opposite to her was staring at her, looking closely at her face. Then he glanced at her shoes, which were still red with dust, because she had forgotten to wipe them. Looking grieved, but at the same time shocked, even scandalized, he said that the job had been filled already, and that he was sorry. She felt, again, outraged; for all that time she had worked here, it had been part of herself, this office, and now he would not take her back. 'I am sorry, Mary,' he said, avoiding her eyes; and she saw that the job had not been filled and that he was putting her off. There was a long moment of silence, while Mary saw the dreams of the last few weeks fade and vanish. Then he asked her if she had been ill.

'No,' she said bleakly.

Back in the hotel bedroom she looked at herself in the glass. Her frock was a faded cotton; and she could see, comparing it with the clothes of the girls in the office, that it was very out of fashion. Still, it was decent enough. True that her skin had become dried and brown, but when she relaxed her face, she could not see much difference in herself. Holding it smoothed and still, there were little white marks raying out from her eyes, like brush strokes. It was a bad habit to get into, she thought, screwing up one's eyes. And her hair was not very smart. But then, did he think one had hairdressers on farms? She was suddenly viciously, revengefully angry against him, against the matron, against everyone. What did they expect? That she should have gone through all those sufferings and disappointments and yet remain unchanged? But it was the first time that she admitted to herself that she had changed, in herself, not in her circumstances. She thought that she would go to a beauty shop and get at least her appearance restored to normal; then she would not be refused the job that was hers by right. But she remembered she had no money. Turning out her purse she found half a crown and a sixpence. She would not be able to pay her hotel bill. Her moment of panic faded; she sat down stiffly on a chair against the wall, and remained still, wondering what to do. But the effort of thought was too great; she seemed faced by innumerable humiliations and obstacles. She appeared to be waiting for something. After a while, her body slumped into itself, and there was a dogged patient look about her shoulders. When there was a knock on the door, she looked up as if she had been expecting it, and Dick's entrance did not change her face. For a moment they said nothing. Then he appealed to her, holding out his arms: 'Mary, don't leave me.' She sighed, stood up, automatically adjusted her skirt and smoothed her hair. She gave the impression of starting off for a planned journey. Seeing her pose, and her face, which showed no opposition or hatred, only resignation, Dick dropped his arms. There was to be no scene: her mood forbade it.

In his turn he came to his senses, and, as she had done, glanced at himself in the mirror. He had come in his farm clothes, without stopping even to eat, after reading the note which had seemed to stab him with pain and humiliation. His sleeves flapped over spare burnt arms; his feet were sockless and thrust into hide boots. But he said, as if they had come in together for a trip, that they might go and have lunch and on to a cinema, if she felt like it. He was trying to make her feel as if nothing had happened, she thought; but looking at him she saw it was a response to her acceptance of the situation that made him speak as he did. Seeing her awkwardly, painfully, smooth her dress, he said that she should go and buy herself some clothes.

She replied, speaking for the first time, in her usual tart and offhand way, 'What shall I use for money?'

They were back together again, not even the tones of their voices changed.

After they had eaten, in a restaurant that Mary chose because it looked too out of the way for any of her old friends to see her there, they went back to the farm, as if everything were quite normal, and her running away a little thing, and one that could be easily forgotten.

But when she got home, and she found herself back in her usual routine, with now not even day-dreams to sustain her, facing her future with a tired stoicism, she found she was exhausted. It was an effort for her to do anything at all. It seemed as if the trip into town had drained her reserves of strength and left her with just enough each day to do what had to be done, but nothing more. This was the beginning of an inner disintegration in her. It began with this numbness, as if she could no longer feel or fight.

And perhaps, if Dick had not got ill when he did, the end would have come quickly after all, one way or another. Perhaps she might have died quite soon, as her mother had done, after a brief illness, simply because she did not want particularly to live. Or she might have run away again, in another desperate impulse towards escape, and this time done it sensibly, and learned how to live again, as she was made to live, by nature and upbringing, alone and sufficient to herself. But there was a sudden and unexpected change in her life, which staved off the disintegration for a little while. A few months after she had run away, and six years after she had married him, Dick got ill, for the first time.

7

It was a brilliant, cool, cloudless June. This was the time of the year Mary liked best: warm during the day, but with a tang in the air; and several months to go before the smoke from the veld fires thickened into the sulphurous haze that dimmed the colours of the bush. The coolness gave her back some of her vitality: she was tired, yes, but it was not unbearable; she clutched at the cold months as if they were a shield to ward off the dreaded listlessness of the heat that would follow.

In the early mornings, when Dick had gone to the lands, she would walk gently over the sandy soil in front of the house, looking up into the high blue dome that was fresh as ice crystals, a marvellous clear blue, with never a cloud to stain it, not for months and months. The cold of the night was still in the soil. She would lean down to touch it, and touched, too, the rough brick of the house, that was cool and damp against her fingers. Later, when it grew warm, and the sun seemed as hot as in summer, she would go out into the front and stand under a tree on the edge of the clearing (never far into the bush where she was afraid) and let the deep shade rest her. The thick olive-green leaves overhead let through chinks of clear blue, and the wind was sharp and cold. And then, suddenly, the whole sky lowered itself into thick grey blanket, and for a few days it was a different world, with a soft dribble of rain, and it was really cold: so cold she wore a sweater and enjoyed the sensation of shivering inside it. But this never lasted long. It seemed that from one half hour to the next the heavy grey would grow thin, showing blue behind, and then the sky would seem to lift, with layers of dissolving cloud in the middle air; all at once, there would be a high blue sky again, all the grey curtains gone. The sunshine dazzled and glittered, but held no menace; this was not the sun of October, that insidiously sapped from within. There was a lift in the air, an exhilaration. Mary felt healed – almost. Almost, she became as she had been, brisk and energetic, but with a caution in her face and in her movements that showed she had not forgotten the heat would return. She tenderly submitted herself to this miraculous three months of winter, when the country was purified of its menace. Even the veld looked different, flaming for a few brief weeks into red and gold and russet, before the trees became solid masses of heavy green. It was as if this winter had been sent especially for her, to send a tingle of vitality into her, to save her from her helpless dullness. It was *her* winter; that was how she felt. Dick noticed it; he was attentively solicitous to her after her running away – for her return had bound him to her in gratitude for ever. If he had been a spiteful sort of man, he might have gone cold against her because it had really been such an easy way to win mastery over him, the sort of trick women use to defeat their men. But it never occurred to him. And after all, her running away had been genuine enough; though it had had the results that any calculating woman could have foreseen. He was gentle and tolerant, curbing his rages; and he was pleased to see her with new life, moving around the house with more zest, a softened, rather pathetic look on her face, as if she were clinging to a friend she knew must leave her. He even asked her again to come down on the farm with him; he felt a need to be near her, for he was secretly afraid she might vanish again one day when he was away. For although their marriage was all wrong, and there was no real understanding between them, he had become accustomed to the double solitude that any marriage, even a bad one, becomes. He could not imagine returning to a house where there was no Mary. And even her rages against her servants seemed to him, during that short time, endearing; he was grateful for the resurgence of vitality that showed itself in an increased energy over the shortcomings and laziness of her houseboy.

But she refused to help him on the farm. It seemed to her a

cruelty that he should suggest it. Up here, on the rise, even
with the tumbled heap of big boulders behind the house that
blocked the sweeping winds, it was cool compared with the
fields shut down between ridges of rock and trees. Down there,
one would not be able to tell it was winter! Even now, looking
down into the hollow one could see the heat shimmering over
buildings and earth. No, let her stay where she was: she
wouldn't go down with him. He accepted it, grieved and
snubbed as always; but still, happier than he had been for a
long time. He liked to see her at night, sitting peacefully with
her hands folded, on the sofa, cuddling herself luxuriously
inside her sweater, shivering cheerfully with the cold. For these
nights the roof cracked and crinkled like a thousand fireworks,
because of the sharp alternations between the day's hot sun
and the frosts of night. He used to watch her reaching up her
hand to touch the icy-cold iron of the roof, and felt disconsolate
and helpless against this mute confession of how much she
hated the summer months. He even began to think of putting
in ceilings. He secretly got out his farm books and calculated
what they would cost. But the last season had been a bad one
for him; and the end of his impulse to protect her from what
she dreaded was a sigh, and a determination to wait until next
year, when things might be better.

Once she did go down with him to the lands. It was when he
told her there had been frost. She stood over the cold earth in
the vlei one morning before the sun rose, laughing with
pleasure, because of the crusty film of white over the earth.
'Frost!' she said. 'Who would believe it, in this baked, god-
forsaken spot!' She picked up pieces of the crackling flimsy
stuff and rubbed them between blue hands, inviting him to do
the same, sharing with him this moment of delight. They were
moving gently towards a new relation; they were more truly
together than they had ever been. But then it was that he
became ill; and the new tenderness between them, which might
have grown into something strong enough to save them both,
was not yet strong enough to survive this fresh trouble.

For one thing, Dick had never been ill before, although this
was a malaria district and he had lived in it so long. Perhaps he

had had malaria in his blood for years and never known it? He always took quinine, every night, during the wet season, but not when it grew cold. Somewhere on the farm there must be, he said, a tree trunk filled with stagnant water, in a warm enough spot for mosquitoes to breed; or perhaps an old rusting tin in a shady place where the sun could not reach the water to evaporate it. In any event, weeks after one could expect fever in the usual way, Mary saw Dick come up from the lands one evening, pale and shivering. She offered him quinine and aspirin, which he took, and afterwards fell into bed, without eating his supper. The next morning, angry with himself and refusing to believe he was ill, he was off to work as usual, wearing a heavy leather jacket as a futile prophylactic against violent shivering fits. At ten in the morning, with the fever sweat pouring down his face and neck and soaking his shirt, he crawled up the hill and got between blankets, half-unconscious already.

It was a very sharp attack, and because he was not used to illness, he was querulous and difficult. Mary sent a letter over to Mrs Slatter – though she hated having to ask favours of her – and later that day Charlie brought the doctor in his car; he had driven thirty miles to fetch him. The doctor made the usual pronouncements, and when he had finished with Dick, told Mary the house was dangerous as it was, and should be wired for mosquitoes. Also, he said, the bush should be cut back for another hundred yards about the house. Ceilings should be put in at once, otherwise there was danger of their both getting sunstroke. He looked shrewdly at Mary, informed her she was anaemic, run down and in bad nervous condition and she should go for at least three months to the coast at once. He then left, while Mary stood on the verandah and watched the car drive off, with a grim little smile on her face. She was thinking, with hate, that it was all very well for rich professionals to talk. She hated that doctor, with his calm way of shrugging off their difficulties; when she had said they could not afford a holiday, he had said sharply, 'Nonsense! Can you afford to be really ill?' And he had asked how long it had been since she had been to the coast? She had never seen the sea!

But the doctor had understood their position better than she imagined, for the bill she awaited with dread, did not come. After a while she wrote to know how much they owed, and the answer came back: 'Pay me when you can afford it.' She was miserable with frustrated pride; but let it go – they literally did not have the money.

Mrs Slatter sent over a sack of citrus from her orchard for Dick, and many offers of assistance. Mary was grateful for her presence there, only five miles away, but decided not to call her save in an emergency. She wrote one of those dry little notes of hers in thanks for the citrus, and said that Dick was better. But Dick was not at all better. There he lay, in all the helpless terror of a person suffering his first bad illness, with his face turned to the wall and a blanket over his head. 'Just like a nigger!' said Mary in sharp scorn over his cowardice; she had seen sick natives lie just like that, in a kind of stoical apathy. But from time to time Dick roused himself to ask about the farm. Every conscious moment he worried about the things that would be going wrong without his supervision. Mary nursed him like a baby for a week, conscientiously, but with impatience because of his fear for himself. Then the fever left him, and he was weak and depressed, hardly able to sit up. He now tossed and kicked and fretted, talking all the time about his farmwork.

She saw that he wanted her to go down and see to things, but did not like to suggest it. For a while she did not respond to the appeal she saw in his weakened and querulous face; then, realizing he would get out of bed before he was fit to walk, she said she would go.

She had to crush down violent repugnance to the idea of facing the farm natives herself. Even when she had called the dogs to her and stood on the verandah with the car keys in her hand, she turned back again to the kitchen for a glass of water; sitting in the car with her foot resting on the accelerator, she jumped out again, on an excuse that she needed a handkerchief. Coming out of the bedroom she noticed the long sjambok that rested on two nails over the kitchen door, like an ornament: it was a long time since she had remembered its existence. Lifting it down, looping it over her wrist, she went to the car with more confidence. Because of it, she opened the back door of the car and let out the dogs; she hated the way they breathed down the back of her neck as she drove. She left them whining with disappointment outside the house, and drove herself down to the lands where the boys were supposed to be working. They knew of Dick's illness, and were not there, having dispersed, days before, to the compound. She took the car along the rough and rutted road as near as she could get to the compound, and then walked towards it along the native path that was trodden hard and smooth, but with a soft littering of glinting slippery grass over it, so that she had to move carefully to save herself from sliding. The long pale grass left sharp needles in her skirts, and the bushes shook red dust into her face.

The compound was built on a low rise above the vlei, about half a mile from the house. The system was that a new labourer presenting himself for work was given a day without pay to build a hut for himself and his family before taking his place with the workers. So there were always new huts, and always empty old ones that slowly collapsed and fell down unless somebody thought of burning them. The huts were closely clustered over an acre or two of ground. They looked like natural growths from the ground, rather than man-made dwellings. It was as though a giant black hand had reached down from the sky, picked up a handful of sticks and grass, and dropped them magically on the earth in the form of huts. They were grass-roofed, with pole walls plastered with mud, and single low doors, but no windows. The smoke from the fires inside percolated through the thatch or drifted in clouds from the doorways, so that each had the appearance of smouldering slowly from within. Between the huts were irregular patches of ill-cultivated mealies, and pumpkin vines trailed everywhere through plants and bushes and up over the walls and roofs, with the big amber-coloured pumpkins scattered among the leaves. Some of them were beginning to rot, subsiding into a sour festering ooze of pinky stuff, covered with flies. Flies were everywhere. They hummed round Mary's head in a cloud as she walked, and they were clustered round the eyes of the dozen small black children who were pot-bellied and mostly naked, staring at her as she picked her way through the vines and mealies past the huts. Thin native mongrels, their bones ridging through their hides, bared their teeth and cringed. Native women, draped in dirty store-stuff, and some naked above the waist with their slack black breasts hanging down, gazed at her from doorways with astonishment at her queer appearance, commenting on her among themselves, laughing, and making crude remarks. There were some men: glancing through doorways she could see bodies huddled asleep; some sat on their haunches on the ground in groups, talking. But she had no idea which were Dick's labourers, which were merely visiting here, or perhaps passing through the place on their way somewhere else. She stopped before one of them and told him to fetch the headboy, who soon came stooping out of one of the better huts that were ornamented on the walls with patterns of daubed red and yellow clay. His eyes were inflamed: she could see he had been drinking.

She said in kitchen kaffir: 'Get the boys on to the lands in ten minutes.'

'The boss is better?' he asked with hostile indifference.

She ignored the question, and said, 'You can tell them that I will take two and six off the ticket of every one of them that isn't at work in ten minutes.' She held out her wrist and pointed to the watch, showing him the time interval.

The man slouched and stooped in the sunshine, resenting her presence; the native women stared and laughed; the filthy, underfed children crowded around, whispering to each other; the starved dogs slunk in the background among the vines and mealies. She hated the place, which she had never entered before. 'Filthy savages!' she thought vindictively. She looked straight into the reddened, beer-clouded eyes of the headman, and repeated, 'Ten minutes.' Then she turned and walked off down the winding path through the trees, listening for the sounds of the natives turning out of the huts behind her.

She sat in the car waiting, beside the land where she knew they were supposed to be reaping maize. After half an hour a few stragglers arrived, the headboy among them. At the end of an hour not more than half of the labourers were present: some had gone visiting to neighbouring compounds without permission, some lay drunk in their huts. She called the headboy to her, and took down the names of those who were absent, writing them in her big awkward hand on a scrap of paper, spelling the unfamiliar names with difficulty. She remained there the whole morning, watching the straggling line of working boys, the sun glaring down through the old canvas hood on to her bare head. There was hardly any talking among them. They worked reluctantly, in a sullen silence; and she knew it was because they resented her, a woman, supervising them. When the gong rang for the lunch interval, she went up to the house and told Dick what had happened, but toning it down so that he would not worry. After lunch she drove down again, and curiously enough without repugnance for this work from which she had shrunk so long. She was exhilarated by the unfamiliar responsibility, the sensation of pitting her will against the farm. Now she left the car standing on the road, as the gang of natives moved into the middle of the field where the pale gold maize stood high above their heads, and where she could not see them from outside. They were tearing off the heavy cobs, and putting them into the halfsacks tied round their waists, while others followed cutting down the pillaged stalks and leaning them in small pyramids that regularly dotted the field. She moved steadily along the land with them, standing in the cleared part among the rough stubble, and watched them ceaselessly. She still carried the long thong of leather looped round one wrist. It gave her a feeling of authority, and braced her against the waves of hatred that she could feel coming from the gang of natives. As she walked steadily along beside them, with the hot yellow sunlight on her head and neck, making her shoulders ache, she began to understand how it was that Dick could stand it, day after day. It was difficult to sit still in the car with the heat filtering through the roof; it was another thing to move along with the workers, in the rhythm of their movement, concentrated on the work they were doing. As the long afternoon passed, she watched, in a kind of alert stupor, the naked brown backs bend, steady and straighten, the ropes of muscle sliding under the dusty skin. Most of them wore pieces of faded stuff as loincloths; some, khaki shorts; but nearly all were naked above the waist. They were a short thin crowd of men, stunted by bad feeding, but muscular and tough. She was oblivious to anything outside of this field, the work to be done, the gang of natives. She forgot about the heat, the beating sun, the glare. She watched the dark hands stripping cobs, and leaning the ragged gold stems together, and thought of nothing else. When one of the men paused for a moment in his work to rest, or to wipe the running sweat from his eyes, she waited one minute by her watch, and then called sharply to him to begin again. He would look slowly round at her, then bend back to the mealies, slowly, as if in protest. She did not know that Dick made a habit of calling a general rest of five minutes each hour; he had learned they worked better for it; it seemed to her an insolence directed against her authority over them when they stopped, without permission, to straighten their backs and wipe off the sweat. She kept them at it until sundown, and went back to the house satisfied with herself, not even tired. She was exhilarated and light-limbed, and swung the sjambok jauntily on her wrist.

Dick was lying in bed in the low-roofed room that was as chilly in the cool months as soon as the sun went down as it was hot in summer, anxious and restless, resenting his helplessness. He did not like to think of Mary close to those natives all day; it was not a woman's job. And besides, she was so bad with natives, and he was short of labour. But he was relieved and rested when she told him how the work was progressing. She said nothing of how she disliked the natives, of how the hostility that she could feel as something palpable coming from them against her, affected her; she knew he could be in bed for days yet, and that she would have to do it whether she liked it or not. And, really, she liked it. The sensation of being boss over perhaps eighty black workers gave her new confidence; it was a good feeling, keeping them under her will, making them do as she wanted.

At the week's end it was she who sat behind the small table set out on the verandah among the pot plants while the gangs of boys stood outside, under dark overshadowing trees waiting to be paid. This was the monthly ritual.

It was already dusk, the first stars coming out in the sky; and on the table was set a hurricane lamp, whose low dull flame looked a doleful bird caught in a glass cage. The bossboy beside her called out the names as she turned them up on her list. As she came to those who had not obeyed her summons that first day, she deducted half a crown, handing over the balance in silver; the average wage was about fifteen shillings, for the month. There were sullen murmurings amongst the natives; and as there was a small storm of protest brewing, the bossboy moved to the low wall and began arguing with them in his own language. She could only understand an odd word here or there, but she disliked the man's attitude and tone; he seemed, from his manner, to be telling them to accept an unalterable evil fate, not scolding them, as she would have liked to do, for their negligence and laziness. After all, for several days they had done no work at all. And if she did what she had threatened, the whole lot of them would be docked two and sixpence, because none had obeyed her and appeared on the lands within the specified ten minutes. They were in the wrong; she was in the right; and the bossboy should be telling them so, not persuasively arguing with them and shrugging his shoulders – and even, once, laughing. At last he turned back to her, told her they were dissatisfied and demanded what was due. She said shortly and finally that she had said she would deduct that amount and she intended to keep her word. She would not change her mind. Suddenly angry, she added, without reflecting, that those who did not like it could leave. She went on with the business of arranging the little piles of notes and silver, taking no notice of the storm of talk outside. Some of them walked off to the compound, accepting the position. Others waited in groups till she had finished the paying, and then came up to the wall. One after another spoke to the bossboy, saying they wanted to leave. She felt a little afraid, because she knew how hard it was to get labour, and how this was Dick's most persistent worry. Nevertheless, even while she turned her head to listen for Dick's movements in the bed that was behind her through one thickness of wall, she was filled with determination and resentment, because they expected to be paid for work they had not done, and had gone visiting when Dick was ill; above all, that they had not come to the lands in that interval of ten minutes. She turned to the waiting group and told them that those of them who were contracted natives could not leave.

These had been recruited by what is the South African equivalent of the old press gang: white men who lie in wait for the migrating bands of natives on their way along the roads to look for work, gather them into large lorries, often against their will (sometimes chasing them through the bush for miles if they try to escape), lure them by the fine promises of good employment and finally sell them to the white farmers at five pounds or more per head for a year's contract.

Of these boys she knew that some would be found to have run away from the farm during the next few days; and some would not be recovered by the police, for they would escape through the hills to the border and so out of reach. But she was not going to be swayed now by fear of their going and Dick's labour troubles; she would rather die than show weakness. She dismissed them, using the police as a threat. The others, who were working on a monthly basis, and whom Dick kept with him by a combination of coaxing and good-humoured threats, she said could leave at the month's end. She spoke to them directly – not through the medium of the bossboy – in cold clear tones, explaining with admirable logic how they were in the wrong, and how she was justified in acting as she did. She ended with a short homily on the dignity of work, which is a doctrine bred into the bones of every white South African. They would never be any good, she said (speaking in kitchen kaffir which some of them did not understand, being fresh from their kraals) until they learned to work without supervision, for the love of it, to do as they were told, to do a job for its own sake, not thinking about the money they would be paid for it. It was this attitude towards work that had made the white man what he was: the white man worked because it was good to work, because working without reward was what proved a man's worth.

The phrases of this little lecture came naturally to her lips: she did not have to look for them in her mind. She had heard them so often from her father, when he was lecturing his native servants, that they welled up from the part of her brain that held her earliest memories.

The natives listened to her with what she described to herself as 'cheeky' faces. They were sullen and angry, listening to her (or what they could understand of her speech) with inattention, simply waiting for her to finish.

Then, brushing away their protests, which broke out as soon as her voice stopped, she got up with an abrupt dismissing gesture, lifted the little table with the paper bags of money stacked on it, and carried it inside. After a while she heard them moving off, talking and grumbling among themselves, and looking through the curtains saw their dark bodies mingling with the shadows of the trees before they disappeared. Their voices floated back: angry shouts now and imprecations against her. She was filled with vindictiveness and a feeling of victory. She hated them all, every one of them, from the headboy whose subservience irritated her, to the smallest child; there were some children working among the others who could be no more than seven or eight years old.

She had learned, standing in the sun watching them all day, to hide her hatred when she spoke to them, but she did not attempt to hide it from herself. She hated it when they spoke to each other in dialects she did not understand, and she knew they were discussing her and making what were probably obscene remarks against her – she knew it, though she could only ignore it. She hated their half-naked, thick-muscled black bodies stooping in the mindless rhythm of their work. She hated their sullenness, their averted eyes when they spoke to her, their veiled insolence: and she hated more than anything, with a violent physical repulsion, the heavy smell that came from them, a hot, sour animal smell.

'How they stink,' she said to Dick, in an explosion of anger that was the reaction from setting her will against theirs.

Dick laughed a little. He said, 'They say we stink.'

'Nonsense!' she exclaimed, shocked that these animals should so presume.

'Oh yes,' he said, not noticing her anger. 'I remember talking to old Samson once. He said: "You say we smell. But to us there is nothing worse than a white man's smell."'

'Cheek!' she began indignantly; but then she saw his still pale and hollowed face, and restrained herself. She had to be very careful, because he was liable to be touchy and irritable in his present stage of weakness.

'What were you talking to them about?' he asked.

'Oh, nothing much,' she said warily, turning away. She had decided not to tell him about the boys that were leaving until later, when he was really well.

'I hope you are being careful with them,' he said anxiously. 'You have to go slow with them these days, you know. They are all spoilt.'

'I don't believe in treating them soft,' she said scornfully. 'If I had my way, I'd keep them in order with the whip.'

'That's all very well,' he said irritably, 'but where would you get the labour?'

'Oh, they all make me sick,' she said, shuddering.

During this time, in spite of the hard work and her hatred of the natives, all her apathy and discontent had been pushed into the background. She was too absorbed in the business of controlling the natives without showing weakness, of running the house and arranging things so that Dick would be comfortable when she was out. She was finding out, too, about every detail of the farm: how it was run and what was grown. She spent several evenings over Dick's books when he was asleep. In the past she had taken no interest in this: it was Dick's affair. But now she was analysing figures – which wasn't difficult with only a couple of cash books – seeing the farm whole in her mind. She was shocked by what she found. For a little while she thought she must be mistaken; there must be more to it than this. But there was not. She surveyed what crops were grown, what animals there were, and analysed without difficulty the causes of their poverty. The illness, Dick's enforced seclusion and her enforced activity, had brought the farm near to her and made it real. Before it had been an alien and rather distasteful affair from which she voluntarily excluded herself, and which she made no attempt to understand as a whole, thinking it more complicated than it was. She was now annoyed with herself that she had not tried to appreciate these problems before.

Now, as she followed the gang of natives up the field, she thought continually about the farm, and what should be done. Her attitude towards Dick, always contemptuous, was now bitter and angry. It was not a question of bad luck, it was simply incompetence. She had been wrong in thinking that those outbursts of wishful thinking over turkeys, pigs, etc., had been a kind of escape from the discipline of his work on the farm. He was all of a piece, everything he did showed the same traits. Everywhere she found things begun and left unfinished. Here it was a piece of land that had been half-stumped and then abandoned so that the young trees were growing up over it again; there it was a cowshed made half of brick and iron and half of bush timber and mud. The farm was a mosaic of different crops. A single fifty-acre land had held sunflowers, sunhemp, maize, monkeynuts and beans. Always he reaped twenty sacks of this and thirty sacks of that with a few pounds profit to show on each crop. There was not a single thing properly done on the whole place, nothing! Why was he incapable of seeing it? Surely he must see that he would never get any further like this?

Sun-dazed, her eyes aching with the glare, but awake to every movement of the boys, she contrived, schemed and planned, deciding to talk to Dick when he was really well, to persuade him to face clearly where he would end if he did not change his methods. It was only a couple of days before he would be well enough to take over the work: she would allow him a week to get back to normal, and then give him no peace till he followed her advice.

But on that last day something happened that she had not foreseen.

Down in the vlei, near the cowsheds, was where Dick stacked his mealiecobs each year. First sheets of tin were laid down, to protect them from white ants; then the sacks of cobs were emptied on to it, and there slowly formed a low pile of white, slippery-sheathed mealies. This was where she remained these days, to supervise the proper emptying of the sacks. The natives unloaded the dusty sacks from the waggon, holding them by the corners on their shoulders, bent double under the weight. They were like a human conveyor-belt. Two natives standing on the waggon swung the heavy sack on to the waiting bent back. The men moved steadily forward in a file, from the waggon's side to the mealie-dump, staggering up its side on the staircase of wedged full sacks, to empty the cobs in white flying shower down the stack. The air was gritty and prickly with the tiny fragments of husk. When Mary passed her hand over her face, she could feel it rough, like fine sacking.

She stood at the foot of the heap, which rose before her in a great shining white mountain against the vivid sky, her back to the patient oxen which were standing motionless with their heads lowered, waiting till the waggon should be emptied and they free to move off on another trip. She watched the natives, thinking about the farm, and swinging the sjambok from her wrist so that it made snaky patterns in the red dust. Suddenly she noticed that one of the boys was not working. He had fallen out of line, and was standing by, breathing heavily, his face shining with sweat. She glanced down at her watch. One minute passed, then two. But still he stood, his arms folded, motionless. She waited till the hand of the watch had passed the third minute, in growing indignation that he should have the temerity to remain idle when he should know by now her rule that no one should exceed the allowed one-minute pause. Then she said, 'Get back to work.' He looked at her with the expression common to African labourers: a blank look, as if he hardly saw her, as if there was an obsequious surface with which he faced her and her kind, covering an invulnerable and secret hinterland. In a leisurely way he unfolded his arms and turned away. He was going to fetch himself some water from the petrol tin that stood under a bush for coolness, nearby. She said again, sharply, her voice rising: 'I said, get back to work.'

At this he stopped still, looked at her squarely and said in his own dialect which she did not understand, 'I want to drink.'

'Don't talk that gibberish to me,' she snapped. She looked around for the bossboy who was not in sight.

The man said, in a halting ludicrous manner, 'I . . . want . . . water.' He spoke in English, and suddenly smiled and opened his mouth and pointed his finger down his throat. She could hear the other natives laughing a little from where they stood on the mealie-dump. Their laughter, which was good-humoured, drove her suddenly mad with anger: she thought it was aimed at her, whereas these men were only taking the opportunity to laugh at something, anything at all, in the middle of their work; one of themselves speaking bad English and sticking his finger down his throat was as good a thing to laugh at as any other.

But most white people think it is 'cheek' if a native speaks English. She said, breathless with anger, 'Don't speak English to me,' and then stopped. This man was shrugging and smiling and turning his eyes up to heaven as if protesting that she had forbidden him to speak his own language, and then hers – so what was he to speak? That lazy insolence stung her into an inarticulate rage. She opened her mouth to storm at him, but remained speechless. And she saw in his eyes that sullen resentment, and – what put the finishing touch to it – amused contempt. Involuntarily she lifted her whip and brought it down across his face in a vicious swinging blow. She did not know what she was doing. She stood quite still, trembling; and when she saw him put his hand, dazedly, to his face, she looked down at the whip she held in stupefaction, as if the whip had swung out of its own accord, without her willing it. A thick weal pushed up along the dark skin of the cheek as she looked, and from it a drop of bright blood gathered and trickled down and off his chin, and splashed to his chest. He was a great hulk of a man, taller than any of the others, magnificently built, with nothing on but an old sack tied round his waist. As she stood there, frightened, he seemed to tower over her. On his big chest another red drop fell and trickled down to his waist. Then she saw him make a sudden movement and recoiled, terrified;

she thought he was going to attack her. But he only wiped the blood off his face with a big hand that shook a little. She knew that all the natives were standing behind her stock-still, watching the scene. In a voice that sounded harsh from breathlessness, she said, 'Now get back to work.' For a moment the man looked at her with an expression that turned her stomach liquid with fear. Then, slowly, he turned away, picked up a sack and rejoined the conveyor-belt of natives. They all began work again quite silently. She was trembling with fright, at her own action, and because of the look she had seen in the man's eyes.

She thought: he will complain to the police that I struck him? This did not frighten her, it made her angry. The biggest grievance of the white farmer is that he is not allowed to strike his natives, and that if he does, they may – but seldom do – complain to the police. It made her furious to think that this black animal had the right to complain against her, against the behaviour of a white woman. But it is significant that she was not afraid for herself. If this native had gone to the police station, she might have been cautioned, since it was her first offence, by a policeman who was a European, and who came on frequent tours of the district, when he made friends with the farmers, eating with them, staying the night with them, joining their social life. But he, being a contracted native, would have been sent back to this farm; and Dick was hardly likely to make life easy for a native who had complained of his wife. She had behind her the police, the courts, the jails; he, nothing but patience. Yet she was maddened by the thought he had even the right to appeal; her greatest anger was directed against the sentimentalists and theoreticians, whom she thought of as 'They' – the law-makers and the Civil Service – who interfered with the natural right of a white farmer to treat his labour as he pleased.

But mingled with her anger was that sensation of victory, a satisfaction that she had won in this battle of wills. She watched him stagger up the sacks, his great shoulders bowed under his load, taking a bitter pleasure in seeing him subdued thus. And nevertheless her knees were still weak: she could have sworn that he nearly attacked her in that awful moment after she struck him. But she stood there unmoving, locking her conflicting feelings tight in her chest, keeping her face composed and severe; and that afternoon she returned again, determined not to shrink at the last moment, though she dreaded the long hours of facing the silent hostility and dislike.

When night came at last, and the air declined swiftly into the sharp cold of a July night, and the natives moved off, picking up old tins they had brought to drink from, or a ragged coat, or the corpse of some rat or veld creature they had caught while working and would cook for their evening meal, and she knew her task was finished, because tomorrow Dick would be here, she felt as if she had won a battle. It was a victory over these natives, over herself and her repugnance of them, over Dick and his slow, foolish shiftlessness. She had got far more work out of these savages than he ever had. Why, he did not even know how to handle natives!

But that night, facing again the empty days that would follow, she felt tired and used-up. And the argument with Dick, that she had been planning for days, and that had seemed such a simple thing when she was down on the lands, away from him, considering the farm and what should be done with it without him, leaving him out of account, seemed now a weary heart-breaking task. For he was preparing to take up the reins again as if her sovereignty had been nothing, nothing at all. He was absorbed and preoccupied again, that evening, and not discussing his problems with her. And she felt aggrieved and insulted; for she did not care to remember that for years she had refused all his pleas for her help and that he was acting as she had trained him to act. She saw, that evening, as the old fatigue came over her and weighted her limbs, that Dick's well-meaning blunderings would be the tool with which she would have to work. She would have to sit like a queen bee in this house and force him to do what she wanted.

The next few days she bided her time, watching his face for the returning colour and the deepening sunburn that had been washed out by the sweats of fever. When he seemed fully himself again, strong, and no longer petulant and irritable, she broached the subject of the farm.

They sat one evening under the dull lamplight, and she sketched for him, in her quick emphatic way, exactly how the farm was running, and what money he could expect in return, even if there were no failures and bad seasons. She demonstrated to him, unanswerably, that they could never expect to get out of the slough they were in, if they continued as they were: a hundred pounds more, fifty pounds less, according to the variations of weather and the prices, would be all the difference they could anticipate.

As she spoke her voice became harsh, insistent, angry. Since he did not speak, but only listened uneasily, she got out his books and supported her contentions with figures. From time to time he nodded, watching her finger moving up and down the long columns, pausing as she emphasized a point, or did rapid calculations. As she went on he said to himself that he ought not to be surprised, for he knew her capacity; had it not been for this reason that he had asked for her help?

For instance, she ran chickens on quite a big scale now, and made a few pounds every month from eggs and table birds; but all the work in connection with this seemed to be finished in a couple of hours. That regular monthly income had made all the difference to them. Nearly all day, he knew, she had nothing to do; yet other women who ran poultry on such a scale found it heavy work. Now she was analysing the farm, and the organization of crops, in a way that made him feel humble, but also provoked him to defend himself. For the moment, however, he remained silent, feeling admiration, resentment and self-pity; the admiration temporarily gaining upper hand. She was making mistakes over details, but on the whole she was quite right: every cruel thing she said was true! While she talked, pushing the roughened hair out of her eyes with her habitual impatient gesture, he felt hurt too; he recognized the justice of her remarks, he was prevented from defensiveness because of the impartiality of her voice; but at the same time the impartiality stung him and wounded him. She was looking at the farm from outside, as a machine for making money: that was how she regarded it. She was critical entirely from this angle. But she left so much out of account. She gave him no credit for the way he looked after his soil, for that hundred acres of trees. And he could not look at the farm as she did. He loved it and was part of it. He liked the slow movement of the seasons, and the complicated rhythm of the 'little crops' that she kept describing with contempt as usual.

When she had finished, his conflicting emotions kept him silent, searching for words. And at last he said, with that little defeated smile of his: 'Well, and what shall we do?' She saw that smile and hardened her heart: it was for the good of them both; and she had won! He had accepted her criticisms. She began explaining, in detail, exactly what it was they should do. She proposed they grew tobacco: people all about them were growing it and making money. Why shouldn't they? And in everything she said, every inflection of her voice, was one implication: that they should grow tobacco, make enough money to pay their debts, and leave the farm as soon as they could.

His realization, at last, of what she was planning, stunned his responses. He said bleakly: 'And when we have made all that money, what shall we do?'

For the first time she looked unconfident, glanced down at the table, could not meet his eyes. She had not really thought of it. She only knew that she wanted him to be a success and make money, so that they would have the power to do what they wanted, to leave the farm, to live a civilized life again. The stinting poverty in which they lived was unbearable; it was destroying them. It did not mean there was not enough to eat: it meant that every penny must be watched, new clothes forgone, amusements abandoned, holidays kept in the never-never-land of the future. A poverty that allows a tiny margin for spending, but which is shadowed always by a weight of debt that nags like a conscience, is worse than starvation itself. That was how she had come to feel. And it was bitter because it was a self-imposed poverty. Other people would not have understood Dick's proud self-sufficiency. There were plenty of farmers in the district, in fact all over the country, who were as poor as they, but who lived as they pleased, piling up debts, hoping for some windfall in the future to rescue them. (And, in parentheses, it must be admitted that their cheerful shiftlessness was proved to be right: when the war came and the boom in tobacco, they made fortunes from one year to the next – which occurrence made the Dick Turners appear even more ridiculous than ever.) And if the Turners had decided to abandon their pride, to take an expensive holiday and to buy a new car, their creditors, used to these farmers, would have agreed. But Dick would not do this. Although Mary hated him for it, considering he was a fool, it was the only thing in him she still respected: he might be a failure and a weakling, but over this, the last citadel of his pride, he was immovable.

Which was why she did not plead with him to relax his conscience and do as other people did. Even then fortunes were being made out of tobacco. It seemed so easy. Even now, looking across the table at Dick's weary, unhappy face, it seemed so easy. All he had to do was to make up his mind to it. And then? That was what he was asking – what was their future to be?

When she thought of that hazy, beautiful time in the future, when they could live as they pleased, she always imagined herself back in town, as she had been, with the friends she had known then, living in the Club for young women. Dick did not fit into the picture. So when he repeated his question, after her long evasive silence, during which she refused to look into his eyes, she was silenced by their inexorably different needs. She shook the hair again from her eyes, as if brushing away something she did not want to think about, and said, begging the question, 'Well, we can't go on like this, can we?'

And now there was another silence. She tapped on the table with the pencil, twirling it around between finger and thumb, making a regular irritating noise that caused him to tauten his muscles against it.

So now it was up to him. She had handed the whole thing over to him again and left him to do as he could – but she would not say towards what goal she wanted him to work. And he began to feel bitter and angry against her. Of course they could not go on like this: had he ever said they should? Was he not working like a nigger to free them? But then, he had got out of the habit of living in the future; this aspect of her worried him. He had trained himself to think ahead to the next season. The next season was always the boundary of his planning. Yet she had soared beyond all that and was thinking of other people, a different life – and without him: he knew it, though she did not say so. And it made him feel panicky, because it was so long now since he had been with other people that he did not need them. He enjoyed an occasional grumble with Charlie Slatter, but if he was denied that outlet, then it did not matter. And it was only when he was with other people that he felt useless, and a failure. He had lived for so many years with the working natives, planning a year ahead, that his horizons had narrowed to fit his life, and he could not imagine anything else. He certainly could not think of himself anywhere but on this farm: he knew every tree on it. This is no figure of speech: he knew the veld he lived from as the natives know it. His was not the sentimental love of the townsman. His senses had been sharpened to the noise of the wind, the song of the birds, the feel of the soil, changes in weather – but they had been dulled to everything else. Off this farm he would wither and die. He wanted to make good so that they continue living on the farm, but in comfort, and so that Mary could have the things she craved. Above all, so that they could have children. Children, for him, were an insistent need. Even now, he had not given up hope that one day . . . And he had never understood that she visualized a future off the farm, and with his concurrence! It made him feel lost and blank, without support for his life. He looked at her almost with horror, as an alien creature who had no right to be with him, dictating what he should do.

But he could not afford to think of her like that: he had realized, when she ran away, what her presence in his house meant to him. No; she must learn to understand his need for the farm, and when he had made good, they would have children. She must learn that his feeling of defeat was not really caused by his failure as a farmer at all: his failure was her hostility towards him as a man, their being together as they were. And when they could have children even this would be healed, and they would be happy. So he dreamed, his head on his hands, listening to that tap-tap-tap of the pencil.

But in spite of this comfortable conclusion to his meditation, his sense of defeat was overwhelming. He hated the thought of tobacco; he always had, it seemed to him an inhuman crop. His farm would have to be run in a different way; it would mean standing for hours inside buildings in steamy temperatures; it would mean getting up at nights to watch thermometers.

So he fiddled with his papers on the table, pressed his head into his hands, and rebelled miserably against his fate. But it was no good, with Mary sitting opposite him, forcing him to do as she willed. At last he looked up, smiled a twisted unhappy smile, and said, 'Well, boss, can I think it over for a few days?' But his voice was strained with humiliation. And when she said irritably, 'I do wish you wouldn't call me boss!' he did not answer, though the silence between them said eloquently what they were afraid to say. She broke it at last by rising briskly from the table, sweeping away the books, and saying, 'I am going to bed.' And left him there, sitting with his thoughts.

Three days later he said quietly, his eyes averted, that he was aranging with native builders to put up two barns.

When he looked at her at last, forcing himself to face her uncontrollable triumph, he saw her eyes bright with new hope, and thought with disquiet what it would mean to her if he failed this time.

8

Once she had exerted her will to influence him, she withdrew, and left him alone. Several times he made an attempt to draw her into his work by asking advice, suggesting she should help him with something that was troubling him, but she refused these invitations as she had always done, for three reasons. The first was calculated: if she were always with him, always demonstrating her superior ability, his defensiveness would be provoked and he would refuse, in the end, to do anything she wanted. The other two were instinctive. She still disliked the farm and its problems and shrank from becoming, as he had resigned to its little routine. And the third reason, though she was not aware of it, was the strongest. She needed to think of Dick, the man to whom she was irrevocably married, as a person on his own account, a success from his own efforts. When she saw him weak and goal-less, and pitiful, she hated him, and the hate turned in on herself. She needed a man stronger than herself, and she was trying to create one out of Dick. If he had genuinely, simply, because of the greater strength of his purpose, taken the ascendency over her, she would have loved him, and no longer hated herself for becoming tied to a failure. And this was what she was waiting for, and what prevented her, though she itched to do it, from simply ordering him to do the obvious things. Really, her withdrawal from the farm was to save what she thought was the weakest point of his pride, not realizing that she was his failure. And perhaps she was right, instinctively right: material success she would have respected and given herself to. She was right, for the wrong reasons. She would have been right if Dick had been a different kind of man. When she noticed that he was again behaving foolishly, spending money on unnecessary things, skimping expenses on essentials, she refused to let herself think about it. She could not: it meant too much, this time. And Dick, rebuffed and let down because of her withdrawal, ceased to appeal to her. He stubbornly went his own way, feeling as if she had encouraged him to swim in deep waters beyond his strength, and then left him to his own devices.

She retired to the house, to the chickens and that ceaseless struggle with her servants. Both of them knew they were facing a challenge. And she waited. For the first years she had been waiting and longing in the belief, except for short despairing intervals, that somehow things would change. Something miraculous would happen and they would win through. Then she had run away, unable to bear it, and, returning, had realized there would be no miraculous deliverance. Now, again, there was hope. But she would do nothing but wait until Dick had set things going. During those months she lived like a person with a certain period to endure in a country she disliked: not making definite plans, but taking it for granted that once transplanted to a new place, things would settle themselves. She still did not plan what would happen when Dick made this money, but she day-dreamed continually about herself working in an office, as the efficient and indispensable secretary, herself in the Club, the popular elder confidante, herself welcomed in a score of friendly houses, or 'taken out' by men who treated her with the comradely affection that was so simple and free from danger.

Time passed quickly, rushing upwards, as it does in those periods when the various crises that develop and ripen in each life show like hills at the end of a journey, setting a boundary to an era. As there is no limit to the amount of sleep to which the human body can be made to accustom itself, she slept hours every day, so as to hasten time, so as to swallow great gulps of it, waking always with the satisfactory knowledge that she was another few hours nearer deliverance. Indded, she was hardly awake at all, moving about what she did in a dream of hope, a hope that grew so strong as the weeks passed that she would wake in the morning with a sensation of release and excitement, as if something wonderful was going to happen that very day.

She watched the progress of the block of tobacco barns that were being built in the vlei below as she might have watched a ship constructed that would carry her from exile. Slowly they took shape; first an uneven outline of brick, like a ruin; then a divided rectangle, like hollow boxes pushed together; and then the roof went on, a new shiny tin that glinted in the sunlight and over which the heat waves swam and shimmered like glycerine. Over the ridge, out of sight, near the empty potholes of the vlei, the seedbeds were being prepared for when the rains would come and transform the eroded valley-bottom into a running stream. The months went past until October. And though this was the time of the year she dreaded, when the heat was like an enemy, she endured it quite easily, sustained by hope. She said to Dick that the heat wasn't so bad this year, and he replied that it had never been worse, glancing at her as he spoke with concern, even distrust. He could never understand her fluctuating dependence on the weather, an emotional attitude towards it that was alien to him. Since he submitted himself to heat and cold and dryness, they were no problems to him. He was their creature, and did not fight against them as she did.

And this year she felt the growing tension in the smoke-dimmed air with excitement, waiting for the rains to fall which would start the tobacco springing in the fields. She used to ask Dick with an apparent casualness that did not deceive him, about other farmers' crops, listening with bright-eyed anticipation to his laconic accounts of how this one had made ten thousand pounds in a good season, and that one cleared off all his debts. And when he pointed out, refusing to respect her pretence at disinterestedness, that he had only two barns built, instead of the fifteen or twenty of a big farmer, and that he could not expect to make thousands, even if the season were good, she brushed this warning aside. It was necessary for her to dream of immediate success.

The rains came – unusually enough – exactly as they should, and settled comfortably into a soaking December. The tobacco looked healthy and green and fraught – for Mary – with promise of future plenty. She used to walk round the fields with Dick just for the pleasure of looking at its sturdy abundance, and thinking of those flat green leaves transformed into a cheque of several figures.

And then the drought began. At first Dick did not worry: tobacco can stand periods of dryness once the plants have settled into the soil. But day after day the great clouds banked up, and day after day the ground grew hotter and hotter. It was past Christmas, then well into January. Dick became morose and irritable, with the strain, Mary curiously silent. Then, one afternoon, there was a slight shower that fell, perversely, on only one of the two pieces of land which held the tobacco. Again the drought began, and the weeks passed without a sign of rain. At last the clouds formed, piled up, dissolved. Mary and Dick stood on their verandah and saw the heavy veils pass along the hills. Thin curtains of rain advanced and retreated over the veld; but on their farm it did not fall, not for several days after other farmers had announced the partial salvation of their crops. One afternoon there was a warm drizzle, fat gleaming drops falling through sunlight where a brilliant rainbow arched. But it was not enough to damp the parched ground. The withered leaves of the tobacco hardly lifted. Then followed days of bright sun.

'Well,' said Dick, his face screwed up in chagrin, 'it is too late in any case.' But he was hoping that the field which had caught the first shower, might survive. By the time the rain fell as it should, most of the tobacco was ruined: there would be a little. A few mealies had come through: this year they would not cover expenses. Dick explained all this to Mary quietly, with an expression of suffering. But at the same time she saw relief written in his face. It was because he had failed through no fault of his own. It was sheer bad luck that could have happened to anyone: she could not blame him for it.

They discussed the situation one evening. He said he had applied for a fresh loan to save them from bankruptcy, and that next year he would not rely on tobacco. He would prefer to plant none; he would put in a little if she insisted. If they had another failure like this year, it would mean bankruptcy for certain.

In a last attempt Mary pleaded for another year's trial; they could not have two bad seasons running. Even to him, 'Jonah' (she made herself use this name for him, with an effort at sympathetic laughter), it would be impossible to send two bad seasons, one after another. And why not, in any case, get into debt properly? Compared with some others, who owed thousands, they were not in debt at all. If they were going to fail, let them fail with a crash, in a real attempt to make good. Let them build another twelve barns, plant out all the lands they had with tobacco, risk everything on one last try. Why not? Why should he have a conscience when no one else did?

But she saw the expression on his face she had seen before, when she had pleaded they might go on holiday to restore themselves to real health. It was a look of bleak fear that chilled her. 'I'm not getting a penny more into debt that I can help,' he said finally. 'Not for anyone.' And he was obdurate; she could not move him.

And next year, what then?

If it was a good year, he said, and all the crops did well, and there was no drop in prices, and the tobacco was a success, they would recover what they had lost that year. Perhaps it would mean a bit more than that. Who knew? His luck might turn. But he was not going to risk everything on one crop again until he was out of debt. Why, he said, his face grey, if they went bankrupt the farm would be lost to them! She replied, though she knew it was what wounded him most, that she would be glad if that did happen: then they would be forced to do something vigorous to support themselves; and that the real reason for his complacency was that he knew, always, that even if they did reach the verge of bankruptcy, they could live on what they grew and their own slaughtered cattle.

The crises of individuals, like the crises of nations, are not realized until they are over. When Mary heard that terrible 'next year' of the struggling farmer, she felt sick; but it was not for some days that the buoyant hope she had been living on died, and she felt what was ahead. Time, through which she had been living half-consciously, her mind on the future, suddenly lengthened out in front of her. 'Next year' might mean anything. It might mean another failure. It would certainly mean no more than a partial recovery. The miraculous reprieve was not going to be granted. Nothing would change: nothing ever did.

Dick was surprised she showed so few signs of disappointment. He had been bracing himself to face storms of rage and tears. With the habit of long years, he easily adapted himself to the thought of 'next year', and began planning accordingly. Since there were no immediate indications of despair from Mary, he ceased looking for them: apparently the blow had not been as hard as he had thought it would be.

But the effects of mortal shocks only manifest themselves slowly. It was some time before she no longer felt strong waves of anticipation and hopefulness that seemed to rise from the depths of herself, out of a region of her mind that had not yet heard the news about the tobacco failure. It took a long time before her whole organism was adjusted to what she knew was the truth: that it would be years, if ever, before they got off the farm.

Then followed a time of dull misery: not the sharp bouts of unhappiness that were what had attacked her earlier. Now she felt as if she were going soft inside at the core, as if a soft rottenness was attacking her bones.

For even day-dreams need an element of hope to give satisfaction to the dreamer. She would stop herself in the middle of one of her habitual fantasies about the old days, which she projected into her future, saying dully to herself that there would be no future. There was nothing. Nil. Emptiness.

Five years earlier she would have drugged herself by the reading of romantic novels. In towns women like her live vicariously in the lives of the film stars. Or they take up religion, preferably one of the more sensuous Eastern religions. Better educated, living in the town with access to books, she would have found Tagore perhaps, and gone into a sweet dream of words.

Instead, she thought vaguely that she must get herself something to do. Should she increase the number of her chickens? Should she take in sewing? But she felt numbed and tired, without interest. She thought that when the next cold season came and stung her into life again, she would do something. She postponed it: the farm was having the same effect on her that it had had on Dick; she was thinking in terms of the next season.

Dick, working harder than ever on the farm, realized at last that she was looking worn, with a curious puffy look about her eyes, and patches of red on her cheeks. She looked really very unhealthy. He asked her if she were feeling ill. She replied, as if only just becoming aware of it, that she was. She was suffering from bad headaches, a lassitude that might mean she was ill. She seemed to be pleased, he noted, to think that illness could be the cause.

He suggested, since he could not afford to send her for a holiday, that she might go into town and stay with some of her friends. She appeared horrified. The thought of meeting people, and most particularly those people who had known her when she was young and happy, made her feel as if she were raw all over, her nerves exposed on a shrinking surface.

Dick went back to work, shrugging his shoulders at her obstinacy, hoping that her illness would pass.

Mary was spending her days moving restlessly about the house, finding it difficult to sit still. She slept badly at nights. Food did not nauseate her, but it seemed too much trouble to eat. And all the time it was as if there were thick cottonwool in her head, and a soft dull pressure on it from outside. She did her work mechanically, attending to her chickens and the store, keeping things running out of habit. During this time she hardly ever indulged in her old fits of temper against her servant. It was as if, in the past, these sudden storms of rage had been an outlet for an unused force, and that, as the force died, they became unnecessary to her. But she still nagged: that had become a habit, and she could not speak to a native without irritation in her voice.

After a while, even her restlessness passed. She would sit for hours at a time on the shabby old sofa with the faded chintz curtains flapping above her head, as if she were in a stupor. It seemed that something had finally snapped inside of her, and she would gradually fade and sink into darkness.

But Dick thought she was better.

Until one day she came to him with a new look on her face, a desperate, driven look, that he had never seen before, and asked if they might have a child. He was glad: it was the greatest happiness he had ever known from her because she asked it, of her own accord, turning to him – so he thought. He thought she was turning to him at last, and expressing it this way. He was so glad, filled with a sharp delight, that for a moment he nearly agreed. It was what he wanted most. He still dreamed that one day, 'when things were better', they could have children. And then his face became dull and troubled, and he said, 'Mary, how can we have children?'

'Other people have them, when they are poor.'

'But Mary, you don't know how poor we are.'

'Of course I know. But I can't go on like this. I must have something. I haven't anything to do.'

He saw she was desiring a child for her own sake, and that he still meant nothing to her, not in any real way. And he replied obdurately that she had only to look around her to see what happened to children brought up as theirs would be brought up.

'Where?' she asked vaguely, actually looking around the room as if these unfortunate children were visible there, in their house.

He remembered how isolated she was, how she had never become part of the life of the district. But this irritated him again. It had been years before she stirred herself to find out about the farm; after all this time she still did not know how people lived all around them – she hardly knew the names of their neighbours. 'Have you never seen Charlie's Dutchman?'

'What Dutchman?'

'His assistant. Thirteen children! On twelve pounds a month. Slatter is hard as nails with him. Thirteen children! They run round like puppies, in rags, and they live on pumpkin and mealiemeal like kaffirs. They don't go to school . . .'

'Just one child?' persisted Mary, her voice weak and plaintive. It was a wail. She felt she needed one child to save her from herself. It had taken weeks of slow despair to bring her to this point. She hated the idea of a baby, when she thought of its helplessness, its dependence, the mess, the worry. But it would give her something to do. It was extraordinary to her that things had come to this; that it was she pleading with Dick to have a child, when she knew he longed for them, and she disliked them. But after thinking about a baby through those weeks of despair, she had come to cling to the idea. It wouldn't be so bad. It would be company. She thought of herself, as a child, and her mother; she began to understand how her mother had clung to her, using her as a safety-valve. She identified herself with her mother, clinging to her most passionately and pityingly after all these years, understanding now something of what she had really felt and suffered. She saw herself, that barelegged, bareheaded, silent child, wandering in and out of the chicken-coop house – close to her mother, wrung simultaneously by love and pity for her, and by hatred for her father; and she imagined her own child, a small daughter, comforting her as she had comforted her mother. She did not think of this child as a small baby; that was a stage she would have to get through as quickly as posible. No, she wanted a little girl as a companion; and refused to consider that the child, after all, might be a boy.

But Dick said: 'And what about school?'

'What about it?' said Mary angrily.

'How are we going to pay school fees?'

'There aren't any school fees. My parents didn't pay fees.'

'There are boarding fees, books, train fares, clothes. Is the money going to come out of the sky?'

'We can apply for a Government grant.'

'*No*,' said Dick, sharply, wincing. 'Not on your life! I've had enough of going hat in hand into fat men's offices, asking for money, while they sit on their fat arses and look down their noses. Charity! I won't do it. I won't have a child growing up knowing I can't do anything for it. Not in this house. Not living this way.'

'It's all right for me to live this way, I suppose,' said Mary grimly.

'You should have thought of that before you married me,' said Dick, and she blazed into fury because of his callous injustice. Or rather, she almost blazed into anger. Her face went beef-red, her eyes snapped – and then she subsided again, folding trembling hands over each other, shutting her eyes. The anger vanished: she was feeling too tired for real temper. 'I am getting on for forty,' she said wearily. 'Can't you see that very soon I won't be able to have a child at all? Not if I go on like this.'

'Not now,' he said inexorably. And that was the last time a child was ever mentioned. She knew as well as he did that it was folly, really, Dick being what he was, using his pride over borrowing as a last ditch for his self-respect.

Later, when he saw she had lapsed back into that terrible apathy, he appealed again: 'Mary, please come to the farm with me. Why not? We could do it together.'

'I hate your farm,' she said in a stiff, remote voice. 'I hate it, I want nothing to do with it.'

But she did make the effort, in spite of her indifference. It was all the same to her what she did. For a few weeks she accompanied Dick everywhere he went, and tried to sustain him with her presence. And it filled her with despair more than ever. It was hopeless, hopeless. She could see so clearly what was wrong with him, and with the farm, and could do nothing to help him. He was so obstinate. He asked her for advice, looked boyishly pleased when she picked up a cushion and trailed after him off to the lands; yet, when she made suggestions his face shut into dark obstinacy, and he began defending himself.

Those weeks were terrible for Mary. That short time, she looked at everything straight, without illusions, seeing herself and Dick and their relationship to each other and to the farm, and their future, without a shadow of false hope, as honest and stark as the truth itself. And she knew she could not bear this sad clear-sightedness for long; that, too, was part of the truth. In a mood of bitter but dreamy clairvoyance she followed Dick around, and at last told herself she should give up making suggestions and trying to prod him into commonsense. It was useless.

She took to thinking with a dispassionate tenderness about Dick himself. It was a pleasure to her to put away bitterness and hate against him, and to hold him in her mind as a mother might, protectively, considering his weaknesses and their origins, for which he was not responsible. She used to take her cushion to the corner of the bush, in the shade, and sit on the ground with her skirts well tucked up, watching for ticks to crawl out of the grass, thinking about Dick. She saw him standing in the middle of the big red land, balanced among the huge clods, a spare, fly-away figure with his big flopping hat and loose clothing, and wondered how people came to be born without that streak of determination, that bit of iron, that clamped the personality together. Dick was so nice – so nice! she said to herself wearily. He was so decent; there wasn't an ugly thing in him. And she knew, only too well, when she made herself face it (which she was able to do, in this mood of dispassionate pity) what long humiliation he had suffered on her account, as a man. Yet he had never tried to humiliate her: he lost his temper, yes, but he did not try to get his own back. He was so nice! But he was all to pieces. He lacked that thing in the centre that should hold him together. And had he always been like that? Really, she didn't know. She knew so little about him. His parents were dead; he was an only child. He had been brought up somewhere in the suburbs of Johannesburg, and she guessed, though he had not said so, that his childhood had been less squalid than hers, though pinched and narrow. He had said angrily that his mother had had a hard time of it; and the remark made her feel kin to him, for he loved his mother and had resented his father. And when he grew up he had tried a number of jobs. He had been clerk in the post office, something on the railways, had finally inspected watermeters for the municipality. Then he had decided to become a vet. He had studied for three months, discovered he could not afford it; and, on an impulse, had come to Southern Rhodesia to be a farmer, and to 'live his own life'.

So here he was, this hopeless, decent man, standing on his 'own' soil, which belonged to the last grain of sand to the Government, watching his natives work, while she sat in the shade and looked at him, knowing perfectly well that he was doomed: he had never had a chance. But even then it seemed impossible to her, that such a good man should be a failure. And she would get up from the cushion, and walk across to him, determined to have one more try.

'Look, Dick,' she said one day, timidly, but firmly, 'look, I have an idea. Next year, why not try to stump another hundred acres or so, and get a really big crop in, all mealies. Plant mealies on every acre you have, instead of all these little crops.'

'And what if it is a bad season for mealies?'

She shrugged: 'You don't seem to be getting very far as you are.'

And then his eyes reddened, and his face set, and the two deep lines scored from cheekbones to chin deepened.

'What more can I do than I am doing?' he shouted at her. 'And how can I stump a hundred acres more? The way you talk! Where am I to get the labour from? I haven't enough labour to do what I have got to do now. I can't afford to buy niggers at five pounds a head any longer. I have to rely on voluntary labour. And it just isn't coming any more. It's partly your fault. You lost me twenty of my best boys, and they'll never come back. They are out somewhere else giving my farm a bad name, at this moment, because of your damned temper. They are just not coming to me now as they used. No, they all go into the towns where they loaf about doing nothing.'

And then, this familiar grievance carried him away, and he began to storm against the Government, which was under the influence of the nigger-lovers from England, and would not force the natives to work on the land, would not simply send out lorries and soldiers and bring them to the farmers by force. The Government never understood the difficulties of farmers! Never! And he stormed against the natives themselves, who refused to work properly, who were insolent – and so on. He talked on and on, in a hot, angry, bitter voice, the voice of the white farmer, who seems to be contending, in the Government, with a force as immovable as the skies and seasons themselves. But, in this storm of resentment, he forgot about the plans for next year. He returned to the house preoccupied and bitter, and snapped at the houseboy, who temporarily represented the genus native, which tormented him beyond all endurance.

Mary was worried by him at this time, so far as she could be worried in her numbed state. He would return with her at sundown tired and irritable, to sit in a chair smoking endlessly. By now he was a chain-smoker, though he smoked native cigarettes which were cheaper, but which gave him a perpetual cough and stained his fingers yellow to the middle joints. And he would fidget and jig about in the chair, as if his nerves simply would not relax. And then, at last, his body slackened and he lay limp, waiting for supper to come in, so that he could go to bed at last and sleep.

But the houseboy would enter and say there were farm boys waiting to see him, for permission to go visiting, or something of that kind, and Mary would see that tense look return to Dick's face, and the explosive restlessness of his limbs. It seemed that he could not bear natives any more. And he would shout at the houseboy to get out and leave him alone and tell the farm natives to get to hell back to the compound. But in half an hour the servant would return, saying patiently, bracing himself against Dick's irritation, that the boys were still waiting. And Dick would stub out the cigarette, immediately light another and go outside, shouting at the top of his voice.

Mary used to listen, her own nerves tense. Although this exasperation was so familiar to her, it annoyed her to see it in him. It irritated her extremely, and she would be sarcastic when he came back, and said, 'You can have your troubles with the natives, but I am not allowed to.'

'I tell you,' he would say, glaring at her from hot, tormented eyes, 'I can't stand them much longer.' And he would subside, shaking all over, into his chair.

But in spite of this perpetual angry undercurrent of hate, she was disconcerted when she saw him talking to his bossboy perhaps, on the lands. Why, he seemed to be growing into a native himself, she thought uneasily. He would blow his nose on his fingers into a bush, the way they did; he seemed, standing beside them, to be one of them; even his colour was not so different, for he was burned a rich brown, and he seemed to hold himself the same way. And when he laughed with them, cracking some joke to keep them good-humoured, he seemed to have gone beyond her reach into a crude horse-humour that shocked her. And what was to be the end of it, she wondered? And then an immense fatigue would grip her, and she thought dimly: 'What does it matter, after all?'

At last she said to him that she saw no point spending all her time sitting under a tree with ticks crawling up her legs, in order to watch him. Especially when he took no notice of her.

'But, Mary, I like you being there.'

'Well, I've had enough of it.'

And she lapsed into her former habits, ceasing to think about the farm. The farm was the place from which Dick returned to eat and sleep.

And now she gave way. All day she sat numbly on the sofa with her eyes shut, feeling the heat beating in her brain. She was thirsty: it was too much of an effort to get a glass of water or to call the boy to fetch it for her. She was sleepy; but to get up from where she sat and climb on the bed was an exhausting labour. She slept where she was. Her legs felt, as she walked, that they were too heavy for her. To make a sentence was an overwhelming effort. For weeks on end she spoke to no one but Dick and the servant; and even Dick she saw for five minutes in the morning and for half an hour at night, before he dropped exhausted into bed.

The year moved through the cold bright months towards the heat; and, as it advanced the wind drove a rain of fine dust through the house, so that surfaces were gritty to the touch; and spiralling dust-devils rose in the lands below, leaving a shining wreckage of grass and maize husks hanging in the air like motes. She thought of the heat ahead with dread, but not able to summon up enough energy to fight it. She felt as if a touch would send her off balance into nothingness; she thought of a full complete darkness with longing. Her eyes closed, she

140

imagined that the skies were blank and cold, without even stars to break their blackness.

It was at this time, when any influence would have directed her into a new path, when her whole being was poised, as it were, waiting for something to propel her one way or the other, that her servant, once again, gave notice. This time there was no row over a broken dish or a badly-washed plate; quite simply, he wanted to go home; and Mary was too indifferent to fight. He left, having brought in his place a native whom Mary found so intolerable that she discharged him after an hour's work. She was left servantless for a while. Now she did not attempt to do more than was essential. Floors were left unswept, and they ate tinned food. And a new boy did not present himself. Mary had earned such a bad name among them as a mistress that it became increasingly difficult as time went on to replace those who left.

Dick, unable to stand the dirt and bad food any longer, said he would bring up one of the farm natives for training as a houseboy. When the man presented himself at the door, Mary recognized him as the one she had struck with the whip over the face two years before. She saw the scar on his cheek, a thin darker weal across the black skin. She stood irresolute in the doorway, while he waited outside, his eyes bent down. But the thought of sending him back to the lands and waiting for somebody else to be sent up; even this postponement tired her. She told him to come in.

That morning, because of some inward prohibition she did not try to explain, she could not work with him as was usually her custom on these occasions. She left him alone in the kitchen; and when Dick came up, said, 'Isn't there another boy that will do?'

Dick, without looking at her, and eating as he always did these days, in great gulps, as if there was no time, said: 'He's the best I could find. Why?' He sounded hostile.

She had never told him about the incident of the whip, for fear of his anger. She said: 'He doesn't seem a very good type to me.' As she spoke she saw that look of exasperation grow on his face, and added hastily, 'But he will do, I suppose.'

Dick said, 'He is clean and willing. He's one of the best boys I have ever had. What more do you want?' He spoke brusquely, almost with brutality. Without speaking again he went out. And so the native stayed.

She began on the usual routine of instruction, as cold-voiced and methodical as always, but with a difference. She was unable to treat this boy as she had treated all the others, for always, at the back of her mind, was that moment of fear she had known just after she had hit him and thought he would attack her. She felt uneasy in his presence. Yet his demeanour was the same as in all the others; there was nothing in his attitude to suggest that he remembered the incident. He was silent, dogged and patient under her stream of explanations and orders. His eyes he always kept lowered, as if afraid to look at her. But she could not forget it, even if he had; and there was a subtle difference in the way she spoke to him. She was as impersonal as she knew how to be; so impersonal that her voice was free, for a while, even of the usual undertone of irritation.

She used to sit quite still, watching him work. The powerful, broad-built body fascinated her. She had given him white shorts and shirts to wear in the house, that had been used by her former servants. They were too small for him; as he swept or scrubbed or bent to the stove, his muscles bulged and filled out the thin material of the sleeves until it seemed they would split. He appeared even taller and broader than he was because of the littleness of the house.

He was a good worker, one of the best she had had. She used to go round after him trying to find things that he had left undone, but she seldom did. So, after a while, she became used to him, and the memory of that whip slashing across his face faded. She treated him as it was natural to her to treat natives, and her voice grew sharp and irritated. But he did not answer back, and accepted her often unjust rebukes without even lifting his eyes off the ground. He might have made up his mind to be as neutral as he knew how.

And so they proceeded, with everything apparently as it

should be, a good routine established, that left her free to do nothing. But she was not quite as indifferent as she had been.

By ten in the morning, after he had brought her tea, he would go off to the back behind the chicken-runs under a big tree, carrying a tin of hot water; and from the house she sometimes caught a glimpse of him bending over it, sluicing himself, naked from the waist up. But she tried not to be around when it was time for his bath. After this was over, he came back to the kitchen and remained quite still, leaning against the back wall in the sun, apparently thinking of nothing. He might have been asleep. Not until it was time to prepare lunch did he start work again. It annoyed her to think of him standing idly there, immobile and silent for hours, under the unshaded force of the sun which seemed not to affect him. There was nothing she could do about it, though instead of sinking into a dreary lethargy that was almost sleep, she would rack her brains to think of work she could give him.

One morning she went out to the fowl-runs, which she often forgot to do these days; and when she had finished a perfunctory inspection of the nesting-boxes, and her basket was filled with eggs, she was arrested by the sight of the native under the trees a few yards off. He was rubbing his thick neck with soap, and the white lather was startlingly white against the black skin. He had his back to her. As she looked, he turned by some chance, or because he sensed her presence, and saw her. She had forgotten it was his time to wash.

A white person may look at a native, who is no better than a dog. Therefore she was annoyed when he stopped and stood upright, waiting for her to go, his body expressing resentment of her presence there. She was furious that perhaps he believed she was there on purpose; this thought, of course, was not conscious; it would be too much presumption, such unspeakable cheek for him to imagine such a thing, that she would not allow it to enter her mind; but the attitude of his still body as he watched her across the bushes between them, the expression on his face, filled her with anger. She felt the same impulse that had once made her bring down the lash across his face. Deliberately she turned away, loitered round the chicken-runs, and threw out handfuls of grain; and then slowly stooped out through the low wire door. She did not look at him again; but knew he was standing there, a dark shape, quite motionless, seen out of the corner of her eye. She went back to the house, for the first time in many months jerked clean out of her apathy, for the first time in months seeing the ground she walked over, and feeling the pressure of the sun against the back of her bare neck, the sharp, hot stones pressing up under her soles.

She heard a strange angry muttering, and realized she was talking to herself, out aloud, as she walked. She clapped her hand over her mouth, and shook her head to clear it; but by the time that Moses had come back into the kitchen, and she heard his footsteps, she was sitting in the front room rigid with an hysterical emotion; when she remembered the dark resentful look of that native as he stood waiting for her to leave, she felt as if she had put her hand on a snake. Impelled by a violent nervous reaction she went to the kitchen, where he stood in clean clothes, putting away his washing things. Remembering that thick black neck with the lather frothing whitely on it, the powerful back stooping over the bucket, was like a goad to her. And she was beyond reflecting that her anger, her hysteria, was over nothing, nothing that she could explain. What had happened was that the formal pattern of black-and-white, mistress-and-servant, had been broken by the personal relation; and when a white man in Africa by accident looks into the eyes of a native and sees the human being (which it is his chief preoccupation to avoid), his sense of guilt, which he denies, fumes up in resentment and he brings down the whip. She felt that she must do something, and at once, to restore her poise. Her eyes happened to fall on a candle-box under the table, where the scrubbing brushes and soap were kept, and she said to the boy: 'Scrub this floor.' She was shocked when she heard her own voice, for she had not known she was going to speak. As one feels when in an ordinary social conversation, kept tranquil by banalities, some person makes a remark that strikes below the surface, perhaps in error letting slip what he really thinks of you, and the shock sweeps one off one's balance, causing a nervous giggle or some stupid sentence that makes everyone present uncomfortable, so she felt: she had lost her balance; she had no control over her actions.

'I scrubbed it this morning,' said the native slowly, looking at her, his eyes smouldering.

She said, 'I said scrub it. Do it at once.' Her voice rose on the last words. For a moment they stared at each other, exposing their hatred; then his eyes dropped, and she turned and went out, slamming the door behind her.

Soon she heard the sound of the wet brush over the floor. She collapsed on the sofa again, as weak as if she had been ill. She was familiar with her own storms of irrational anger, but she had never known one as devastating as this. She was shaking, the blood throbbed in her ears, her mouth was dry. After a while, more composed, she went to the bedroom to fetch herself some water; she did not want to face the native Moses.

Yet, later, she forced herself to rise and go to the kitchen; and, standing in the doorway, surveyed the wet streaked floor as if she had truly come to inspect it. He stood immobile just outside the door, as usual gazing out to the clump of boulders where the euphorbia tree stuck out its grey-green, fleshy arms into vivid blue sky. She made a show of peering behind cupboards, and then said, 'It is time to lay the table.'

He turned, and began laying out glass and linen, with slow and rather clumsy movements, his great black hands moving among the small instruments. Every movement he made irritated her. She sat tensed, wound up, her hands clenched. When he went out, she relaxed a little, as if a pressure had been taken off her. The table was finished. She went to inspect it; but everything was in its right place. But she picked up a glass and took it to the back room.

'Look at this glass, Moses,' she commanded.

He came across and looked at it politely: it was only an appearance of looking, for he had already taken it from her to wash it. There was a trace of white fluff from the drying towel down one side. He filled the sink with water, and whisked in soapsuds, just as she had taught him, and washed the glass while she watched. When it was dry she took it from him and returned to the other room.

'She imagined him again standing silent at the door in the sun, looking at nothing, and she could have screamed or thrown a glass across the room to smash on the wall. But there was nothing, absolutely nothing, that she could give him to do. She began a quiet prowl through the house: everything, though shabby and faded, was clean and in its place. That bed, the great connubial bed which she had always hated, was smooth and uncrumpled, the coverlets turned back at the corners in a brave imitation of the inviting beds in modern catalogues. The sight of it gritted on her, reminding her of the hated contact in the nights with Dick's weary muscular body, to which she had never been able to accustom herself. She turned from it, clenching her hands, and saw her face suddenly in the mirror. Faded, tousled, her lips narrowed in anger, her eyes hot, her face puffed and blotched with red, she hardly recognized herself. She gazed, shocked and pitiful; and then she cried, weeping hysterically in great shuddering gasps, trying to smother the sound for fear the native at the back might hear her. She cried for some time; then, as she lifted her eyes to dry them, saw the clock. Dick would be home soon. Fear of his seeing her in this state stilled her convulsing muscles. She bathed her face, combed her hair, powdered the dark creased skin round the eyes.

That meal was as silent as all their meals were, these days. He saw her reddened, crumpled face, and her blood-suffused eyes, and knew what was wrong. It was always because of rows with her servants that she cried. But he was weary and disappointed; it had been quite a long time since the last fight, and he had imagined she might be getting over her weakness. She ate nothing, keeping her head bent down; and the native moved about the table through the meal like an automaton, his body serving them because it must, his mind not there. But the thought of this man's efficiency, and the sight of Mary's swollen face, suddenly goaded Dick. He said, when the native was out of the room: 'Mary, you must keep this boy. He is the best we have ever had.' She did not look up, even then, but remained, quite still, apparently deaf. Dick saw that her thin, sun-crinkled hand was shaking. He said again, after a silence, his voice ugly with hostility: 'I can't stand any more changing of servants. I've had enough. I'm warning you, Mary.' And again she did not reply; she was weak with the tears and anger of the morning, and afraid that if she opened her mouth she might weep anew. He looked at her in some astonishment, for as a rule she would have snapped back some complaint of theft, or bad behaviour. He had been braced to meet it. Her continued silence, which was pure opposition, drove him to insist on an assent from her. 'Mary,' he said, like a superior to a subordinate, 'did you hear what I said?' 'Yes,' she said at last, sullenly, with difficulty.

When he left, she went immediately to the bedroom so as to avoid the sight of the native clearing the table, and slept away four hours of unendurable time.

9

And so the days passed, through August and September, hot hazy days with slow winds blowing in sultry, dusty gusts from the encircling granite kopjes. Mary moved about her work like a woman in a dream, taking hours to accomplish what would formerly have taken her a few minutes. Hatless under the blazing sun, with the thick cruel rays pouring on to her back and shoulders, numbing and dulling her, she sometimes felt as if she were bruised all over, as if the sun had bruised her flesh to a tender swollen covering for aching bones. She would turn giddy as she stood, and send the boy for her hat. Then, with relief, as if she had been doing hard physical labour for hours, instead of wandering aimlessly among the chickens without seeing them, she would collapse into a chair, and sit unmoving, thinking of nothing; but the knowledge of that man alone in the house with her lay like a weight at the back of her mind. She was tight and controlled in his presence; she kept him working as long as she could, relentless over every speck of dust and every misplaced glass or plate – that she noticed. The thought of Dick's exasperation, and his warning that he could stand no more changes of servants, a challenge which she had not the vitality to face, caused her to hold herself like a taut-drawn thread, stretched between two immovable weights: that was how she felt, as if she were poised, a battleground for two contending forces. Yet what the forces were, and how she contained them, she could not have said. Moses was indifferent and calm against her as if she did not exist, except in so far as he obeyed her orders; Dick, formerly so good-natured and easy to please, now complained continually over her bad management; for she would nag at the boy in that high nervous voice of hers over a chair that was two inches out of its right place, and fail to notice that the ceiling was shrouded in cobwebs.

She was letting everything slide, except what was forced on her attention. Her horizon had been narrowed to the house. The chickens began to die; she murmured something about disease; and then understood that she had forgotten to feed them for a week. Yet she had wandered, as usual, through the runs, with a basket of grain in her hand. As they died, the scrawny fowls were cooked and eaten. For a short while, shocked at herself, she made an effort and tried to keep her mind on what she was doing. Yet, not long after, the same thing happened: she had not noticed the drinking troughs were empty. Fowls were lying over the baked earth, twitching feebly in death for lack of water. And then she could no longer be troubled. For weeks they lived on chicken, till the big wire runs were empty. And now there were no eggs. She did not order them from the store, because they were so expensive. Her mind, nine-tenths of the time, was a soft aching blank. She would begin a sentence and forget to finish it. Dick became accustomed to the way she would say three words, and then, her face becoming suddenly null and empty, lapse into silence. What she had been going to say had gone clean out of her head. If he gently prompted her to continue, she looked up, not seeing him, and did not answer. It grieved him so that he could not protest over the abandonment of her chickens, which had kept them going with a little ready money up till now.

But as far as the native was concerned, she was still responsive. This was the small part of her mind that was awake. All those scenes she would have liked to stage, but did not dare, for fear of the boy's leaving and Dick's anger, she acted out in her mind. Once she was roused by a noise and realized it was herself, talking out loud in the living-room in a low angry voice. In her fantasy, the native had forgotten to clean the bedroom that morning, and she was raging at him, thinking up cruel cutting phrases in her own language that he could not possibly have understood, even if she had said them to him. The sound of that soft, disjointed, crazy voice was as terrifying as the sight of herself in the mirror had been. She was afraid, jerked back into herself, shrinking from the vision of herself talking like a mad woman in the corner of the sofa.

She got up softly and went to the door between the living-room and the kitchen, looking through to see if the boy was near and could have heard. There he stood, as always, leaning against the outer wall; and she could see only his big shoulder bulging underneath the thin cloth, and his hand hanging idly down, the fingers curled softly inwards over the pinkish-brown palm. And he did not move. She told herself he could not have heard; and pushed the thought of the two open doors between herself and him out of her mind. She avoided him all that day, moving restlessly about the rooms as if she had forgotten how to remain still. She wept all that afternoon lying on the bed, with a hopeless convulsive sobbing; so that she was worn out when Dick came home. But this time he noticed nothing; he was worn out himself, wanting only to sleep.

The next day, when she was giving out supplies from the cupboard in the kitchen (which she tried to remember to keep locked, but which, more often than not, remained open without her noticing it, so that this business of putting out the amounts needed for the day was really futile), Moses, who was standing beside her with the tray, said he wanted to leave at the end of the month. He spoke quietly and directly, but with a trace of hesitation, as if he were setting himself to face opposition. She was familiar with this note of nervousness, for whenever a boy gave notice, although she always felt a sharp relief because the tensions that were created between herself and every servant would be dissolved by his going, she also felt indignant, as if it were an insult to herself. She never let one go without long argument and expostulation. And now, she opened her mouth to remonstrate, but became silent; her hand dropped from the door of the cupboard, and she found herself thinking of Dick's anger. She could not face it. She simply could not go through scenes with Dick. And it was not her fault this time; had she not done everything she could to keep this boy, whom she hated, who frightened her? To her horror she discovered she was shaking with sobs again, there, in front of the native! Helpless and weak, she stood beside the table, her back towards him, sobbing. For some time neither of them moved; then he came round where he could see her face, looking at her curiously, his brows contracted in speculation and wonder. She said at last, wild with panic: 'You mustn't go!' And she wept on, repeating over and over again, 'You must stay! You must stay!' And all the time she was filled with shame and mortification because he was seeing her cry.

After a while she saw him go across to the shelf where the water-filter stood to fill a glass. The slow deliberation of his movements galled her, because of her own lost control; and when he handed the glass to her she did not lift her hand to take it, feeling that his action was an impertinence which she should choose to ignore. But in spite of the attitude of dignity she was striving to assume, she sobbed out again, 'You mustn't go,' and her voice was an entreaty. He held the glass to her lips, so that she had to put up her hand to hold it, and with the tears running down her face she took a gulp. She looked at him pleadingly over the glass. and with renewed fear saw an indulgence for her weakness in his eyes.

'Drink,' he said simply, as if he were speaking to one of his own women; and she drank.

Then he carefully took the glass from her, put it on the table, and seeing that she stood there dazed, not knowing what to do, said: 'Madame lie down on the bed.' She did not move. He put out his hand reluctantly, loathe to touch her, the sacrosanct white woman, and pushed her by the shoulder; she felt herself gently propelled across the room towards the bedroom. It was like a nightmare where one is powerless against horror: the touch of this black man's hand on her shoulder filled her with nausea; she had never, not once in her whole life, touched the flesh of a native. As they approached the bed, the soft touch still on her shoulder, she felt her head beginning to swim and her bones going soft. 'Madame lie down,' he said again, and his voice was gentle this time, almost fatherly. When she dropped to a sitting position on the bedside, he gently held her shoulder and pushed her down. Then he took her coat off the door where it hung, and placed it over her feet. He went out, and the horror retreated; she lay there numbed and silent, unable to consider the implications of the incident.

After a while she slept, and it was late afternoon when she woke. She could see the sky outside the square of window, banked with thunderous blue clouds, and lit with orange light from the sinking sun. For a moment she could not remember what had happened; but when she did the fear engulfed her again, a terrible dark fear. She thought of herself weeping helplessly, unable to stop; of drinking at that black man's command; of the way he had pushed her across the two rooms to the bed; of the way he had made her lie down and then tucked the coat in round her legs. She shrank into the pillow with loathing, moaning out loud, as if she had been touched by excrement. And through her torment she could hear his voice, firm and kind, like a father commanding her.

After a while, when the room was quite dark, and only the pale walls glimmered, reflecting the light that still glowed in the tops of the trees, though their lower boughs held the shadows of dusk, she got up, and put a match to the lamp. It flared up, steadied, glowed quietly. The room was now a shell of amber light and shadows, hollowed out of the wide tree-filled night. She powdered her face, and sat a long time before the mirror, feeling unable to move. She was not thinking, only afraid, and of what she did not know. She felt she could not go out till Dick returned and supported her against the presence of the native. When Dick came, he said, looking at her with dismay, that he had not woken her at lunch-time, and that he hoped she was not ill. 'Oh no,' she said. 'Only tired. I am feeling . . .' Her voice tailed off, the blank look settled on her face. They were sitting in the dim arc of light from the swinging lamp, the boy quietly moving about the table. For a long time she kept her eyes lowered, though an alertness came back to her features with his entrance. When she made herself look up, and peer hurriedly into his face, she was reassured, for there was nothing new in his attitude. As always, he behaved as if he were an abstraction, not really there, a machine without a soul.

Next morning she made herself go into the kitchen and speak normally; and waited fearfully for him to say again that he wanted to leave. But he did not. For a week things went on until she realized he was not going; he had responded to her tears and appeal. She could not bear to think she had got her way by these methods; and because she did not want to remember it, she slowly recovered. Relieved, released from the torturing thought of Dick's anger, with the memory of her shameful collapse gone from her mind, she began again to use that cold biting voice to make sarcastic comments on the native's work. One day he turned to her in the kitchen, looked at her straight in the face and said in a voice that was disconcertingly hot and reproachful: 'Madame asked me to stay. I stay to help Madame. If Madame cross, I go.'

The note of finality checked her; she felt helpless. Particularly as she had been forced to remember why he was here at all. And then, the resentful heat of his voice said that he considered she was unjust. Unjust! She did not see it like that.

He was standing beside the stove, waiting for something to finish cooking. She did not know what to say. He moved over to the table, while he waited for her reply, he picked up a cloth with which to grasp the hot iron of the oven door-handle. Without looking at her, he said: 'I do the work well, yes?' he spoke in English, which as a rule she would have flamed into temper over; she thought it impertinence. But she answered in English, 'Yes.'

'Then why Madame always cross?'

He spoke, this time, easily, almost familiarly, good-humouredly, as if he were humouring a child. He bent to open the oven, with his back to her, and took out a tray of the crisp light scones, that were so much better than she could make herself. He began turning them out, one by one, on to a wire tray to cool. She felt as if she should go at once, but did not move. She was held, helpless, watching his big hands flip those little scones on to the tray. And she said nothing. She felt the usual anger rise within her, at the tone he used to her; at the same time she was fascinated, and out of her depth; she did not know what to do with this personal relation. So, after a while, since he did not look at her, and moved quietly about his work, she went away without replying.

When the rains broke in late October, after six weeks of destroying heat, Dick, as always at this time of the year stayed away for the midday meal because of the pressure of work. He left about six in the morning and returned at six at night, so there was only one meal to be cooked: breakfast and lunch were sent to him on the fields. As she had done before in previous years. Mary told Moses that she would not take lunch, and that he could bring her tea: she felt she could not be troubled to eat. On the first day of Dick's long absences, instead of the tray of tea, Moses brought her eggs, jam and toast. These he set carefully down on the small table beside her.

'I told you I only wanted tea,' she said sharply.

He answered quietly: 'Madame ate no breakfast, she must eat.' On the tray there was even a handleless cup with flowers in it: crude yellows and pinks and reds, bush flowers, thrust together clumsily, but making a strong burst of colour on the old stained cloth.

As she sat there, her eyes bent down, and he straightened himself after setting down the tray, what troubled her most was this evidence of his desire to please her, the propitiation of the flowers. He was waiting for a word of approval and pleasure from her. She could not give it; but the rebuke that sprang to her lips remained unspoken, and she pulled the tray to her and began to eat, without a word.

There was now a new relation between them. For she felt helplessly in his power. Yet there was no reason why she should. Never ceasing for one moment to be conscious of his presence about the house, or standing silently at the back against the wall in the sun, her feeling was one of a strong and irrational fear, a deep uneasiness, and even – though this she did not know, would have died rather than acknowledge – of some dark attraction. It was as though the act of weeping before him had been an act of resignation – resignation of her authority; and he had refused to hand it back. Several times the quick rebukes had come to her lips, and she had seen him look at her deliberately, not accepting it, but challenging her. Only once, when he had really forgotten to do something and was in the wrong, had he worn his old attitude of blank submissiveness. Then he accepted, because he was at fault. And now she began to avoid him. Whereas before she had made herself follow up his work, and had inspected everything he did, now she hardly went to the kitchen and left the care of the house to him. Even the keys she left on a shelf in the storeroom, where he could find them to open the grocery cupboard as he needed. And she was held in balance, not knowing what this new tension was that she could not break down.

Twice he asked her questions, in that new familiar friendly voice of his.

Once it was about the war. 'Did Madame think it would be over soon?' She was startled. To her, living out of contact with everything, not even reading the weekly newspaper, the war was a rumour, something taking place in another world. But she had seen him poring over the old newsprint spread on the kitchen table as covering. She answered stiffly that she did not know. And again, some days later, as if he had been thinking in the interval, he asked: 'Did Jesus think it right that people should kill each other?' This time she was angry at the implied criticism, and she answered coldly that Jesus was on the side of the good people. But all day she burned with her old resentment, and at night asked Dick: 'Where does Moses come from?'

'Mission boy,' he replied. 'The only decent one I've ever had.' Like most South Africans, Dick did not like mission boys, they 'knew too much'. And in any case they should not be taught to read and write: they should be taught the dignity of labour and general usefulness to the white man.

'Why?' he asked suspiciously. 'No trouble again, I hope?'

'No.'

'Has he been cheeky?'

'No.'

But the mission background explained a lot: that irritatingly well-articulated 'madame', for instance, instead of the usual 'missus', which was somehow in better keeping with his station in life.

That 'madame' annoyed her. She would have liked to ask him to drop it. But there was nothing disrespectful in it: it was only what he had been taught by some missionary with foolish ideas. And there was nothing in his attitude towards her she could take hold of. But although he was never disrespectful, he forced her now to treat him as a human being; it was impossible for her to thrust him out of her mind like something unclean, as she had done with all the others in the past. She was being forced into contact, and she never ceased to be aware of him. She realized, daily, that there was something in it that was dangerous, but what it was she was unable to define.

Now she dreamed through her broken nights, horrible, frightening dreams. Her sleep, once an instantaneous dropping of a black curtain, had become more real than her waking. Twice she dreamed directly of the native, and on each occasion she woke in terror as he touched her. On each occasion in her dream he had stood over her, powerful and commanding, yet kind, but forcing her into a position where she had to touch him. And there were other dreams, where he did not enter directly, but which were confused, terrifying, horrible, from which she woke sweating in fear, trying to put them out of her mind. She became afraid to go to sleep. She would lie in the dark, tense beside Dick's relaxed sleeping body, forcing herself to remain awake.

Often, during the day, she watched him covertly, not like a mistress watching a servant work, but with a fearful curiosity, remembering those dreams. And every day he looked after her, seeing what she ate, bringing her meals without her ordering them, bringing her little gifts of a handful of eggs from the compound fowls, or a twist of flowers from the bush.

Once, when it was long past sundown and Dick had not returned, she said to Moses, 'Keep the dinner hot, I am going to see what has happened to the boss.'

When she was in the bedroom fetching her coat, Moses knocked at the door, and said he would go and find out; Madame should not walk around in the dark bush by herself.

'All right,' she said helplessly, and took her coat off.

But there was nothing wrong with Dick. He had been held

up over an ox that had broken its leg. And when, a week later, he was again long after his time in coming, and she was worried, she made no effort to find out what was wrong, fearing that the native might again, quite simply and naturally, take the responsibility for her welfare. It had come to this: that she watched her actions from one point of view only; would they allow Moses to strengthen that new human relationship between them, in a way she could not counter, and which she could only try to avoid.

In February, Dick fell ill again with malaria. As before, it was a short, sudden attack, and bad while it lasted. As before, she reluctantly sent a note by bearer to Mrs Slatter, asking them to fetch the doctor. He looked at the slatternly little house with raised eyebrows, and asked Mary why she had taken no notice of his former prescriptions. She did not answer. 'Why have you not cut down the bush round the house where mosquitoes can breed?' 'My husband could not spare the boys.' 'But he can spare the time to be ill, eh?' The doctor's manner was bluff, easy, but at bottom indifferent; he had learned after years in a farming district, when to cut his losses as a doctor. Not his money, which he knew he would never see, but the patients themselves. These people were hopeless. The window-curtains faded by the sun to a dingy grey, torn and not mended, proclaimed it. Everywhere there was evidence of breakdown in will. It was a waste of time even coming. But from habit he stood over the shivering, burning Dick and prescribed. He said Dick was worn out, a shell of a man, liable to get any disease going. He spoke as strongly as he could, trying to frighten Mary into action. But her attitude said listlessly, 'What is the use.' He left at last with Charlie Slatter, who was sardonically disapproving; but unable to prevent himself from thinking that when he took over this place he would remove the wire from the chicken runs for his own, and that the corrugated iron of the house and buildings might come in useful some time.

Mary sat up with Dick the first two nights of his illness, on a hard chair, to keep herself awake, holding the blankets close over the restless limbs. But Dick was not as bad as the last time; he was not afraid now, knowing that the attack would run its course.

Mary made no effort to supervise the farm work; but twice a day, so as to calm him, she drove herself round the farm on a formal and useless inspection. The boys were in the compound loafing. She knew it, and did not care. She hardly looked at the fields: the farm had become something that did not concern her.

In the daytime, when she had finished preparing Dick's cool drinks, which were all that he took, she sat idly by the bed and sank into her usual apathetic state. Her mind wandered incoherently, dwelling on any scene from her past life that might push itself to the surface. But now it was without nostalgia or desire. And she had lost all sense of time. She set the alarm clock in front of her, to remind her of the regular intervals at which she must go and fetch Dick his drinks. Moses brought her the usual trays of food at the usual times, and she ate mechanically, not noticing what she ate, not noticing, even, that she sometimes put down her knife and fork after a couple of mouthfuls and forgot to finish what was before her. It was on the third morning that he asked, as she whisked an egg he had brought from the compound as a gift, into milk: 'Did Madame go to bed last night?' He spoke with that simple directness that always left her disarmed, not knowing how to reply.

She answered, looking down at the frothing milk, avoiding his eyes: 'I must stay up with the boss.'

'Did Madame stay up the other night?'

'Yes,' she answered, and quickly went into the bedroom with the drink.

Dick lay still, half delirious with fever, in an uncomfortable doze. His temperature had not dropped. He was taking this bout very hard. The sweat poured off him; and then his skin became dry and harsh and burning hot. Every afternoon the slender rod of quicksilver mounted in a trice up the frail glass tube, so she had hardly to keep it in his mouth at all, higher every time she looked at it, until by six in the evening it stood at 105. There it stayed until about midnight, while he tossed and muttered and groaned. In the early hours it dropped rapidly below normal, and he complained he was cold and needed more blankets. But he had all the blankets in the place piled over him. She heated bricks in the oven and wrapped them in cloth and put them by his feet.

That night Moses came to the bedroom door and knocked on the wood frame as he always did. She confronted him through the parted folds of the embroidered hessian curtain.

'Yes?' she asked.

'Madame stay in room tonight. I stay with boss.'

'No,' she said, thinking of the long night spent in intimate vigil with this native. 'No, you go back to the compound and sleep. I will stay with the boss.'

He came forward through the curtains, so that she shrank back a little, he was so close to her. She saw that he held a folded mealie sack in one hand, presumably his preparation for the night. 'Madame must sleep,' he said. 'She is tired, yes?' She could feel the skin round her eyes drawn tight with strain and weariness; but she insisted in a hard nervous voice: 'No, Moses. I must stay.' He moved to the wall where he placed his sack carefully in a space between two cupboards. Then he stood up and said, sounding wounded, even reproachful: 'Madame not thinks I look after boss right, huh? I too sick sometimes. I keep blankets over boss, yes?' He moved to the bed, but not too close, and looked down at Dick's flushed face. 'I give him this drink when he wakes, yes?' And the half-humorous, half-reproachful voice left her disarmed against him. She looked at his face once, quickly, avoiding the eyes, then away. But it would not do to seem afraid to look at him; she glanced down at his hand, the big hand with the lighter palm hanging loosely at his side. He insisted again: 'Madame think I not look after boss well?'

She hesitated, and then said nervously, 'Yes, but I must stay.'

As if her nervousness and hesitation had been answer enough, the man stooped and straightened out the blankets over the sleeping man. 'If boss is very sick, I call Madame,' he said.

She saw him standing by the window, blocking the square of star-strewn, bough-crossed sky, waiting for her to go. 'Madame will be sick too, if she does not sleep,' he said.

She went to the cupboard where she took out her big coat. Before she left the room, she said, in order to assert her authority: 'You will call me if he wakes.'

She went instinctively to her refuge, the sofa, next door, where she spent so many of her waking hours, and sat helplessly, squeezed into one corner. She could not bear to think of the black man there all night, next door, so close to her, with nothing but the thin brick wall separating them.

After a while she pushed a cushion to the head of the sofa, and lay down, covering her feet with the coat. It was a close night, and the air in the little room hardly stirred. The dull flame in the hanging lamp burned low, making a little intimate glimmer of light that sent up broken arcs of light into the darkness under the roof, illuminating a slope of corrugated metal, and a beam. In the room itself there was only a small yellow circle on the table beneath. Everything else was dark, there were only vague elongated shapes. She turned her head slightly to see the curtains at the window; they hung quite still; and listening intently, the tiny night noises from the bush outside sounded suddenly as loud as her own thudding heart. From the trees a few yards away a bird called once, and insects creaked. She heard the movement of branches, as if something heavy was pushing its way through them; and thought with fear of the low crouching trees all about. She had never become used to the bush, never felt at home in it. Still, after all this time, she felt a stirring of alarm when she realized the strangeness of the encircling veld where little animals moved, and unfamiliar birds talked. Often in the night she woke and thought of the small brick house, like a frail shell that might crush inwards under the presence of the hostile bush. Often she thought how, if they left this place, one wet fermenting season would swallow the small cleared space, and send the young trees thrusting up from the floor, pushing aside brick and cement, so that in a few months there would be nothing left but heaps of rubble about the trunks of trees.

She lay tense on the sofa, every sense alert, her mind quivering like a small hunted animal turned to face its pursuers. She ached all over with the strain. She listened to the night outside, to her own heart, and for sounds from the room next door. She heard the dry sound of horny feet moving over thin matting, a clink of glasses being moved, a low mutter from the sick man. Then she heard the feet move close, and a sliding movement as the native settled himself down on the sack between the cupboards. He was there, just through the thin wall, so close that if it had not been there his back would have been six inches from her face! Vividly she pictured the broad muscular back, and shuddered. So clear was her vision of the native that she imagined the hot acrid scent of native bodies. She could smell it, lying there in the dark. She turned her head over, and buried her face in a cushion.

For a long time she could hear nothing, only the soft noise of steady breathing. She wondered, was it Dick? But then he muttered again, and as the native rose to adjust the coverings, the sound of breathing ceased. Moses returned, and again she heard the sliding of his back down the wall; and the regular breathing began again: it was he! Several times she heard Dick stir and call out, in that thick voice which was not his, but which came from his sick delirium, and each time the native roused himself to cross to the bed. In between she listened intently for the soft breathing which seemed, as she turned restlessly, to come from all over the room, first from just near her beside the sofa, then from a dark corner opposite. It was only when she turned and faced the wall that she could localize the sound. She fell asleep in that position, bent against the wall as if listening to a keyhole.

It was a troubled, unrestful sleep, visited by dreams. Once she started awake at a movement, and saw the dark bulk of the man part the curtains. She held her breath, but at the sound of her movement he turned his eyes quickly towards her, and away; then he passed soundlessly out of the other door into the kitchen. He was only going out for a few minutes on his own business. Her mind followed him as he crossed the kitchen, opened the door and vanished into the dark alone. Then she turned her head to the cushion again, shuddering, as she had when she imagined that native smell. She thought: soon he will be coming back. She lay still, so as to seem asleep. But he did not come immediately, and after a few minutes' waiting she went to the dim bedroom where Dick lay motionless, in a tormented jumble of limbs. She felt his forehead: it was damp and cold, so she knew it must be well after midnight. The native had taken all the blankets off a chair, and heaped them over the sick man. Now the curtains moved behind her, and a cool breeze struck her neck. She shut the pane nearest the bed, and stood still, listening to the suddenly loud ticking of the clock. Leaning down to gaze at its faintly illuminated dial, she saw it was not yet two o'clock, but she felt that the night had been continuing for a very long time. She heard a noise from the back and quickly, as if guilty, went to lie down. Then she heard again the hard feet on the floor as Moses passed her to his station on the other side of the wall, and saw him looking at her to see if she was asleep. Now she felt she was wide awake, and could not sleep. She was chilly, but did not want to rise to look for further coverings. Again she imagined she smelt the warm odour, and to dispel the sensation turned her head softly to see the curtains blowing as the fresh night air poured in. Dick was quite still now; there was no sound from the other room except that faint rhythm of breathing.

She drifted off to sleep, and this time dreamed immediately, horribly.

She was a child again, playing in the small dusty garden in front of the raised wood-and-iron house, with playmates who in her dream were faceless. She was first in the game, a leader, and they called her name and asked her how they should play. She stood by the dry-smelling geranium plants, in the sun, with the children all about her. She heard her mother's sharp voice call for her to come in, and went slowly out of the garden up on to the verandah. She was afraid. Her mother was not there, so she went to the room inside. At the bedroom door she stopped, sickened. There was her father, the little man with the plump juicy stomach, beer-smelling and jocular, whom she hated, holding her mother in his arms as they stood by the window. Her mother was struggling in mock protest, playfully expostulating. Her father bent over her mother, and at the sight, Mary ran away.

Again, she was playing, this time with her parents and her brother and sister, before she went to bed. It was a game of hide-and-seek, and it was her turn to cover her eyes while her mother hid herself. She knew that the two older children were standing on one side watching; the game was too childish for them, and they were losing interest. They were laughing at her, who took the game so seriously. Her father caught her head and held it in his lap with his small hairy hands, to cover up her eyes, laughing and joking loudly about her mother hiding. She smelt the sickly odour of beer, and through it she smelt too – her head held down in the thick stuff of his trousers – the unwashed masculine smell she always associated with him. She struggled to get her head free, for she was half-suffocating, and her father held it down, laughing at her panic. And the other children laughed too. Screaming in her sleep she half-woke, fighting off the weight of sleep on her eyes, filled with the terror of the dream.

She thought she was still awake and lying stiffly on the sofa listening intently for the breathing next door. It continued for a long time, while she waited for each soft expulsion of breath. Then there was silence. She gazed in growing terror round the room, hardly daring to move her head for fear of disturbing the native through the wall, seeing the dull light fall in a circle on the table, illuminating its rough surface. In her dream the conviction grew that Dick was dead – that Dick was dead, and that the black man was waiting next door for her coming. Slowly she sat up, disentangling her feet from the clinging weight of the coat, trying to control her terror. She repeated to herself that there was nothing to fear. At last she gathered her legs close, and let them down over the edge of the sofa, very quietly, not daring to make a sound. Again she sat trembling, trying to calm herself, until she forced her body to raise itself and stand in the middle of the room, measuring the distance between herself and the bedroom, seeing the shadows in the skins on the floor with terror, because they seemed to move up at her in the swaying of the lamplight. The skin of a leopard near the door seemed to take shape and fill out, its little glassy eyes staring at her. She fled to the door to escape it. She stood cautiously, putting out a hand to part the heavy curtain. Slowly she peered through. All she could see was the shape of Dick lying still under the blankets. She could not see the African, but she knew he was waiting for her there in the shadow. She parted the curtains a little more. Now she saw one leg stretching from the wall into the room, an enormous, more than life-size leg, the limb of a giant. She went forward a little; now she could see him properly. Dreaming, she felt irritated and let down, for the native was asleep, crouched against the wall, exhausted after long wakefulness. He sat as she had seen him sit sometimes in the sun, with one knee up, his arm resting on it loosely, so that the palm turned over and the fingers curled limply. The other leg, the one she had first seen, stretched almost to where she stood, and at her feet she saw the thick skin of the sole, cracked and horny. His head was bent forward on his chest, showing his thick neck. She felt as she sometimes did when, awake, she expected to find that he had left undone something he was paid to do, and taking herself to look, found everything in order. Her annoyance with herself turned into anger against the native; and now she looked towards the bed again where Dick lay stretched and motionless. She stepped over the giant leg lying over the floor, and moved silently round the bed with her back to the window. Bending over Dick she felt the night air coolly on her shoulders, and with sharp anger said to herself that the native had opened the window again, and had caused Dick's death through chill. Dick looked ugly. He was dead, yellow-faced, his mouth fallen open and his eyes staring. In her dream she put out her hand to touch his skin. It was cold, and she felt only relief and exultation. At the same time she felt guilty because of her gladness, and tried to arouse in herself the sorrow she ought to feel. As she stood, bending forward over Dick's stillness, she knew the native had silently awakened and was watching her. Without turning her head, she saw at the edge of her vision the great leg softly withdrawn, and she knew he was standing in the shadow. Then he was coming towards her. It seemed as if the room were very big, and he was approaching her slowly from an immense distance. She stood rigid with fear, the chill sweat running down her body, waiting. He approached slowly, obscene and powerful, and it was not only he, but her father who was threatening her. They advanced together, one person, and she could smell, not the native smell, but the unwashed smell of her father. It filled the room, musty, like animals; and her knees went liquid as her nostrils distended to find clean air and her head became giddy. Half-conscious, she leaned back against the wall for support, and nearly fell through the open window. He came near and put his hand on her arm. It was the voice of the African she heard. He was comforting her because of Dick's death, consoling her protectively; but at the same time it was her father menacing and horrible, who touched her in desire.

She screamed, knowing suddenly she was asleep and in nightmare. She screamed and screamed desperately, trying to wake herself from the horror. She thought: my screams must be waking Dick; and she struggled in the sands of sleep. Then she was awake and sitting up, panting. The African was standing beside her, red-eyed and half-asleep, holding out to her a tray with tea. The room was filled with a thick grey light, and the still burning lamp sent a thin beam to the table. Seeing the native, with the terror of the dream still in her, she shrank back into the corner of the sofa, breathing fast and irregularly, watching him in a paroxysm of fright. He put the tray down, clumsily, because of his weariness, and she struggled in her mind to separate dream from reality.

The man said, watching her curiously, 'The boss is asleep.' And her knowledge that Dick lay dead next door faded. But still she watched the black man, warily, unable to speak. She saw in his face surprise at her posture of fear, and she watched grow there that look she had so often seen lately, half sardonic, speculative, brutal, as if he were judging her. Suddenly he said softly: 'Madame afraid of me, yes?' It was the voice of the dream, and as she heard it, her body went weak and she trembled. She fought to control her voice, and spoke after a few minutes in a half whisper: 'No, no, no. I am not afraid.'

And then she was furious with herself for denying something whose possibility should never even be admitted.

She saw him smile, and watched his eyes drop to her hands, which lay on her lap trembling. His eyes travelled up her body slowly to her face, taking in the hunched shoulders, the way her body was pressed into the cushions for support.

He said easily, familiarly, 'Why is Madame afraid of me?'

She said half-hysterically, in a high-pitched voice, laughing nervously: 'Don't be ridiculous. I am not afraid of you.' She spoke as she might have done to a white man, with whom she was flirting a little. As she heard the words come from her mouth, and saw the expression on the man's face, she nearly fainted. She saw him give her a long, slow, imponderable look; then turn, and walk out of the room.

When he had gone, she felt released from an inquisition. She sat weak and shaking, thinking of the dream, trying to clear away the fog of horror.

After a while she poured out some tea, spilling it into the saucer. Again, as she had done in her dream, she forced herself to stand up and walk into the room next door. Dick was sleeping quietly, and looked better. Without touching him she left him, passing to the verandah, where she leant forward against the chilly bricks of the balustrade, breathing in drafts of cool morning air. It was not sunrise yet. All the sky was clear and colourless, flushed with rosy streaks of light, but there was darkness still among the silent trees. She could see faint smoke rising in drifts from the small clustering huts of the compound, and knew that she must go and beat the gong for the day's work to begin.

All that day she sat in the bedroom as usual, watching Dick grow better hourly, although he was very weak still, and not yet well enough to be irritable.

She did not go around the farm at all that day. And she avoided the native; she felt that she was too unsure of herself, had not the strength to face him. When he had left after lunch for his time off, she went hastily to the kitchen, almost furtively, made cold drinks for Dick, and returned looking behind her as if pursued.

That night she locked all the doors of the house, and went to bed beside Dick, thankful, perhaps for the first time in their marriage, for his closeness.

He was back at work in a week.

Again, falling swiftly, one after the other, the days passed, the long days spent alone in the house while Dick was on the lands, alone with the African. She was fighting against something she did not understand. Dick became to her, as time went by, more and more unreal; while the thought of the African grew obsessive. It was a nightmare, the powerful black man always in the house with her, so that there was no escape from his presence. She was possessed by it, and Dick was hardly there to her.

From the time she woke in the morning to find the native bending over them with the tea, his eyes averted from her bare shoulders, until the time he was out of the house altogether, she could never relax. Fearfully, she did her work in the house, trying to keep out of his way; if he was in one room she went to another. She would not look at him; she knew it would be fatal to meet his eyes, because now there was always the memory of her fear, of the way she had spoken to him that night. She used to give her orders hurriedly, in a strained voice, then hastily leave the kitchen. She dreaded hearing him speak, because now there was a new tone in his voice: familiar, half-insolent, domineering. A dozen times she was on the point of saying to Dick, 'He must go.' But she never dared. Always she stopped herself, unable to bear the anger that would follow. But she felt as if she were in a dark tunnel, nearing something final, something she could not visualize, but which waited for her inexorably, inescapably. And in the attitude of Moses, in the way he moved or spoke, with that easy, confident, bullying insolence, she could see he was waiting too. They were like two antagonists, silently sparring. Only he was powerful and sure of himself, and she was undermined with fear, by her terrible dream-filled nights, her obsession.

10

People who live to themselves, whether from necessity or choice, and who do not trouble themselves about their neighbours' affairs, are always disquieted and uneasy if by some chance they come to know that other people discuss them. It is as though a sleeping man should wake and find round his bed a circle of strangers staring at him. The Turners, who might have been living on the moon for all the thought they gave to 'the district', would have been astonished if they had known that for years they had provided the staple of gossip among the farmers round about. Even people they knew by name only, or those they had never heard of, discussed them with an intimate knowledge that was entirely due to the Slatters. It was all the Slatters' fault – yet how can one blame them? No one really believes in the malignancy of gossip, save those who know how they themselves have suffered from it; and the Slatters would have cried, had they been challenged: 'We have told people nothing but the truth' – but with that self-conscious indignation that confesses guilt. Mrs Slatter would have had to be a most extraordinary woman to remain perfectly impartial and fair to Mary, after having been snubbed so many times. For she had made repeated attempts to 'get Mary out of herself', as she put it. Sensing Mary's fierce pride (she had plenty of her own), she had asked her time and time again to a party, or a tennis afternoon, or an informal dance. Even after the second of Dick's illnesses she had tried to make Mary break her isolation: the doctor had been frighteningly cynical about the Turner ménage. But always came back those curt little notes from Mary (the Turners had not had a telephone installed when everyone else did, because of the expense) that were like the deliberate ignoring of an offered hand. When Mrs Slatter came across Mary in the store on post-days, she had always asked her, with unfailing kindness, to come over some time. And Mary had always replied stiffly that she would like to, but that 'Dick was so busy just now'. But it was a long time now since anyone had seen Mary or Dick at the station.

'What did they *do*?' people asked. At the Slatters' people always asked what the Turners *did*. And Mrs Slatter, whose good humour and patience had at long last given out, was prepared to tell them. There was that time Mary ran away from her husband – but that must be a good six years ago now. And Charlie Slatter would chip in, telling his story how Mary had arrived hatless and shabby, after having walked *alone* over the veld (although she was a woman), and asked him to drive her in to the station. 'How was I to know she was running off from Turner? She didn't tell me. I thought she was going in for a day's shopping, and Turner was too busy. And when Turner came over, half-batty with worry, I had to tell him I had taken her in. She shouldn't have done it. It was not the right thing to do.' The story had by now become monstrously distorted. Mary had run away from her husband in the middle of the night because he had locked her out, had found refuge with the Slatters, had borrowed money from them to leave. Dick had come after her next morning and promised never to illtreat her again. That was the story, told all over the district to the accompaniment of headshaking and tongue-clickings. But when people started saying that Slatter had horsewhipped Turner, it was too much: Charlie got annoyed. He liked Dick, though he despised him. Dick he was sorry for. He began to put people right about the affair. He repeated continually that Dick should have let Mary go. It was good riddance. He had been well out of it and didn't know when he was lucky. So, slowly, because of Charlie, the thing was reversed. Mary was execrated; Dick exonerated. But of all this interest and talk, Mary and Dick remained ignorant. Necessarily so, since for years they had been confined to the farm.

The real reason why the Slatters, particularly Charlie, maintained their interest in the Turners, was that they wanted Dick's farm still: more even than they had. And, since it was Charlie's intervention that precipitated the tragedy, though he cannot be blamed for it, it is necessary to explain about his farming. Just as World War II produced its fabulously wealthy tobacco barons, so the First World War enriched many farmers because of the sharp rise in the price of maize. Until World War I, Slatter had been poor; after it, he found himself rich. And once a man is rich, when he has the temperament of a Slatter, he gets richer and richer. He was careful not to invest his money in farming: farming he did not trust as an investment. Any surplus went into mining shares; and he did not improve his farm more than was essential for the purpose of making money from it. He had five hundred acres of the most beautiful rich dark soil, which in the old days had produced twenty-five and thirty bags of mealies to the acre. Year after year he had squeezed that soil, until by now he got five bags an acre if he was lucky. He never dreamed of fertilizing. He cut down his trees (such as remained when the mining companies had done) to sell as firewood. But even a farm as rich as his was not inexhaustible; and while he no longer needed to make his thousands every year, his soil was played out, and he wanted more. His attitude to the land was fundamentally the same as that of the natives whom he despised; he wanted to work out one patch of country and move on to the next. And he had cultivated all the cultivable soil. He needed Dick's farm badly, because the farms that bounded his on the other sides were taken up. He knew exactly what he wanted to do with it. Dick's farm consisted of a little bit of everything. He had a hundred acres of that wonderful dark soil; and it was not played out, because he had looked after it. He had a little soil suitable for tobacco. And the rest was good for grazing.

It was the grazing Charlie wanted. He did not believe in pampering cattle by feeding them in winter. He turned them out to fend for themselves, which was all very well when the grass was good, but he had so many cattle and the grazing was thin and poor. So Dick provided the only outlet. For years Charlie had been planning for when Dick would be bankrupt. But then Dick obstinately refused to go bankrupt. 'How does he *do* it?' people asked irritably; for everyone knew that he never seemed to make any money, always had bad seasons, was always in debt. 'Bcause they live like pigs and they never buy anything,' said Mrs Slatter tartly; by now she felt that Mary could go and drown herself, for all she cared.

Perhaps they would not have been so indignant and as irritated if Dick had been suitably conscious of his failure. If he had come to Charlie and asked for advice, and pleaded incapacity, it would have been different. But he did not. He sat tight on his debts and his farm, and ignored Charlie. To whom it occurred one day that he had not seen Dick at all for over a year. 'How time flies!' said Mrs Slatter, when he pointed this out; but after working it out, they agreed it was nearer two years; time, on a farm, has a way of prolonging itself unnoticed. That same afternoon Charlie drove over to the Turners. He was feeling a little guilty. He had always considered himself as Dick's mentor, as a man with much longer experience and greater knowledge. He felt responsible for Dick, whom he had watched right from the time he first began to farm. As he drove, he kept a sharp eye for signs of neglect. Things seemed neither better nor worse. The fireguards along the boundary were there, but they would protect the farm from a small slow-burning fire, not a big one with the wind behind it. The cowsheds, while not actually falling down, had been propped up by poles, and the thatched roofs were patched like darned stockings, the grass all different colours and stages of newness, reaching untidily to the ground in untrimmed swathes. The roads needed draining: they were in a deplorable state. The big plantation of gum trees past which the road went had been burnt by a veld-fire in one corner; they stood pale and spectral in the strong yellow afternoon sunlight, their leaves hanging stiffly down, their trunks charred black.

Everything was just the same: ramshackle, but not exactly hopeless.

He found Dick sitting on a big stone by the tobacco barns, which were now used as store-sheds, watching his boys stack the year's supply of meal out of reach of the ants on strips of iron supported by bricks. Dick's big floppy farm hat was pulled over his face, and he looked up to nod at Charlie, who stood beside him, watching the operations, his eyes narrowed; he was noting that the sacks in which the meal was held were so rotten with age that they were unlikely to last out the season.

'What can I do for you?' asked Dick, with his usual defensive politeness. But his voice was uncertain; it sounded unused. And his eyes, peering painfully out of the shadow of the hat, were bright and anxious.

'Nothing,' said Charlie curtly, giving him a slow, irritated look. 'Just came to see how you were doing. Haven't seen you for months.'

To which there came no reply. The natives were finishing work. The sun had gone down, leaving a wake of sultry red over the kopjes, and the dusk was creeping over the fields from the edges of the bush. The compound, visible among the trees half a mile away as a group of conical shapes, was smoking gently, and there was a small glow of fire behind dark trunks. Someone was beating a drum; the monotonous tom-tom noise sounded the end of the day. The boys were swinging their tattered jackets over their shoulders and filing away along the edge of the lands. 'Well,' said Dick, getting up with a painful stiff movement, 'that's another day finished.' He shivered sharply. Charlie examined him: big trembling hands as thin as spines; thin hunched shoulders set in a steady shiver. And it was very hot: the ground was glowing out warmth and the red flush in the sky was fiery. 'Got fever?' asked Charlie.

'No, don't think so. Blood getting thin after all these years.'

'More than thin blood is wrong with you,' retorted Charlie, who seemed to find it a personal triumph that Dick should have fever. Yet he looked at him kindly, his big bristly face with its little squashed-looking features intent and steady. 'Get fever much these days? Had it since I brought the quack to see you?'

'I get it quite often these days,' said Dick. 'I get it every year. I had it twice last year.'

'Wife look after you?'

A worried look came on Dick's face. 'Yes,' he said.

'How is she?'

'Seems much the same.'

'Has she been ill?'

'No, not ill. But she's not too good. Seems nervy. She's run down. Been on the farm too long.' And then, in a rush, as if he could not keep it to himself another moment, 'I am worried sick about her.'

'But what's the trouble?' Charlie sounded neutral; yet he never took his eyes off Dick's face. The two men were still standing in the dusk under the tall shape of the barn. A sweetish moist smell came from the open door; the smell of freshly-ground mealies. Dick shut the door, which was half off its hinges, by lifting it into place with his shoulder. He locked it. There was one screw in the triangular flange of the hasp: a strong man could have wrenched it off the frame. 'Come up to the house?' he asked Charlie, who nodded, and then inquired, looking around: 'Where's your car?'

'Oh, I walk these days.'

'Sold it?'

'Yes. Cost too much to run. I send in the waggon now to the station when I want something.'

They climbed into Charlie's monster of a car, which balanced and clambered over the rutted tracks too small for it. The grass was growing back over the roads now that Dick had no car.

Between the low, tree-covered rise where the house was, and where the barns stood among bush, were lands which had not been cultivated. It looked as if they had been allowed to lie fallow, but Charlie, looking closely through the dusk, could see that among the grass and low bushes were thin, straggling mealies. He thought at first they had seeded themselves; but they seemed to be regularly planted. 'What's this?' he asked, 'what's the idea?'

'I was trying out a new idea from America.'

'What idea?'

'The bloke said there was no need to plough or to cultivate. The idea is to plant the grain among ordinary vegetation and let it grow of itself.'

'Didn't work out, hey?'

'No,' said Dick, blankly. 'I didn't bother to reap it. I thought

I might as well leave it to do the soil some good . . .' His voice tailed off.

'Experiment,' said Charlie briefly. It was significant that he sounded neither exasperated nor angry. He seemed detached; but kept glancing curiously, with an undercurrent of uneasiness, at Dick, whose face was obstinately set and miserable. 'What was that you were saying about your wife?'

'She's not well.'

'Yes, but why, man?'

Dick did not answer for a while. They passed from the open lands, where the golden evening glow still lingered on the leaves, to the bush, where it was dense dusk. The big car zoomed up the hill, which was steep, its bonnet reaching up into the sky. 'I don't know,' said Dick at last. 'She's different lately. Sometimes I think she's much better. It's difficult to tell with women how they are. She's not the same.'

'But in what way?' persisted Charlie.

'Well, for instance. Once, when she first came to the farm she had more go in her. She doesn't seem to care. She doesn't care about anything. She simply sits and does nothing. She doesn't even trouble about the chickens and things like that. You know she used to make a packet out of them every month or so. And she doesn't care what the boy does in the house. Once she used to drive me mad nagging. Nag, nag, nag, all day. You know how women get when they've been too long on the farm. No self-control.'

'No woman knows how to handle niggers,' said Charlie.

'Well, I am quite worried,' stated Dick, laughing miserably. 'I should be quite pleased if she did nag.'

'Look here, Turner,' said Charlie abruptly. 'Why don't you give up this business and get off the place? You are not doing yourself or your wife any good.'

'Oh, we rub along.'

'You are ill, man.'

'I am all right.'

They stopped outside the house. A glimmer of light came from within, but Mary did not appear. A second light sprang up in the bedroom. Dick had his eyes on it. 'She's changing her

174

dress,' he said; and he sounded pleased. 'No one has been here for so long.'

'Why don't you sell out to me? I'll give you a good price for it.'

'Where should I go?' asked Dick in amazement.

'Get into town. Get off the land. You are no good on the land. Get yourself a steady job somewhere.'

'I keep my end up,' said Dick resentfully.

The thin shape of a woman appeared against the light, on the verandah. The two men got out of the car and went inside.

' 'Evening, Mrs Turner.'

'Good evening,' said Mary.

Charlie examined her closely when they were inside the lighted room, more closely because of the way she had said, 'Good evening.' She remained standing uncertainly in front of him, a dried stick of a woman, her hair that had been bleached by the sun into a streaky mass falling round a scrawny face and tied on the top of her head with a blue ribbon. Her thin, yellowish neck protruded out of a dress that she had apparently just put on. It was a frilled raspberry-coloured cotton; and in her ears were long red ear-rings like boiled sweets, that tapped against her neck in short swinging jerks. Her blue eyes, which had once told anyone who really took the trouble to look into them that Mary Turner was not really 'stuck-up', but shy, proud, and sensitive, had a new light in them. 'Why, good evening!' she said girlishly. 'Why, Mr Slatter, we haven't had the pleasure of seeing you for a long time.' She laughed, twisting her shoulder in a horrible parody of coquetry.

Dick averted his eyes, suffering. Charlie stared at her rudely: stared and stared until at last she flushed and turned away, tossing her head. 'Mr Slatter doesn't like us,' she informed Dick socially, 'or otherwise, he would come to see us more often.'

She sat herself down in the corner of the old sofa, which had gone out of shape and become a thing of lumps and hollows with a piece of faded blue stuff stretched over it.

Charlie, his eyes on that material, asked: 'How is the store going?'

'We gave it up, it didn't pay,' said Dick brusquely. 'We are using up the stock ourselves.'

Charlie looked at Mary's ear-rings, and at the sofa-cover, which was of the material always sold to natives, an ugly patterned blue that has become a tradition in South Africa, so much associated with 'kaffir-truck' that it shocked Charlie to see it in a white man's house. He looked round the place, frowning. The curtains were torn; a windowpane had been broken and patched with paper; another had cracked and not been mended at all; the room was indescribably broken down and faded. Yet everywhere were little bits of stuff from the store, roughly-hemmed, draping the back of a chair, or tucked in to form a chair seat. Charlie might have thought that this small evidence of a desire to keep up appearances was a good sign; but all his rough and rather brutal good humour was gone; he was silent, his forehead dark.

'Like to stay to supper?' asked Dick at last.

'No thanks,' said Charlie; then changed his mind out of curiosity. 'Yes, I will.'

Unconsciously the two men were speaking as if in the presence of an invalid; but Mary scrambled out of her seat, and shouted from the doorway: 'Moses! Moses!'

Then, since the native did not appear, she turned and smiled at them with social coyness, and said: 'Excuse me, but you know what these boys are.'

She went out. The men were silent. Dick's face was averted from Charlie, who since he had never become convinced of the necessity for tact, gazed intently at Dick, as if trying to force him into some explanation or statement.

Supper, when it was brought in by Moses, consisted of a tray of tea, some bread and rather rancid butter, and a chunk of cold meat. There was not a piece of crockery that was whole; and Charlie could feel the grease on the knife he held. He ate with distaste, making no effort to hide it, while Dick said nothing, and Mary made abrupt, unrelated remarks about the weather with that appalling coyness, shaking her ear-rings, writhing her thin shoulders, ogling Charlie with a conventional flirtatiousness.

To all this Charlie made no response. He said, 'Yes, Mrs Turner. No, Mrs Turner.' And looked at her coldly, his eyes hard with contempt and dislike.

When the native came to clear away the dishes there was an incident that caused him to grind his teeth and go white with anger. They were sitting over the sordid relics of the meal, while the boy moved about the table, slackly gathering dishes together. Charlie had not even noticed him. Then Mary asked: 'Like some fruit, Mr Slatter? Moses, fetch the oranges. You know where they are.' Charlie looked up, his jaws moving slowly over the food in his mouth, his eyes alert and bright; it was the tone of Mary's voice when she spoke to the native that jarred him: she was speaking to him with exactly the same flirtatious coyness with which she had spoken to himself.

The native replied, with a rough offhand rudeness: 'Oranges finished.'

'I know they are not finished. There were two left. I *know* they are not.' Mary was appealing, looking up at the boy, almost confiding in him.

'Oranges finished,' he repeated in that tone of surly indifference, but with a note of self-satisfaction, of conscious power that took Charlie's breath away. Literally, he could not find words. He looked at Dick, who was sitting staring down at his hands; and it was impossible to see what he was thinking, or whether he had noticed anything at all. He looked at Mary: her wrinkled yellow skin had an ugly flush under the eyes, and the expression on her face was unmistakably one of fear. She appeared to have understood that Charlie had noticed something: she kept glancing at him guiltily, smiling.

'How long have you had that boy?' asked Charlie at last, jerking his head at Moses, who was standing at the doorway with the tray, openly listening. Mary looked helplessly at Dick.

Dick said tonelessly, 'About four years, I think.'

'Why do you keep him?'

'He's a good boy,' sid Mary, tossing her head. 'He works well.'

'It doesn't seem like it,' said Charlie bluntly, challenging her with his eyes. But hers were evasive and uneasy. At the same time they held a gleam of secret satisfaction that sent the blood to Charlie's head. 'Why don't you get rid of him? Why do you let him speak to you like that?'

Mary did not reply. She had turned her head, and was looking over her shoulder at the doorway where Moses stood; and in her face was an ugly brainlessness that caused Charlie to shout out suddenly at the native: 'Get away from there. Get on with your work.'

The big native disappeared, responding at once to the command. And then there was a silence. Charlie was waiting for Dick to speak, to say something that showed he had not completely given in. But his head was still bent, his face dumbly suffering. At last Charlie appealed direct to him, ignoring Mary as if she were not present at all. 'Get rid of that boy,' he said. 'Get rid of him, Turner.'

'Mary likes him,' was the slow, blank response.

'Come outside, I want to talk to you.'

Dick lifted his head and looked resentfully at Charlie; he resented that he was being forced to take notice of something he wanted to ignore. But he obediently hoisted his body out of the chair and followed Charlie outside. The two men went down the verandah steps, and as far as the shadow of the trees.

'You've got to get away from here,' said Charlie curtly.

'How can I?' said Dick listlessly. 'How can I when I am still in debt?' And then, as if it were still a question of money, with nothing else involved, he said: 'I know other people don't seem to worry. I know there are plenty of farmers who are as hard up as I am and who buy cars and go for holidays. But I just can't do it, Charlie. I can't do it. I am not made that way.'

Charlie said: 'I'll buy your farm from you and you can stay here as manager, Turner. But you must go away first for a holiday, for at least six months. You must get your wife away.'

He spoke as if there could be no question of a refusal; he had been shocked out of self-interest. It was not even pity for Dick that moved him. He was obeying the dictate of the first law of white South Africa, which is: 'Thou shalt not let your fellow whites sink lower than a certain point; because if you do, the nigger will see he is as good as you are.' The strongest

178

emotion of a strongly organized society spoke in his voice, and it took the backbone out of Dick's resistance. For, after all, he had lived in the country all his life; he was undermined with shame; he knew what was expected of him, and that he had failed. But he could not bring himself to accept Charlie's ultimatum. He felt that Charlie was asking him to give up life itself, which for him, was the farm and his ownership of it.

'I'll take this place over as it stands, and give you enough to clear your debts. I'll engage a manager to run it till you get back from the coast. You must go away for six months at the very least, Turner. It doesn't matter where you go. I'll see that you have the money to do it. You can't go on like this, and that is the end of it.'

But Dick did not give in so easily. He fought for four hours. For four hours they argued, walking up and down beneath the trees.

Charlie drove away at last without going back to the house. Dick returned to it walking heavily, almost staggering, the spring of his living destroyed. He would no longer own the farm, he would be another man's servant. Mary was sitting in a lump in the corner of the sofa; the manner she had instinctively assumed in Charlie's presence, to preserve appearances and to hold her own, had gone. She did not look at Dick when he came in. For days at a time she did not speak to him. It was as if he did not exist for her. She seemed to be sunk fathoms deep in some dream of her own. She only came to life, only noticed what she was doing, when the native came in to do some little thing in the room. Then she never took her eyes off him. But what this meant Dick did not know: he did not want to know; he was beyond fighting it now.

Charlie Slatter did not waste time. He drove round the district from farm to farm, trying to find someone who would take over the Turners' place for a few months. He gave no explanations. He was extraordinarily reticent; he said merely that he was helping Turner to take his wife away. At last he heard of a young man just out from England, who wanted a job. Charlie did not mind who it was: anyone would do; the thing was too urgent. He at last drove into town himself to find him. He was not particularly impressed with the youth one way or the other; he was the usual type; the self-contained, educated Englishman who spoke in a la-di-da way as if he had a mouthful of pearls. He brought the young man back with him. He told him little; he did not know what to tell him. The arrangement was that he should take over the farm at once, within a week, letting the Turners go off to the coast; Charlie would arrange about the money; Charlie would tell him what to do on the farm: that was the plan. But when he went over to Dick, to tell him, he found that while he had become reconciled to the necessity of leaving, he could not be persuaded to leave at once.

Charlie, Dick, and the young man, Tony Marston, stood in the middle of a field; Charlie hot and angry and impatient (for he could not bear to be thwarted at the best of times), Dick stubborn and miserable, Marston sensitive to the situation and trying to efface himself.

'Damn it, Charlie, why kick me off like this? I've been here fifteen years!'

'For God's sake, man, I am not kicking you off. I want you to get off before – you should get off at once. You must see that for yourself.'

'Fifteen years!' said Dick, his lean dark face flushed, 'fifteen years!' He even bent down, unconsciously, and picked up a handful of earth, and held it in his hand, as if claiming his own. It was an absurd gesture. Charlie's face put on a jeering little smile.

'But, Turner, you will be coming back to it.'

'It won't be mine,' said Dick, and his voice broke. He turned away, still clutching his soil. Tony Marston also turned away, and pretended to be inspecting the condition of the field; he did not want to intrude on this grief. Charlie, who had no such scruples, looked impatiently at Dick's working face. Yet with a tinge of respect. He respected the emotion he could not understand. Pride of ownership, yes: that he knew; but not this passionate attachment to the soil, as such. He did not understand it; but his voice softened.

'It will be as good as yours. I won't upset your farm. You can go on with it, when you come back, just as you like.' He spoke with his usual rough good-humour.

'Charity,' said Dick, in that remote grieved voice.

'It's not charity. I'm buying it as a business concern. I want the grazing. I will run my cattle here with yours, and you can go on with your crops as you like.'

Yet he was thinking it was charity, was even a little surprised at himself for this complete betrayal of his business principles. In the minds of all three of them the word 'charity' was written in big black letters, obscuring everything else. And they were all wrong. It was an instinctive self-preservation. Charlie was fighting to prevent another recruit to the growing army of poor whites, who seem to respectable white people so much more shocking (though not pathetic, for they are despised and hated for their betrayal of white standards, rather than pitied) than all the millions of black people who are crowded into the slums or on to the dwindling land reserves of their own country.

At last, after much argument, Dick agreed to leave at the end of a month, when he had shown Tony how he liked things done on 'his' land. Charlie, cheating a little, booked the railway journey for three weeks ahead. Tony went back to the house with Dick, agreeably surprised that he had not been in the country more than a couple of months before finding a job. He was given a thatched, mud-walled hut at the back of the house. It had been a store-hut at one stage, but was now empty. There were scattered mealies on the floor still, which had escaped the broom; on the walls were ant tunnels of fine red granules which had not been brushed away. There was an iron bedstead, supplied by Charlie, a cupboard made of boxes and curtained over with that peculiarly ugly, blue native stuff, and a mirror over a basin on a packing-case. Tony did not mind these things in the least. He was in a mood of elation, a fine romantic mood, and things like bad food or sagging mattresses were quite unimportant to him. Standards that would have shocked him in his own country seemed more like exciting indications of a different sense of values, here.

He was twenty. He had had a good, conventional education, and had faced the prospect of becoming some kind of a clerk in his uncle's factory. To sit on an office stool was not his idea of life; and he had chosen South Africa as his home because a remote cousin of his had made five thousand pounds the year before out of tobacco. He intended to do the same, and better, if he could. In the meantime he had to learn. The only thing he had against this farm was that it had no tobacco; but six months on a mixed farm would be experience, and good for him. He was sorry for Dick Turner, whom he knew to be unhappy; but even this tragedy seemed to him romantic; he saw it, impersonally, as a symptom of the growing capitalization of farming all over the world, of the way small farmers would inevitably be swallowed by the big ones. (Since he intended to be a big one himself, this tendency did not distress him.) Because he had never yet earned his own living, he thought entirely in abstractions. For instance, he had the conventionally 'progressive' ideas about the colour bar, the superficial progressiveness of the idealist that seldom survives a conflict with self-interest. He had brought with him a suitcase full of books, which he stacked round the circular wall of his hut: books on the colour question, on Rhodes and Kruger, on farming, on the history of gold. But, a week later, he picked up one of them and found the back eaten out by white ants. So he put them back in the suitcase and never looked at them again. A man cannot work twelve hours a day and then feel fresh enough for study.

He took his meals with the Turners. Otherwise, he was expected to pick up enough knowledge in a month to keep this place running for six, until Dick returned. He spent all day with Dick on the lands, rising at five, and going to bed at eight. He was interested in everything, well-informed, fresh, alive – a charming companion. Or perhaps Dick might have found him so ten years before. As it was he was not responsive to Tony, who would start a comfortable discussion on miscegenation, perhaps, or the effects of the colour bar on industry only to find Dick staring, with abstract eyes. Dick was concerned, in Tony's presence, only to get through these last days without losing his last shreds of self-respect by breaking down, by refusing to go. And he knew he had to go. Yet his feelings were so violent, he was in such a turmoil of unhappiness, that he had to restrain crazy impulses to set fire to the long grass and watch the flames destroy the veld he knew so well that each bush and tree was a personal friend; or to pull down the little house he had built with his own hands and lived in so long. It seemed a violation that someone else would give orders here, someone else would farm his soil and perhaps destroy his work.

As for Mary, Tony hardly saw her. He was disturbed by her, when he had time to think about the strange, silent, dried-out woman who seemed as if she had forgotten how to speak. And then, it would appear that she realized she should make an effort, and her manner would become odd and gauche. She would talk for a few moments with a grotesque sprightliness that shocked Tony and made him uncomfortable. Her manner had no relation to what she was saying. She would suddenly break into one of Dick's slow, patient explanations about a plough or a sick ox, with an irrelevant remark about the food (which Tony found nauseating) or about the heat at this time of the year. 'I do so like it when the rains come,' she would say conversationally, giggle a little, and relapse suddenly into a blank, staring silence. Tony began to think she wasn't quite all there. But then, these two had had a hard time of it, so he understood; and in any case, living here all by themselves for so long was enough to make anyone a bit odd.

The heat in that house was so great that he could not understand how she stood it. Being new to the country he felt the heat badly; but he was glad to be out and away from that tin-roofed oven where the air seemed to coagulate into layers of sticky heat. Although his interest in Mary was limited, it did occur to him to think that she was leaving for a holiday for the first time in years, and that she might be expected to show symptoms of pleasure. She was making no preparations that he could see; never even mentioned it. And Dick, for that matter, did not talk about it either.

About a week before they were due to leave, Dick said to Mary over the lunch table, 'How about packing?' She nodded, after two repetitions of the question, but did not reply.

'You must pack, Mary,' said Dick gently, in that quiet

hopeless voice with which he always addressed her. But when he and Tony returned that night, she had done nothing. When the greasy meal was cleared away, Dick pulled down the boxes and began to do the packing himself. Seeing him at it, she began to help; but before half an hour was gone, she had left him in the bedroom, and was sitting blankly on the sofa.

'Complete nervous breakdown,' diagnosed Tony, who was just off to bed. He had the kind of mind that is relieved by putting things into words: the phrase was an apology for Mary; it absolved her from criticism. 'Complete nervous breakdown' was something anyone might have; most people did, at some time or another. The next night, too, Dick packed, until everything was ready. 'Buy yourself some material and make a dress or two,' said Dick diffidently, for he had realized, handling her things, that she had, almost literally, 'nothing to wear'. She nodded, and took out of a drawer a length of flowered cotton stuff that had been taken over with the stock from the store. She began to cut it out, then remained still, bent over it, silent, until Dick touched her shoulder and roused her to come to bed. Tony, witness of this scene, refrained from looking at Dick. He was grieved for them both. He had learned to like Dick very much; his feeling for him was sincere and personal. As for Mary, while he was sorry for her, what could be said about a woman who simply wasn't there? 'A case for a psychologist,' he said again, trying to reassure himself. For that matter, Dick would benefit by treatment himself. The man was cracking up, he shivered perpetually, his face was so thin the bone structure showed under the skin. He was not fit to work at all, really; but he insisted on spending every moment of daylight on the fields; he could not bear to leave them when dusk came. Tony had to bring him away; his task now was almost one of a male nurse, and he was beginning to look forward to the Turners' departure.

Three days before they were due to leave, Tony asked to stay behind for the afternoon, because he was not feeling well. A touch of the sun, perhaps; he had a bad headache, his eyes hurt, and nausea moved in the pit of his stomach. He stayed away from the midday meal, lying in his hut which, though warm enough, was cold compared to that oven of a house. At four o'clock in the afternoon he woke from an uneasy aching sleep, and was very thirsty. The old whisky bottle that was usually filled with drinking water was empty; the boy had forgotten to fill it. Tony went out into the yellow glare to fetch water from the house. The back door was open, and he moved silently, afraid to wake Mary, whom he had been told slept every afternoon. He took a glass from a rack, and wiped it carefully, and went into the living-room for the water. A glazed earthenware filter stood on the shelf that served as a sideboard. Tony lifted the lid and peered in: the dome of the filter was slimy with yellow mud, but the water trickled out of the tap clear, though tasting stale and tepid. He drank, and drank again, and, having filled his bottle, turned to leave. The curtain between this room and the bedroom was drawn back, and he could see in. He was struck motionless by surprise. Mary was sitting on an upended candlebox before the square of mirror nailed on the wall. She was in a garish pink petticoat, and her bony yellow shoulders stuck sharply out of it. Beside her stood Moses, and, as Tony watched, she stood up and held out her arms while the native slipped her dress over them from behind. When she sat down again she shook out her hair from her neck with both hands, with the gesture of a beautiful woman adoring her beauty. Moses was buttoning up the dress; she was looking in the mirror. The attitude of the native was of an indulgent uxoriousness. When he had finished the buttoning, he stood back, and watched the woman brushing her hair. 'Thank you, Moses,' she said in a high commanding voice. Then she turned, and said intimately: 'You had better go now. It is time for the boss to come.' The native came out of the room. When he saw the white man standing there, staring at him incredulously, he hesitated for a moment and then came straight on, passing him on silent feet, but with a malevolent glare. The malevolence was so strong, that Tony was momentarily afraid. When the native had gone, Tony sat down on a chair, mopped his face which was streaming with the heat, and shook his head to clear it. For his thoughts were conflicting. He had been in the country long enough to be shocked; at the same time his 'progressiveness' was deliciously flattered by this evidence of white ruling-class hypocrisy. For in a country where coloured children appear plentifully among the natives wherever a lonely white man is stationed, hypocrisy, as Tony defined it, was the first thing that had struck him on his arrival. But then, he had read enough about psychology to understand the sexual aspect of the colour bar, one of whose foundations is the jealousy of the white man for the superior sexual potency of the native; and he was surprised at one of the guarded, a white woman, so easily evading this barrier. Yet he had met a doctor on the boat coming out, with years of experience in a country district, who had told him he would be surprised to know the number of white women who had relations with black men. Tony felt at the time that he would be surprised; he felt it would be rather like having a relation with an animal, in spite of his 'progressiveness'.

And then all these considerations went from his mind, and he was left simply with the fact of Mary, this poor twisted woman, who was clearly in the last stages of breakdown, and who was at this moment coming out of the bedroom, one hand still lifted to her hair. And then he felt, at the sight of her face, which was bright and innocent, though with an empty, half-idiotic brightness, that all his suspicions were nonsense.

When she saw him, she stopped dead, and stared at him with fear. Then her face, from being tormented, became slowly blank and indifferent. He could not understand this sudden change. But he said, in a jocular uncomfortable voice: 'There was once an Empress of Russia who thought so little of her slaves, as human beings, that she used to undress naked in front of them.' It was from this point of view that he chose to see the affair; the other was too difficult for him.

'Was there?' she said doubtfully at last, looking puzzled.

'Does that native always dress and undress you?' he asked.

Mary lifted her head sharply, and her eyes became cunning. 'He has so little to do,' she said, tossing her head. 'He must earn his money.'

'It's not customary in this country, is it?' he asked slowly, out of the depths of his complete bewilderment. And he saw, as he spoke, that the phrase 'this country', which is like a call to solidarity for most white people, meant nothing to her. For her, there was only the farm; not even that – there was only this house, and what was in it. And he began to understand with a horrified pity, her utter indifference to Dick; she had shut out everything that conflicted with her actions, that would revive the code she had been brought up to follow.

She said suddenly, 'They said I was not like that, not like that, not like that.' It was like a gramophone that had got stuck at one point.

'Not like what?' he asked blankly.

'Not like *that*.' The phrase was furtive, sly, yet triumphant. God, the woman is mad as a hatter! he said to himself. And then he thought, but is she, is she? She can't be mad. She doesn't behave as if she were. She behaves simply as if she lives in a world of her own, where other people's standards don't count. She has forgotten what her own people are like. But then, what is madness, but a refuge, a retreating from the world?

Thus the unhappy and bewildered Tony, sitting on his chair beside the water filter, still holding his bottle and glass, staring uneasily at Mary, who began to talk in a sad quiet voice which made him say to himself, as she was speaking, changing his mind again, that she was not mad, at least, not at that moment. 'It's a long time since I came here,' she said, looking straight at him, in appeal. 'So long I can't quite remember . . . I should have left long ago. I don't know why I didn't. I don't know why I came. But things are different. Very different.' She stopped. Her face was pitiful; her eyes were painful holes in her face. 'I don't know anything. I don't understand. Why is all this happening? I didn't mean it to happen. But he won't go away, he won't go away.' And then, in a different voice, she snapped at him, 'Why did you come here? It was all right before you came.' She burst into tears, moaning, 'He won't go away.'

Tony rose to go to her: now his only emotion was pity; his discomfort was forgotten. Something made him turn. In the doorway stood the boy, Moses, looking at them both, his face wickedly malevolent.

'Go away,' said Tony, 'go away at once.' He put his arm round Mary's shoulders, for she was shrinking away and digging her fingers into his flesh.

'Go away,' she said suddenly, over his shoulder at the native. Tony realized that she was trying to assert herself: she was using his presence there as a shield in a fight to get back a command she had lost. And she was speaking like a child challenging a grown-up person.

'Madame want me to go?' said the boy quietly.

'Yes, go away.'

'Madame want me to go because of this boss?'

It was not the words in themselves that made Tony rise to his feet and stride to the door, but the way in which they were spoken. 'Get out,' he said, half-choked with anger. 'Get out before I kick you out.'

After a long, slow, evil look the native went. Then he came back. Speaking past Tony, ignoring him, he said to Mary, 'Madame is leaving this farm, yes?'

'Yes,' said Mary faintly.

'Madame never coming back?'

'No, no, no,' she cried out.

'And is this boss going too?'

'*No*,' she screamed. 'Go *away*.'

'Will you go?' shouted Tony. He could have killed this native: he wanted to take him by his throat and squeeze the life out of him. And then Moses vanished. They heard him walk across the kitchen and out of the back door. The house was empty. Mary sobbed, her head on her arms. 'He's gone,' she cried, 'he's gone, he's gone!' Her voice was hysterical with relief. And then she suddenly pushed him away, stood in front of him like a mad woman, and hissed, 'You sent him away! He'll never come back! It was all right till you came!' And she collapsed in a storm of tears. Tony sat there, his arm round her, comforting her. He was wondering only, 'What shall I say to Turner?' But what could he say? The whole thing was better left. The man was half-crazy with worry as it was. It would be cruel to say anything to him – and in any case, in two days both of them would be gone from the farm.

He decided that he would take Dick aside and suggest, only, that the native should be dismissed at once.

But Moses did not return. He was not there that evening at all. Tony heard Dick ask where the native was, and her answer that she 'had sent him away'. He heard the blank indifference of her voice: saw that she was speaking to Dick without seeing him.

Tony, at last, shrugged in despair, and decided to do nothing. And the next morning he was off to the lands as usual. It was the last day; there was a great deal to do.

11

Mary awoke suddenly, as if some big elbow had nudged her. It was still night. Dick lay asleep beside her. The window was creaking on its hinges, and when she looked into the square of darkness, she could see stars moving and flashing among the tree boughs. The sky was luminous; but there was an undertone of cold grey; the stars were bright; but with a weak gleam. Inside the room the furniture was growing into light. She could see a glimmer that was the surface of the mirror. Then a cock crowed in the compound, and a dozen shrill voices answered for the dawn. Daylight? Moonlight? Both. Both mingled together, and it would be sunrise in half an hour. She yawned, settled back on her lumpy pillows, and stretched out her limbs. She thought, that usually her wakings were grey and struggling, a reluctant upheaval of her body from the bed's refuge. Today she was vastly peaceful and rested. Her mind was clear, and her body comfortable. Cradled in ease she locked her hands behind her head and stared at the darkness that held the familiar walls and furniture. Lazily she created the room in imagination, placing each cupboard and chair; then moved beyond the house, hollowing it out of the night in her mind as if her hand cupped it. At last, from a height, she looked down on the building set among the bush – and was filled with a regretful, peaceable tenderness. It seemed as if she were holding that immensely pitiful thing, the farm with its inhabitants, in the hollow of her hand, which curved round it to shut out the gaze of the cruelly critical world. And she felt as if she must weep. She could feel the tears running down her cheeks, which stung rawly, and she put up her fingers to touch the skin. The contact of rough finger with roughened flesh restored her to herself. She continued to cry, but hopelessly for herself, though still from a forgiving distance. Then Dick stirred and woke, sitting up with a jerk. She knew he was turning his head this way and that, in the dark, listening; and she lay quite still. She felt his hand touch her cheek diffidently. But that diffident, apologetic touch annoyed her, and she jerked her head back. 'What is the matter, Mary?'

'Nothing,' she replied.

'Are you sorry you are leaving?'

The question seemed to her ridiculous; nothing to do with her at all. And she did not want to think of Dick, except with that distant and impersonal pity. Could he not let her live in this last short moment of peace? 'Go to sleep,' she said. 'It's not morning yet.'

Her voice seemed to him normal; even her rejection of him was too familiar a thing to waken him thoroughly. In a minute he was asleep again, stretched out as if he had never stirred. But now she could not forget him; she knew he was lying there beside her, could feel his limbs sprawled against hers. She raised herself up, feeling bitter against him, who never left her in peace. Always he was there, a torturing reminder of what she had to forget in order to remain herself. She sat up straight, resting her head on locked hands, conscious again, as she had not been for a very long time, of that feeling of strain, as if she were stretched taut between two immovable poles. She rocked herself slowly back and forth, with a dim, mindless movement, trying to sink back into that region of her mind where Dick did not exist. For it had been a choice, if one could call such an inevitable thing a choice, between Dick and the other, and Dick was destroyed long ago. 'Poor Dick,' she said tranquilly, at last, from her recovered distance from him; and a flicker of terror touched her, an intimation of that terror which would later engulf her. She knew it: she felt transparent, clairvoyant, containing all things. But not Dick. No; she looked at him, a huddle under blankets, his face a pallid glimmer in the growing dawn. It crept in from the low square of window, and with it came a warm airless breeze. 'Poor Dick,' she said, for the last time, and did not think of him again.

She got out of bed and stood by the window. The low sill cut across her thighs. If she bent forward and down, she could touch the ground, which seemed to rise up outside, stretching to the trees. The stars were gone. The sky was colourless and immense. The veld was dim. Everything was on the verge of colour. There was a hint of green in the curve of a leaf, a shine in the sky that was almost blue, and the clear starred outline of the poinsettia flowers suggested the hardness of scarlet.

Slowly, across the sky, spread a marvellous pink flush, and the trees lifted to meet it, becoming tinged with pink; and bending out into the dawn she saw the world had put on the colour and shape. The night was over. When the sun rose, she thought, her moment would be over, this marvellous moment of peace and forgiveness granted her by a forgiving God. She crouched against the sill, cramped and motionless, clutching on to her last remnants of happiness, her mind as clear as the sky itself. But why, this last morning, had she woken peacefully from a good sleep, and not, as usually, from one of those ugly dreams that seemed to carry over into the day, so that there sometimes seemed no division between the horrors of the night and of the day? Why should she be standing there, watching the sunrise, as if the world were being created afresh for her, feeling this wonderful rooted joy? She was inside a bubble of fresh light and colour, of brilliant sound and birdsong. All around the trees were filled with shrilling birds, that sounded her own happiness and chorused it to the sky. As light as a blown feather she left the room and went outside to the verandah. It was so beautiful: so beautiful she could hardly bear the wonderful flushed sky, streaked with red and hazed against the intense blue; the beautiful still trees, with their load of singing birds; the vivid starry poinsettias cutting into the air with jagged scarlet.

The red spread out from the centre of the sky, seemed to tinge the smoke haze over the kopjes, and to light the trees with a hot sulphurous yellow. The world was a miracle of colour, and all for her, all for her! She could have wept with release and lighthearted joy. And then she heard it, the sound she could never bear, the first cicada beginning to shrill somewhere in the trees. It was the sound of the sun itself, and how she hated the sun! It was rising now; there was a sullen red curve behind a black rock, and a beam of hot yellow light shot up into the blue. One after another the cicadas joined the steady shrilling noise, so that now there were no birds to be heard, and that insistent low screaming seemed to her to be the noise of the sun, whirling on its hot core, the sound of the harsh brazen light, the sound of the gathering heat. Her head was beginning to throb, her shoulders to ache. The dull red disc jerked suddenly up over the kopjes, and the colour ebbed from the sky; a lean, sunflattened landscape stretched before her, dun-coloured, brown and olive-green, and the smoke-haze was everywhere, lingering in the trees and obscuring the hills. The sky shut down over her, with thick yellowish walls of smoke growing up to meet it. The world was small, shut in a room of heat and haze and light.

Shuddering, she seemed to wake, looking about her, touching dry lips with her tongue. She was leaning pressed back against the thin brick wall, her hands extended, palms upwards, warding off the day's coming. She let them fall, moved away from the wall, and looked over her shoulder at where she had been crouching. 'There,' she said aloud, 'it will be there.' And the sound of her own voice, calm, prophetic, fatal, fell on her ears like a warning. She went indoors, pressing her hands to her head, to evade that evil verandah.

Dick was awake, just pulling on his trousers to go and beat the gong. She stood, waiting for the clanging noise. It came, and with it the terror. Somewhere *he* stood, listening for the gong that announced the last day. She could see him clearly. He was standing under a tree somewhere, leaning back against it, his eyes fixed on the house, waiting. She knew it. But not yet, she said to herself, it would not be quite yet; she had the day in front of her.

'Get dressed, Mary,' said Dick, in a quiet urgent voice. Repeated, it penetrated her brain, and she obediently went into the bedroom and began to put on her clothes. Fumbling for buttons she paused, went to the door, about to call for Moses, who would do up her clothes, hand her the brush, tie up her hair, and take the responsibility for her so that she need not think for herself. Through the curtain she saw Dick and that young man sitting at the table, eating a meal she had not prepared. She remembered that Moses had gone: relief flooded her. She would be alone, alone all day. She could concentrate on the one thing left that mattered to her now. She saw Dick rise, with a grieved face, pull across the curtain; she understood that she had been standing in the doorway in her underclothes, in the full sight of that young man. Shame flushed her; but before the saving resentment could countermand the shame, she forgot Dick and the young man. She finished dressing, slowly, slowly, with long pauses between each movement – for had she not all day? – and at last went outside. The table was littered with dishes; the men had gone off to work. A big dish was caked with thick white grease; she thought that they must have been gone some time.

Listlessly she stacked the plates, carried them into the kitchen, filled the sink with water, and then forgot what she was doing. Standing still, her hands hanging idly, she thought, 'Somewhere outside, among the trees, *he* is waiting.' She rushed about the house in a panic, shutting the doors, and all the windows, and collapsed at last on the sofa, like a hare crouching in a tuft of grass, watching the dogs come nearer. But it was no use waiting now: her mind told her she had all day, until the night came. Again, for a brief space, her brain cleared.

What was it all about? she wondered dully, pressing her fingers against her eyes so that they gushed jets of yellow light. I don't understand, she said. I don't understand . . . The idea of herself, standing above the house, somewhere on an invisible mountain peak, looking down like a judge on his court, returned; but this time without a sense of release. It was a torment to her, in that momentarily pitiless clarity, to see herself. That was how they would see her, when it was all over, as she saw herself now: an angular, ugly, pitiful woman, with nothing left of the life she had been given to use but one thought: that between her and the angry sun was a thin strip of blistering iron; that between her and the fatal darkness was a short strip of daylight. And time taking on the attributes of space, she stood balanced in mid-air, and while she saw Mary Turner rocking in the corner of the sofa, moaning, her fists in her eyes, she saw, too, Mary Turner as she had been, that foolish girl travelling unknowingly to this end. I don't understand, she said again. I understand nothing. The evil is there, but of what it consists, I do not know. Even the words were not her own. She groaned because of the strain, lifted in puzzled judgement on herself, who was at the same time the judged, knowing only that she was suffering torment beyond description. For the evil was a thing she could feel: had she not lived with it for many years? How many? Long before she had ever come to the farm! Even that girl had known it. But what had she done? And what was it? What *had* she done? Nothing of her own volition. Step by step, she had come to this, a woman without will, sitting on an old ruined sofa that smelled of dirt, waiting for the night to come that would finish her. And justly – she knew that. But why? Against what had she sinned? The conflict between her judgment on herself, and her feeling of innocence, of having been propelled by something she did not understand, cracked the wholeness of her vision. She lifted her head, with a startled jerk, thinking only that the trees were pressing in round the house, watching, waiting for the night. When she was gone, she thought, this house would be destroyed. It would be killed by the bush, which had always hated it, had always stood around it silently, waiting for the moment when it could advance and cover it, for ever, so that nothing remained. She could see the house, empty, its furnishings rotting. First would come the rats. Already they ran over the rafters at night, their long wiry tails trailing. They would swarm up over the furniture and the walls, gnawing and gutting till nothing was left but brick and iron, and the floors were thick with droppings. And then the beetles: great, black, armoured beetles would crawl in from the veld and lodge in the crevices of the brick. Some were there now, twiddling with their feelers, watching with small painted eyes. And then the rains would break. The sky would lift and clear, and the trees grow lush and distinct, and the air would be shining like water.

But at night the rain would drum down on the roof, on and on, endlessly, and the grass would spring up in the space of empty ground about the house, and the bushes would follow, and by the next season creepers would trail over the verandah and pull down the tins of plants, so that they crashed into pullulating masses of wet growth, and geraniums grew side by side with the blackjacks. A branch would nudge through the broken windowpanes, and slowly, slowly, the shoulders of trees would press against the brick, until at last it leaned and crumbled and fell, a hopeless ruin, with sheets of rusting iron resting on the bushes, and under the tin, toads and long wiry worms like rats' tails, and fat white worms, like slugs. At last the bush would cover the subsiding mass, and there would be nothing left. People would search for the house. They would come across a stone step propped against the trunk of a tree, and say, 'This must be the Turners' old house. Funny how quick the bush covers things over once they are left!' And, scratching round, pushing aside a plant with the point of a shoe, they would come upon a door-handle wedged into the crotch of a stem, or a fragment of china in a silt of pebbles. And, a little further on, there would be a mound of reddish mud, swathed with rotting thatch like the hair of a dead person, which was all that remained of the Englishman's hut; and beyond that, the heap of rubble that marked the end of the store. The house, the store, the chicken runs, the hut – all gone, nothing left, the bush grown over all! Her mind was filled with green, wet branches, thick wet grass, and thrusting bushes. It snapped shut: the vision was gone.

She raised her head and looked about her. She was sitting in that little room with the tin roof overhead, and the sweat was pouring down her body. With all the windows shut it was unbearable. She ran outside: what was the use of sitting there, just waiting, waiting for the door to open and death to enter? She ran away from the house, across the hard, baked earth where the grains of sand glittered towards the trees. The trees hated her, but she could not stay in the house. She entered them, feeling the shade fall on her flesh, hearing the cicadas all about, shrilling endlessly, insistently. She walked straight into the bush, thinking: 'I will come across *him*, and it will all be over.' She stumbled through swathes of pale grass, and the bushes dragged at her dress. She leaned at last against a tree, her eyes shut, her ears filled with noise, her skin aching. There she remained, waiting, waiting. But the noise was unbearable! She was caught up in a shriek of sound. She opened her eyes again. Straight in front of her was a sapling, its greyish trunk knotted as if it were an old gnarled tree. But they were not knots. Three of those ugly little beetles squatted there, singing away, oblivious of her, of everything, blind to everything but the life-giving sun. She came close to them, staring. Such little beetles to make such an intolerable noise! And she had never seen one before. She realized, suddenly standing there, that all those years she had lived in that house, with the acres of bush all around her, and she had never penetrated into the trees, had never gone off the paths. And for all those years she had listened wearily, through the hot dry months, with her nerves prickling, to that terrible shrilling, and had never seen the beetles who made it. Lifting her eyes she saw she was standing in the full sun, that seemed so low she could reach up a hand and pluck it out of the sky: a big red sun, sullen with smoke. She reached up her hand; it brushed against a cluster of leaves, and something whirred away. With a little moan of horror she ran through the bushes and the grass, away back to the clearing. There she stood still, clutching at her throat.

A native stood there, outside the house. She put her hand to her mouth to stifle a scream. Then she saw it was another native, who held in his hand a piece of paper. He held it as illiterate natives always handle printed paper: as if it is something that might explode in their faces. She went towards him and took it. It said: 'Shall not be back for lunch. Too busy clearing things up. Send down tea and sandwiches.' This small reminder from the outer world hardly had the power to rouse her. She thought irritably that here was Dick again; and holding the paper in her hand she went back into the house, opening the windows with an angry jerk. What did the boy mean by not keeping the windows open when she had told him so many times . . . She looked at the paper; where had it come from?

She sat on the sofa, her eyes shut. Through a grey coil of sleep she heard knocking on the door and started up; then she sat down again, trembling, waiting for him to come. The knock sounded again. Wearily she dragged herself up and went to the door. Outside stood the native. 'What do you want?' she asked. He indicated, through the door, the paper lying on the table. She remembered that Dick had asked for tea. She made it, filled a whisky bottle with it, and sent the boy away, forgetting all about the sandwiches. The thought was in her mind that the young man would be thirsty; he was not used to the country. The phrase, 'the country', which was more of a summons to consciousness than even Dick was, disturbed her, like a memory she did not want to revive. But she continued to think about the youth. She saw him, behind shut lids, with his very young, unmarked, friendly face. He had been kind to her; he had not condemned her. Suddenly she found herself clinging to the thought of him. He would save her! She would wait for him to return. She stood in the doorway looking down over the sweep of sere, dry vlei. Somewhere in the trees *he* was waiting; somewhere in the vlei was the young man who would come before the night to rescue her. She stared, hardly blinking, into the aching sunlight. But what was the matter with the big land down there, which was always an expanse of dull red at this time of the year? It was covered over with bushes and grass. Panic plucked at her; already, before she was even dead, the bush was conquering the farm, sending its outriders to cover the good red soil with plants and grass; the bush knew she was going to die! But the young man . . . shutting out everything else she thought of him, with his warm comfort, his protecting arm. She leaned over the verandah wall, breaking off the geraniums, staring at the slopes of bush and vlei for a plume of reddish dust that would show the car was coming. But they no longer had a car; the car had been sold . . . The strength went out of her, and she sat down, breathless, closing her eyes. When she opened them the light had changed, and the shadows were stretching out in front of the house. The feeling of late afternoon was in the air, and there was a sultry, dusty evening glow, a clanging bell of yellow light that washed in her head like pain. She had been asleep. She had slept through this last day. And perhaps while she slept he had come into the house looking for her? She got to her feet in a rush of defiant courage and marched into the front room. It was empty. But she knew, without any doubt at all, that he had been there while she slept, had peered through the window to see her. The kitchen door was open; that proved it. Perhaps that was what had awakened her, his being there, peering at her, perhaps even reaching out to touch her? She shrank and shivered.

But the young man would save her. Sustained by the thought of his coming, which could not be far off now, she left the house by the back door, and walked towards his hut. Stepping over the low brick step, she bent herself into the cool interior. Oh, the coolness was so lovely, lovely on her skin! She sat on his bed, leaning her head on her hands, feeling the small chill from the cement floor strike up against her feet. At last she jerked herself up: she must not sleep again. Along the curving wall of the hut was a row of shoes. She looked at them with wonder. Such good, smart shoes – she hadn't seen anything like them for years. She picked one up, feeling the shiny leather admiringly, peering for the label: 'John Craftsman, Edinburgh,' it said. She laughed, without knowing why. She put it down. On the floor was a big suitcase, which she could hardly lift. She tumbled it open on the floor. Books! Her wonder deepened. She had not seen books for so long she would find it difficult to read. She looked at the titles: *Rhodes and His Influence: Rhodes and the Spirit of Africa: Rhodes and His Mission.* 'Rhodes,' she said vaguely, aloud. She knew nothing about him, except what she had been taught at school, which wasn't much. She knew he had conquered a continent. 'Conquered a continent,' she said aloud, proud that she had remembered the phrase after so long. 'Rhodes sat on an inverted bucket by a hole in the ground, dreaming of his home in England, and of the unconquered hinterland.' She began to laugh; it seemed to her extraordinarily funny. Then she thought, forgetting about the Englishman, and Rhodes, and the books: 'But I haven't been to the store.' And she knew she must go.

She walked along the narrow path towards it. The path now

hardly existed. It was a furrow through the bush, and the grass was under her feet. A few paces from the low brick building, she stopped. There it was, the ugly store. There it was, at her death, even as it had been all her life. But it was empty; if she went in there would be nothing on the shelves, the ants were making red granulated tunnels over the counter, the walls were sheeted with spider-web. But it was still there. In a sudden violent hate she banged on the door. It swung open. The store smell still clung there; it enveloped her, musty and thick and sweet. She stared. There he was, there in front of her, standing behind the counter as if he were serving goods, Moses the black man, standing there, looking out at her with a lazy, but threatening disdain. She gave a little cry and stumbled out, running back down the path, looking over her shoulder. The door was swinging loosely, and he did not come out. So, that was where he was waiting! She knew now that she had expected it all the time. Of course: where else could he wait, but in the hated store? She went back into the thatched hut. There was the young man, looking at her, his face puzzled, stooping over the books she had scattered over the floor, putting them back into the suitcase. No, he could not save her. She sank down on the bed, feeling sick and hopeless. There was no salvation: she would have to go through with it.

And it seemed to her, as she looked at his puzzled, unhappy face, that she had lived through all this before. She wondered, searching through her past. Yes: long, long ago, she had turned towards another young man, a young man from a farm, when she was in trouble and had not known what to do. It had seemed to her that she would be saved from herself by marrying him. And then, she had felt this emptiness when, at last, she had known there was to be no release and that she would live on the farm till she died. There was nothing new even in her death; all this was familiar, even her feeling of helplessness.

She rose to her feet with a queerly appropriate dignity, a dignity that left Tony speechless, for the protective pity with which he had been going to address her, now seemed useless.

She would walk out her road alone, she thought. That was the lesson she had to learn. If she had learned it, long ago, she would not be standing here now, having been betrayed for the second time by her weak reliance on a human being who should not be expected to take the responsibility for her.

'Mrs Turner,' asked the young man awkwardly, 'did you want to see me about something?'

'I was,' she said. 'But it's no good: it's not you . . .' But she could not discuss it with him. She glanced over her shoulder at the evening sky; long trails of pinkish cloud hung there, across the fading blue. 'Such a lovely evening,' she said conventionally.

'Yes . . . Mrs Turner, I have been talking to your husband.'

'Have you?' she asked, politely.

'We thought . . . I suggested that tomorrow, when you get into town, you might go and see a doctor. You are ill, Mrs Turner.'

'I have been ill for years,' she said tartly. 'Inside, somewhere. Inside. Not *ill*, you understand. Everything wrong, somewhere.' She nodded to him, and stepped over the threshold. Then she turned back. '*He* is there,' she whispered secretively. 'In there.' She nodded in the direction of the store.

'Is he?' asked the young man dutifully, humouring her.

She went back to the house, looking round vaguely at the little brick buildings that would soon have vanished. Where she walked, with the warm sand of the path under her feet, small animals would walk proudly through trees and grass.

She entered the house, and faced the long vigil of her death. With deliberation and a stoical pride she sat down on the old sofa that had worn into the shape of her body, and folded her hands and waited, looking at the windows for the light to fade. But after a while she realized that Dick was seated at the table under a lighted lamp, gazing at her.

'Have you finished packing your things?' he asked. 'You know we must be gone by tomorrow morning.'

She began to laugh. 'Tomorrow!' she said. She cackled with laughter; until she saw him get up, abruptly, and go out, his hand over his face. Good, now she was alone.

But later she watched the two men carry in plates and food, and begin to eat, sitting down opposite her. They offered her a cup of liquid which she refused impatiently, waiting for them to go. It would be over soon; soon, in a few hours it would be over. But they would not go. They seemed to be sitting there because of her. She went outside, blindly, feeling with her hands at the edge of the door. There was no lessening of the heat; the invisible dark sky bent over the house, weighing down upon it. Behind her she heard Dick say something about rain. 'It will rain,' she said to herself, 'after I am dead.'

'Bed?' said Dick from the doorway, at last.

The question seemed to have nothing to do with her; she was standing on the verandah, where she knew she would have to wait, watching the darkness for movement.

'Come to bed, Mary!' She saw that she would first of all have to go to bed, because they would not leave her alone until she did. Automatically, she turned the lamp down in the front room, and went to lock the back door. It seemed essential that the back door should be locked; she felt she must be protected from the back; the blow would come from the front. Outside the back door stood Moses, facing her. He seemed outlined in stars. She stepped back, her knees gone to water, and locked the door.

'He's outside,' she remarked breathlessly to Dick, as if this was only to be expected.

'Who is?'

She did not reply. Dick went outside. She could hear him moving, and saw the swinging beams of light from the hurricane lamp he carried. 'There is nothing there, Mary,' he said, when he returned. She nodded, in affirmation, and went again to lock the back door. Now the oblong of night was blank; Moses was not there. He would have gone into the bush, at the front of the house, she thought, in order to wait until she appeared. Back in the bedroom she stood in the middle of the floor. She might have forgotten how to move.

'Aren't you getting undressed?' asked Dick at last, in that hopeless, patient voice.

Obediently she pulled off her clothes and got into bed, lying alertly awake, listening. She felt him put out a hand to touch her, and at once became inert. But he was a long way off, he did not matter to her: he was like a person on the other side of a thick glass wall.

'Mary?' he said.

She remained silent.

'Mary, listen to me. You are ill. You must let me take you to the doctor.'

It seemed to her the young Englishman was speaking; from him had originated this concern for her, this belief in her essential innocence, this absolution from guilt.

'Of course, I am ill,' she said confidingly, addressing the Englishman. 'I've always been ill, ever since I can remember. I am ill *here*.' She pointed to her chest, sitting bolt upright in bed. But her hand dropped, she forgot the Englishman, Dick's voice sounded in her ears like the echo of a voice across a valley. She was listening to the night outside. And, slowly, the terror engulfed her which she had known must come. Once she lay down, and turned her face into the darkness of the pillows; but her eyes were alive with light, and against the light she saw a dark, waiting shape. She sat up again, shuddering. He was in the room, just beside her! But the room was empty. There was nothing. She heard a boom of thunder, and saw, as she had done so many times, the lightning flicker on a shadowed wall. Now it seemed as if the night were closing in on her, and the little house was bending over like a candle, melting in the heat. She heard the crack, crack; the restless moving of the iron above, and it seemed to her that a vast black body, like a human spider, was crawling over the roof, trying to get inside. She was alone. She was defenceless. She was shut in a small black box, the walls closing in on her, the roof pressing down. She was in a trap, cornered and helpless. But she would have to go out and meet him. Propelled by fear, but also by knowledge, she rose out of bed, not making a sound. Gradually, hardly moving, she let her legs down over the dark edge of the bed; and then, suddenly afraid of the dark gulfs of the floor, she ran to the centre of the room. There she paused. A movement of lightning on the walls drove her forward again. She stood in the curtain-folds, feeling the hairy stuff on her skin, like a hide. She shook them off, and stood poised for flight across the darkness of the front room, which was full of menacing shapes. Again the fur of animals; but this time on her feet. The long loose paw of a wildcat caught in her foot as she darted over it, so that she gave a sharp little moan of fear, and glanced over her shoulder at the kitchen door. It was locked and dark. She was on the verandah. She moved backwards till she was pressed against the wall. That was protected; she was standing as she should be, as she knew she had to wait. It steadied her. The fog of terror cleared from her eyes, and she could see, as the lightning flickered, that the two farm dogs were lying with lifted heads, looking at her, on the verandah. Beyond the three slim pillars, and the stiff outlines of the geranium plants, nothing could be seen until the lightning plunged again, when the crowding shoulders of the trees showed against a cloud-packed sky. She thought that as she watched, they moved nearer; and she pressed back against the wall with all her strength, so that she could feel the rough brick pricking through her nightgown into her flesh. She shook her head to clear it, and the trees stood still and waited. It seemed to her that as long as she could fix her attention on them they could not creep up to her. She knew she must keep her mind on three things: the trees, so that they should not rush on her unawares; the door to one side of her where Dick might come; and the lightning that ran and danced, illuminating stormy ranges of cloud. Her feet firmly planted on the tepid rough brick of the floor, her back held against the wall, she crouched and stared, all her senses stretched, rigidly breathing in little gasps.

Then as she heard the thunder growl and shake in the trees, the sky lit up, and she saw a man's shape move out from the dark and come towards her, gliding silently up the steps, while the dogs stood alertly watching, their tails swinging in welcome. Two yards away Moses stopped. She could see his great shoulders, the shape of his head, the glistening of his eyes. And, at the sight of him, her emotions unexpectedly shifted, to create in her an extraordinary feeling of guilt; but towards him, to whom she had been disloyal, and at the bidding of the Englishman. She felt she had only to move forward, to explain, to appeal, and the terror would be dissolved. She opened her mouth to speak; and, as she did so, saw his hand, which held a long curving shape, lifted above his head; and she knew it would be too late. All her past slid away, and her mouth, opened in appeal, let out the beginning of a scream, which was stopped by a black wedge of hand inserted between her jaws. But the scream continued, in her stomach, choking her; and she lifted her hands, clawlike, to ward him off. And then the bush avenged itself: that was her last thought. The trees advanced in a rush, like beasts, and the thunder was the noise of their coming. As the brain at last gave way, collapsing in a ruin of horror, she saw, over the big arm that forced her head back against the wall, the other arm descending. Her limbs sagged under her, the lightning leapt out from the dark, and darted down the plunging steel.

Moses, letting her go, saw her roll to the floor. A steady drumming sound on the iron overhead brought him to knowledge of his surroundings, and he started up, turning his head this way and that, straightening his body. The dogs were growling at his feet, but their tails still swung: this man had fed them and looked after them; Mary had disliked them. Moses clouted them back softly, his open palm to their faces; and they stood watching him, puzzled, and whining softly.

It was beginning to rain; big drops blew in across Moses' back, chilling him. And another dripping sound made him look down at the piece of metal he held, which he had picked up in the bush, and had spent the day polishing and sharpening. The blood trickled off it on to the brick floor. And a curious division of purpose showed itself in his next movements. First he dropped the weapon sharply on the floor, as if in fear; then he checked himself and picked it up. He held it over the verandah wall under the now drenching downpour, and in a few moments withdrew it. Now he hesitated, looking about him. He thrust the metal in his belt, held his hands under the rain, and, cleansed, prepared to walk off through the rain to his hut in the compound, ready to protest his innocence. This purpose, too, passed. He pulled out the weapon, looked at it, and simply tossed it down beside Mary, suddenly indifferent, for a new need possessed him.

Ignoring Dick, who was asleep through one thickness of wall, but who was unimportant, since he had been defeated long ago, Moses vaulted over the verandah wall, alighting squarely on his feet in the squelch of rain which sluiced off his shoulders, soaking him in an instant. He moved off towards the Englishman's hut through the drenching blackness, water to his calves. At the door he peered in. It was impossible to see, but he could hear; holding his own breath, he listened intently, through the sound of the rain, for the Englishman's breathing. But he could hear nothing. He stooped through the doorway, and walked quietly to the bedside. His enemy, whom he had outwitted, was asleep. Contemptuously, the native turned away, and walked back to the house. It seemed he intended to pass it, but as he came level with the verandah he paused, resting his hand on the wall, looking over. It was black, too dark to see. He waited, for the watery glimmer of lightning to illuminate, for the last time, the small house, the verandah, the huddled shape of Mary on the brick, and the dogs who were moving restlessly about her, still whining gently, but uncertainly. It came: a prolonged drench of light, like a wet dawn. And this was his final moment of triumph, a moment so perfect and complete that it took the urgency from thoughts of escape, leaving him indifferent. When the dark returned he took his hand from the wall, and walked slowly off through the rain towards the bush. Though what thoughts of regret, or pity, or perhaps even wounded human affection were compounded with the satisfaction of his completed revenge, it is impossible to say. For, when he had gone perhaps a couple of hundred yards through the soaking bush he stopped, turned aside, and leaned against a tree on an ant-heap. And there he would remain until his pursuers, in their turn, came to find him.